Making New Friends
A New Beginning

Liz Hamilton

Dedicated to...

I dedicate this to my wonderful husband who helped inspire this story.
Thirty three years of marriage and three and a half years of dating
helped to bring this story to life.

Contents

Prologue

With hands gripping her teacup, the lines in Hannah's face tightened and her brow furrowed. Grateful for the life she had, she knew it was not without its struggles and hardships. Her mouth pursed and the corners lifted slightly as she thought back to long ago, remembering how she and Michael fell in love.

Thirty-two years did not erase the sharpness of her memory of what she considered her most pivotal moment; she met the love of her life. My, how it felt like yesterday!

Youth no longer filled her face nor the rest of her body, Michael's neither, but she placed her hand over the steady beat of her heart and she knew that young girl was still inside of her.

She and Michael had their individual moments of difficulty and there had been struggles with their commitment to one another. Two children, a couple of career changes, midlife crises-these were all things they endured together, but they never gave up!

Her mouth tightened again as well as her grip on her teacup as Hannah pondered her internal struggles. It had taken her a lifetime to work past her insecurities. Michael had his own issues as well, but they had not allowed any of these obstacles to get in the way of the beautiful love that developed so many years ago.

Chapter 1

August 1988, a university in East Texas

It was a Monday, and her nerves were making her insides feel like pop-rock firecrackers! Eighteen-year-old Hannah Mathis was battling the feeling of anxiety along with excitement.

Her Dad went with her for move-in day. Her mother was unable to accompany them because teachers had to return to school after the summer break to prepare for their students. After a three-hour drive, her dad went to work helping her unload his truck and her car. Half an hour later, she and her dad finished bringing in their last load.

"Thanks, Dad," Hannah commented as she wiped the perspiration off her brow. It was August in East Texas. It was hot!

"Sure thing, Hannah-bug," her dad said, using his pet name for her. Holding his back as he stood straight to face Hannah, he took his towel out of his pocket to wipe his own brow. Then he continued saying, "I need to get back home."

"So soon?" Hannah asked. "We could get something to eat." Even though Hannah thought she wanted this, she wanted his comforting presence for a while longer.

"It will take three hours to get home," he countered. She studied his face, and Hannah noticed his impassive expression as he glanced away from her. As he shuffled his feet, he wrapped her in a loose hug. However, Hannah clung tightly to him and she dreaded the moment when he would actually leave.

Her dad was trying to make their goodbye short and sweet. He lived most of his adult life across the country from his own family, and he was not one for prolonged and sappy endings.

"Goodbye Hannah-bug," he said softly as he pulled away from the hug. "Call your mother when you can."

"Wait..." Hannah tried to tell him she would walk him out to the front, but he had already exited the room. Feeling slightly bereft at his hasty departure, Hannah sat down in the chair that went with the desk provided for her in the dorm room. She tried to tamp down the tears, and she exhaled loudly at the concept of finally being on her own.

That doesn't mean that she wasn't ready to move out. She definitely was! She had been ready a year ago since visiting the university the summer before and loving the freedom from her parents' overprotection. Those six weeks had caused her to grow up and relinquish the rebellious spirit she possessed during her years of high school. It also helped her to release the pressure she felt from others around her to take part in partying and drinking. It was something that she had no desire to do anymore. Her senior year was spent working and attempting to raise her grade point average. To fight against her parents' smothering, Hannah spent most of her high school years battling low self-esteem, and doing anything and everything to be accepted by others. However, despite her best efforts, much of her time was spent at home as a typical "wallflower."

"Hey!" Her roommate Rhonda Stillman walked into her dorm room, distracting her from her thoughts. "You finally got here!" she exclaimed. A smile lit Hannah's face, and she felt a little more relieved that she was not alone, but she failed to notice the wild look in Rhonda's expression.

"Hey, yourself!" Hannah said. "How long have you been here? And where were you?"

"Just about an hour," Rhonda replied. She flopped on her bed and leaned back against the pillows of her already-made bed. "I went to the student center and the bookstore for something to do because I wasn't sure when you would actually get here."

Rhonda could be described as eccentric. She had a "go with the flow" attitude and she had a deep laugh that caused everyone else around her to join in. At the moment, she was wearing a tie-dyed t-shirt with denim shorts. Her red hair was hanging wildly around her face, and she did not care about styling it at that moment.

Hannah was excited to room with her. My, how those feelings would change in just a few weeks and little did she know that there were some psychological problems below the surface that would cause her to fear for her life!

***

'Finally!' Michael Davis thought to himself. He had everything moved in for his freshman year of college. He was sharing a room with the buddy, Alex Fleming, that Michael met in April when they visited the campus on a weekend designed for incoming students. The two of them formed a strong bond those two days with their shared love of basketball and eighties hair bands! Neither of them wanted to live in a dorm, so they decided to rent an apartment across the street from the university so that they could walk to wherever they needed to go. Their apartment was an old clapboard house that had been renovated into two separate apartments. The rent was cheap and the location was more than convenient.

Michael's mother couldn't come with him for the move-in weekend due to school starting back soon. She was needed for her job as the principal's secretary. She left him on Sunday after accompanying him to his grandparents, on his Dad's side, who lived in a town about half an hour away from the university. It had been a tearful goodbye and Michael humored her when she hugged him tightly and told him to call often.

Michael knew that his mother wanted him to stay strong and focused on his classes that he would begin taking on Monday. He had always been an A student growing up in school, so anything less would not be acceptable in his mind.

He heard the door open, drawing him out of his muse. Alex walked in and he stopped in the doorway of Michael's room. "Hey man! Glad you're here!"

"Hey buddy," Michael said, lifting his chin. However, he didn't move from his sitting position on his bed. "How long have you been here?"

"I got here this morning," Alex commented. He walked to the refrigerator to pull out a pitcher of water that Michael had filled up once he was moved in. Grabbing a glass, Alex filled it and drank all of it before continuing. "I've been out walking around the campus and I have to say that I've noticed some lovely ladies who are attending here!"

Shaking his head, Michael smiled and said, "You've already been checking out the girls?" Michael had no desire for a relationship. He just got out of a messy one and he wanted to focus on his goal of becoming a choral teacher.

"I was bored after unpacking, so I went to the student center to grab a drink," he said, holding up the soda can in his hands.

Chuckling, Michael said, "I plan to steer clear of them. I'm here to focus on school and getting decent grades."

"You can still do that and check out the female population at the same time!" Alex had a silly grin on his face and Michael couldn't help but laugh harder. "How about we change and go see if we can play some basketball?" Alex asked. He walked to his bedroom, leaving the pitcher and the glass sitting on the counter. Michael didn't understand his need for water when he had just drank a soda.

"Sounds good to me," Michael said. "Give me a minute to change and we can go." Michael stood up and took the water pitcher, refilled it, and placed it back on a shelf in the refrigerator. He washed the glass, dried it with a towel before placing it back in the cupboard, believing strongly that things needed to be cleaned up.

***

After spending about an hour unpacking and making up her own bed, Hannah lay on her bed exhausted as she pulled out the schedule for the next few days.

She could hear the deep breathing as Rhonda lay napping opposite her in the bunk beds that were in a row underneath the windows in the room.

The beds were built into a "window seat" of sorts with mattresses on top of them and storage drawers underneath. Rhonda's head was near the opposite wall as Hannah's. Beside each bed was a built-in desk with a wooden chair and a countertop. Above each counter was a mirror for each person to use when getting ready. Across the room were two closets with rolling doors to open each side. This dorm room was quite roomy compared to dorms at other colleges and universities. Hannah's bed was closest to the bathroom that they shared with the room next to them. She could hear music coming from next door as she moved her toiletry items into the bathroom cabinet. The door was open, so Hannah looked in and saw a girl sitting on her bunk across the room.

"Hey," she said, "I'm Hannah." Surprised at herself for initiating the greeting, she almost retreated back into her shell.

However, one of the girls looked up and smiled. "I'm Jackie. It's nice to meet you. This is Michelle." She pointed to the girl sitting in the bunk opposite her. Hannah had not spotted her from her vantage point in the bathroom.

"Hey," Michelle said in a bored voice, but she was smiling.

"Where are you from?" Jackie asked.

"I'm from Montgomery. How about you?" Hannah asked.

"Beaumont," replied Jackie.

"I'm also from Beaumont," answered Michelle.

"Did you guys already know each other before coming?" Hannah asked.

"Yeah, we've been friends since we were little," said Jackie.

The girls were polar opposites from each other. Jackie had a tall, lean, and athletic build with blond hair and blue eyes. Michelle, on the other hand, was short and a little more rounded in several places on her body. She had dark brown hair and brown eyes. Hannah was right in between with light brown hair and hazel eyes. She was what people would describe as average height as well.

"That's nice! Have you met Rhonda? She fell asleep or I would call her in here," said Hannah.

"No, we haven't. What's your major?" asked Michelle.

"I'm going into foreign languages," said Hannah. "I will probably have to transfer somewhere else to complete my degree. What about you?"

"Wow, that sounds difficult," Jackie commented and it made Hannah doubt herself, wondering if she was majoring in the right thing. She often had those kinds of thoughts about herself when she was with other people. Her parents' voices also came back to her as she remembered them telling her not to major in foreign languages. Jackie continued by saying, "I'm going into education. I want to become a softball coach."

"I'm going into business, but I'm not exactly sure what I will do with it quite yet," said Michelle.

"Hey, it's about time for supper," Jackie mentioned. "Do you want to go together?"

"Sure," said Hannah as she was overjoyed with the thought of making friends. "Let me go and see if I can wake up Rhonda to ask if she wants to come with us."

She walked back into their room and said "Hey." Rhonda didn't budge. Uncertain of what to do, she reached down and touched Rhonda on the shoulder.

The response she received was a growl from Rhonda and, "Leave me alone." A feeling came across her gut, but she didn't stop to identify it. *Okay*, she thought to herself, and she murmured, "I'm not going to try to wake her any further."

Hannah quickly grabbed her key and her badge to show for dinner. Her dad paid for her meal ticket, but students had to show their name badge every time they went to eat. She walked back through the connecting bathroom and the three girls walked to the dining hall and went through the line.

Dinner was fried chicken, mashed potatoes, rolls, salad and chocolate cake for dessert. They each got a drink and sat down to eat. Being a small, private school, there was only one main food line with a salad bar, and a snack bar outside of the dining room itself.

As they were getting their drinks, Hannah turned and nearly bumped into someone. "Oh, sorry!" they both said at the same time. Mesmerized by the most beautiful blue-green eyes that she had ever seen, she was speechless. Wow, he was hot!! He bashfully looked away and walked to one of the drink machines.

"Nice to meet you." She muttered to herself. As she turned to walk to the table with her friends, she didn't notice the spill on the floor. As she stepped, she lost her balance as her foot flew out from under her. All of a sudden, strong arms caught her and Hannah looked up into the dreamy guy's face, feeling her face turn a shade of crimson.

"Careful, there. Are you okay?" he asked in a deep voice. He had placed his glass on the counter to help her.

"Yes, thank you," Hannah said as she regained her footing. Then she surprised herself by sticking out her hand. She said, "I'm Hannah Mathis." She knew her face was a deeper red, but she took a breath to push away her fears.

"Nice to meet you. I'm Michael Davis," Michael spoke as he shook her hand, but that was all he said.

"Thank you again," Hannah commented as she gave him a shy grin.

"No problem. See you around," he said then he walked back to the table with several other guys. Once he sat down, he looked across to the table where Hannah was sitting. Unsure of what he was thinking, she moved her gaze downward because she was slightly embarrassed of herself at her bold introduction. He certainly did not seem interested.

Chapter 2

The next morning, Hannah and Rhonda were getting ready for the first day of freshmen orientation. It was three, boring days of learning about the school and where to find their classes. There were also sessions covering good study skills and other knowledge that was supposedly going to help them become scholarly students. Hannah was as excited about these sessions as she was getting a filling in a tooth.! Hannah was not much of a morning person so she typically didn't talk much while she got ready.

Rhonda, on the other hand, was talking non-stop about what sessions she was going to attend that day.

"By the way," said Rhonda, "where did you go last night? I woke up and you were gone." The way that she was speaking so quickly, she reminded Hannah of a wind-up toy where you pulled the string and they talked and moved nonstop!

"I tried waking you," said Hannah in a grumpy tone of voice, "but you didn't seem like you wanted to wake up. I went to supper with Jackie and Michelle next door and then we spent the evening hanging out in the student center. When I came back, you were still asleep, so I took a shower and went to bed."

"I can't believe you went without me," said Rhonda in a "miffy" voice.

"Like I said, you wouldn't wake up." Hannah replied. "I tried and you growled at me and told me to leave you alone."

"Still, you should not have left me here." snarled Rhonda. Hannah's belly felt the uneasy feeling that she felt the night before. However, being a non-confrontational person, Hannah didn't say anything more as she went into the bathroom to shower and get ready.

After coming out, she asked, "Do you want to go to breakfast?"

"Sure," Rhonda replied in a bubbly voice. It was as if the last couple of moments had not happened, which seemed strange to Hannah. Ignoring her feeling of uncertainty, she shrugged it off.

"Let's ask Jackie and Michelle if they want to go with us. That's who I went to supper with last night." She knocked on their adjoining door.

"Hey!" said Jackie after she opened the door.

"Do y'all want to go to breakfast with us?" Hannah asked. "By the way, this is Rhonda," as she pointed to her roommate.

"Hey, nice to meet you," said Jackie. Michelle smiled at her from across their room.

"Hi!' said Rhonda, chuckling a little. "Sorry, I missed joining you guys last night!" She acted as if nothing had just happened. That made Hannah feel better and she assumed everything was fine as they walked out together.

***

As Hannah was getting in the line, there was Michael right in front of her.

"Hi, Michael," she said, shocking herself again at initiating their conversation.

His eyes landed on her and he actually smiled this time. "Hello, Hannah." Then, he turned and walked away, deflating Hannah's momentary confidence.

"Wow!" Rhonda said behind her. "What a dreamy guy!"

"He's very cute!" Hannah agreed. She wondered what it would take to get him to say more than three words to her.

Rhonda continued scouring the line and the dining room for other cute guys. "There's another one!" she exclaimed as she aimed a silly smile toward him. He just looked at her and moved on to sit at a table. Her flirty smile turned into a look that Hannah might describe as evil. It was obvious that Rhonda did not take rejection well.

"Hey, jerk!" she yelled. "How about you smile back next time!?"

Hannah ducked her head with embarrassment as the troubled feeling came over her again. "It's okay," she replied with a slight chuckle. "He doesn't know you, so he may not have understood what you were doing."

"I don't care," said Rhonda. As she walked by his table, she answered in a loud voice "What a jackass! The least he could have done was acknowledge that I was there!"

The guy continued to look at her, but his look changed to annoyance as he still did not reply and turned back to continue the conversation with the guys at his table.

"Hey, calm down," said Hannah. "There are plenty of other guys that will be happy to talk to you."

Rhonda turned her withering glare onto Hannah as she leaned close to her face and snapped, "Are you my friend or not? How about you show some loyalty?"

Quickly backing away, Hannah didn't say anything else as they sat with Jackie and Michelle. The looks on the other girls' faces showed that they were unsure of Rhonda and her disposition as well.

Jackie cleared her throat and began a different conversation. "What sessions did y'all sign up to attend today? Hopefully, they won't be too boring!" Thankfully, it directed the four girls to discuss where they would go for each session throughout the day. By the end of breakfast, Rhonda was back to her normal, cheerful self.

Hannah tried to push away her feeling of unease, and wondered if Rhonda was in a bad mood because she was tired.

***

Hannah and Rhonda walked into Linwood Hall for their first session. As she glanced around the room, she spotted Michael and she was determined to get to know him.

"Let's go sit over there," she said, pointing in his direction. Since moving to college, she was turning into someone she had not ever been before. Hannah liked the boldness that had come over her and she wondered if it had to do with starting completely over where people did not know her family or her jerk of an older brother, who basically ruined high school for her. Peter was a year older than her in school so any of her chances at dating were with people who did not know him.

She and Rhonda walked to the row where Michael was sitting and asked if they could sit beside him. His expression was suspicious as he studied them, but he nodded his head in agreement. Normally, Hannah would have shied away from a situation like this, but she had a compelling need to get to know Michael.

"Hi, Michael," Rhonda said with a loud voice. "I'm Rhonda and Hannah is my awesome roomie!"

Michael mumbled something in response, but he was not impressed by Rhonda at all. He had just met her, and he thought she was downright annoying! He didn't know why she was talking so loudly causing other people to look their way.

"So, Michael, where are you from?" Hannah asked, and again, she was amazed at her boldness in initiating the conversation.

"I'm from Dallas," Michael said and he smiled at her again. Trying not to swoon at how gorgeous he was, Hannah smiled back. He turned the questions around and asked, "What about you? Where are you from?"

Excited that the ice had been broken, she told him where she was from. They began talking about the school and what their majors were going to be.

Hannah made sure to include Rhonda in their conversation because of her negative reactions earlier. She was happy at the moment, so Hannah chalked up her sour attitude at breakfast to being tired and not having enough sleep.

"Do you ever go by 'Mike?'" Rhonda interrupted their conversation with a cackle after she asked. It was weird that this was her comment in response to them talking about their majors.

Glancing at her and then back to Hannah, Michael responded by saying, "I go by 'Michael.'"

The session soon began, and they turned their attention to the professor who was introducing himself.

***

Michael smiled to himself as he was distracted and not listening to the boring lecture about the difficulties of adjusting to college life. Sitting next to Hannah, he realized how beautiful she was up close. She seemed genuine in her desire to get to know him. Yesterday, he wasn't sure if she was just flirting or if she was truly interested in him. Another thing was how good Hannah smelled as he caught a flowery scent as she shifted in her seat. As he told Alex yesterday, Michael wasn't interested in a serious relationship, but maybe they could be friends. There was something about Hannah that made him want to get to know her better. He wasn't so sure about Rhonda. Something about her felt off.

He had spoken to his mom the night before to reassure her that he was doing fine. Communication was something his family did not do well. Even though Michael's mother didn't say out loud her expectations of her son, he knew they were there. Most of his life had been spent following her instructions and wishes for his future. He was a devoted son as he always tried to please her. Michael didn't really follow many of his own passions as she allowed him one year, in middle school, of playing football as a deal that she struck with him to join the choir in high school. As he thought about her, his gut filled with the usual panic that often gripped him. His brow furrowed as he glanced at Hannah sitting next to him knowing that his mom would not be happy with distractions of dating.

Chapter 3

Hannah, Michael and Rhonda were leaving their final session for the day and were heading to the student center.

Once they went inside, Michael asked, "Do you want to play some ping pong?" He was looking more at Hannah than Rhonda.

Both girls answered that they would, so they all walked over to where the ping pong tables were, and people were playing loudly.

Michael walked over to the guy that Hannah had spoken to one afternoon at their "get to know you mixer." It was back in the spring during visitation weekend where incoming freshmen could get a "taste" of college life for a weekend. She and Rhonda had gotten to know each other then, as well. She remembered that his name was Alex. They greeted each other again.

Hannah said, "Please meet my roommate, Rhonda."

Alex shook her hand and told her that it was nice to meet her. With his gaze lingering on Rhonda, he offered each of them a ping pong paddle to begin their game.

The foursome began playing and the ball Rhonda served hit the net. She took her paddle and knocked herself in the head as she laughed and said, "It looks like I don't know how to serve a ball over the net!" Michael found her humor to be extremely strange, but Alex laughed along with her, and he did the same thing with his paddle to add to the joke. Michael couldn't help but laugh at the expression on his roommate's face as he did it and he heard Hannah laugh beside him.

After they finished their game, Michael asked, "Do both of you want to go eat dinner with us?"

Hannah and Rhonda both agreed to join them as she and Michael stood in line together.

Hannah commented, "My family came to Dallas one year when I was eleven to a Cowboys game. It was freezing cold and snowing, believe it or not!"

"I remember that year that it snowed!" Michael exclaimed. "My house isn't very far from Texas Stadium." Michael began getting his meal as they were going through the food line. With a teasing look in his eye, he said, "How come you didn't come visit me if you came all that way?"

Hannah laughed and she said, "Pardon me for overlooking that small error even though I didn't even know you existed!"

Laughing with her, Michael winked and she felt like her heart was doing jumping jacks. Unable to help it, a blush stole over her face. Thankfully, they were through the food line and Hannah moved to get her drink in order to conceal her face.

"Would you and Alex like to join us?" she asked Michael.

"Sounds great." Michael agreed and he turned to point Alex in their direction.

Rhonda was walking beside Alex with a silly, flirtatious smile on her face. Hannah was happy to see that Alex was flirting back because she didn't want a repeat episode like yesterday if he didn't respond to Rhonda. She knew that Rhonda came from a broken home with divorced parents, but she didn't know much more about her. Maybe she needed to spend time getting to know Rhonda a little better.

Shaking her head, Hannah pulled out of her daydream and back to the present with Michael and her new friends.

Jackie got into a conversation with Michael and Alex about basketball and a shared love for the game. All three were planning on joining the intramural basketball teams.

As the group left the dining hall, Michael asked Hannah, "So, what sessions are you going to tomorrow?"

Hannah shared the ones she was interested in, and he replied, "I think I will join you for those."

"Okay," Hannah smiled without knowing what else to say.

Michael and Alex walked the girls part way back to the dorm before waving goodbye then heading to their own apartment across the street.

Michael's glance lingered on Hannah, causing her to blush again. Even though she wanted to get to know him, her inward nature wasn't quite sure what to do when he gave her actual attention.

As they walked away, Rhonda exclaimed rather loudly, "I think he likes you, Hannah!"

Other people were looking in their direction, so Hannah ducked her head in embarrassment as she said, "Maybe."

"Girl, you're about to get you a man!" Rhonda bellowed.

Michelle looked at her and she said, "Do you mind not shouting that so loudly?" She noticed Hannah's embarrassment and was trying to help.

Rhonda glared in her direction, and she snarled, "Shut up! No one asked you!"

Waving a hand toward Hannah, Michelle said, "No, I won't shut up. You're so loud that you are embarrassing her and us!"

Rhonda's glare landed on Hannah, and she said, "Is that true? Am I embarrassing you?"

"Rhonda, it's no big deal." Hannah commented. "I don't even know if Michael likes me, so just let it go."

"Whatever," Rhonda growled and she rolled her eyes. Then, she stalked off in front of the other three girls.

When they got to their room, it almost seemed like Rhonda was going to slam the door in Hannah's face. However, her hand paused, and Hannah walked in after her.

After getting ready for bed, Hannah said, "Rhonda, how about we sit and talk a little before going to sleep. I want us to get to know each other better."

The look Rhonda gave Hannah was intense and filled with an anger Hannah couldn't describe. "If I embarrass you so much, why do you want to get to know me better?"

"I just think it might help us to understand each other better. Let me start." Hannah said. "I come from a small town, and I have an older sister and an older brother. My sister is so smart that I could not ever match her grades in school. My brother is a year older than me and he and I don't get along at all. Now, what about you?"

The rage cooled in Rhonda's eyes a bit and she said, "I'm an only child and I live in the southwest part of Houston. I lived with my mom, after my parents' divorce when I was little. She can be a bitch sometimes and she's angry with me a lot. My dad doesn't pay me much attention other than a few gifts at Christmas and on my birthday." The look on Rhonda's face was troubled.

"I'm really sorry, Rhonda." Hannah didn't really know what else to say to her.

Rhonda's gaze was filled with bitterness as she looked at Hannah and said, "Don't be. I don't need him in my life anyway. My mom is hard enough to live with and he would probably make it worse."

Hannah had been protected all of her life as the youngest of her family and she did not know many people with divorced parents. One of her high school friends came from a broken home and her mother never approved of their friendship. Thinking to herself, Hannah did realize that she got into the most trouble with that friend. Again, she was not sure how to respond to Rhonda, so she changed the subject.

"What made you want to go into music and performing?" Hannah asked. "I love to sing but it's hard for me to get up in front of people unless I'm with someone else or a group."

Rhonda's face changed to joy as she said, "I feel like a different person when I sing for people. It's as if I am living a different life, so that's my plan. I want to get as far away from home as possible when I make it as a famous singer!"

Their conversation was interrupted by the phone ringing. Rhonda answered and it was for her, so Hannah picked up her book to read a little before bed. She wanted to lay down and try to sleep, but Rhonda was extremely loud in her conversation. Hannah wondered if she even knew how loud she actually was. An hour later, she finally hung up and Hannah turned off her lamp. As she laid down, she heard Rhonda say, "Thanks, Hannah."

"You're welcome," Hannah whispered. She felt better and hoped that it was a start to a deeper relationship.

***

The next three days were spent in monotonous sessions, but Michael joined Hannah for many of them and she enjoyed getting to know him. Despite his reminders to himself to keep his distance and just be friends with her, Michael felt an inexplicable connection between them.

She learned that he had a younger sister while she told him about her older brother and sister. She also told him about her love for dogs and how she missed her dog. Her family had to put her down right before she came to college.

After their sessions were over, Hannah, Michael, Rhonda, Michelle, Jackie, Alex and another guy named Danny, ate their meals together. They were becoming fast friends.

As they were walking out of the dining room on Thursday evening, Michael asked, "Hannah, do you want to play some more ping pong?"

"Sure," Hannah said looking at him. "What about Rhonda and Alex?" But the other couple had walked off in the other direction. The four of them had played games the rest of the evenings.

Michael said, "It can just be a twosome this time if you're okay with that."

"Sure," Hannah agreed. They played for about a half hour and then they sat on one of the couches to hang out a while longer. Hannah was growing more and more comfortable with Michael as she got to know him better and he seemed to enjoy her company as well. She felt like someone with confidence when she was with him, and she didn't exactly understand why.

Hannah glanced over at a guy speaking quite loudly on the other side of the student center. "Oh no! It's Lenny!" Hannah complained. "He's a guy that I know from my hometown and he's coming this way."

It was hard not to miss the loud guy talking and joking as he made his way toward Hannah.

"He went to the church where my family goes and he thinks he has a crush on me," Hannah explained, "He saw me at the bookstore yesterday morning. And now he won't leave me alone!"

"Hannah," Lenny drawled as he approached her. "How about we go on a date tomorrow night, and have a French kiss!!" Lenny had a developmental delay and often talked with his volume up too high. He was awkward socially due to his condition.

Hannah's face turned red, and she rolled her eyes, as she thought of how to answer Lenny's insane remark. "Hey Lenny, it's good to see you," she answered him because she wanted to be polite to him despite her embarrassment.

"Hey, Lenny," said Michael in an easygoing voice. "Hannah has already agreed to go out with me tomorrow night. Sorry, buddy!"

Surprised, Hannah smiled at Michael and played along. "Sorry, Lenny," she said. "He asked right before you walked over here, and I told him yes."

"Okay," said Lenny, not seemingly bothered by the rejection. He walked over to a different area of the student center, talking brashly to the people sitting on the couches in that part of the room.

"Bye, Lenny," Hannah said as he walked the other direction. Then, glancing at Michael she said, "Thanks. I appreciate you covering for me so that I didn't have to answer".

"You're welcome," said Michael, "but I also meant it. I would like to go on a date with you tomorrow night. Are you interested?" Trying to remain casual, Michael prepared himself for Hannah to tell him no.

Excitement filled Hannah as she tamped it down to respond to him. Her voice was casual when she responded, "I'd like that." They had finished up their game, so Hannah told Michael she needed to head back.

"Let me walk with you," Michael said.

Hannah started shaking her head as she said, "You don't have to."

Smiling at her, Michael touched Hannah's forearm and he said, "I want to walk with you."

"Okay, thank you," Hannah replied as tingles shot through her from his hand on her arm. It was the first time he had touched her, and her heartbeat went a little haywire.

Feeling the same zing pass through him, Michael looked at Hannah and he said, "I guess I need your room number so that I can call you about tomorrow night."

Hannah was happy to share her information with him.

"Great!" he said as they arrived at the front of the dorm. Touching her arm again, he continued, "See you at six tomorrow."

Hannah smiled at him, and she said, "Okay and thank you for walking me back."

He politely waited for her to walk inside before turning to walk back to his place.

Chapter 4

The next day, nervousness overcame Hannah as she finished getting ready. Michael called a few moments ago to tell her he was on his way. She had gone on a few dates before, but this one was different, and she did not know why.

"Have an awesome time!" Rhonda encouraged. She was also getting ready to go out since it was Friday night, but Hannah did not know what her plans were.

"What are you doing tonight?" she asked.

"Oh, just hanging out with Jackie, Michelle, Alex and Danny at the student center," said Rhonda. "We are trying to figure out where to go and what to do! I'm hoping Alex and I can slip away alone for a little while."

"Okay, well, have fun." Hannah told her. The past few days had been normal with Rhonda without any angry episodes. They had been talking each night before bed, getting to know each other better. Hannah felt bad that Rhonda had such a terrible home life. One day she came in to hear her yelling angrily on the phone. Hannah assumed it was her mom and she immediately went next door to hang out with Jackie and Michelle to give her some space. However, Rhonda was slightly peeved to find Hannah in their room. When she asked

Hannah about it, she couldn't get too mad since Hannah was trying to respect her privacy. Another alarming action was when Hannah touched Rhonda on the arm as she tried to apologize. Rhonda immediately slapped the hand on her shoulder, scaring Hannah to death. She quickly learned not to ever touch her again.

The phone rang and she picked it up. It was Michael and he was waiting for her in the lobby. She grabbed her purse and walked out to meet him.

"Wow, you look amazing!" said Michael. Delight filled his eyes at seeing her and it put Hannah more at ease. She had on black slacks and a silky, blue blouse.

"You look great, too." she replied as butterflies danced in her stomach. Hannah was trying to sound as if she went on dates all the time, which she knew was silly. She was trying not to stare, but he was wearing a green button-down shirt, with acid-wash jeans. His legs looked amazing in those jeans!

Michael walked her to the car and opened the passenger door for her. Hannah had never had a date do that for her in the past and she swooned a bit at the gesture!

***

Dinner was fabulous. Michael took her to a local seafood restaurant and she enjoyed every part of it. She ordered shrimp, with a baked potato, and salad. Michael ordered the same thing except he ordered fries instead of the potato. The waiter also brought out delicious bread to go along with their food. Michael ordered dessert and they shared a hot fudge, brownie sundae, which also was amazing.

And, just as wonderful was their conversation. They talked as if they had known each other forever. Yet, it was great getting to know each other. Hannah told Michael more about her family. "My dad works for a lumber company and my mom is a teacher at the high school," she explained.

Michael told her about his parents and sister. "My dad works for a large company in Dallas and my mom is a secretary at the elementary school near where we live. Jenny, my sister, is two years younger than me and she will be a junior in high school."

As they talked together, Hannah's mind went past "swooning" to becoming smitten with Michael and he seemed to enjoy being with her as well. As they talked, shared and ate great food, both of them leaned closer to each other as their interest continued to grow.

Michael paid the waiter, and as they walked out, he cleverly reached for Hannah's hand. Her heart jumped, and she was even more smitten as he intertwined their fingers.

He opened the car door for her again, having to release her hand. However, after he started the car, he reached for her hand again and he held it the entire drive back to her dorm.

Michael drove up to her dorm and walked around to open the car door for her. As he did, Hannah saw Rhonda sitting on the front porch talking to Alex. They were laughing and flirting with each other. At one point, Alex reached over and kissed Rhonda, which shocked Hannah completely. It seemed a bit soon for that in her mind.

"Thank you! I had a great time!" Hannah gushed.

"I did too," Michael said, glancing toward Rhonda and Alex and looking back at Hannah. "Do you want to go out again tomorrow night?"

"I'd like that." Hannah said before she turned to go inside. However, Michael took her hand again and he pulled her back to him. She couldn't breathe as he leaned toward her. Her heart was thundering so loudly that she was sure that he could hear it! Hannah wasn't sure if he was going to kiss her and when he kissed her cheek, she couldn't help but feel disappointment.

Michael pulled back, smiling and said, "See you tomorrow night!"

"Okay," Hannah responded as she floated toward the door.

"Oh my gosh." Rhonda was right next to her swooning. "He looked like he totally wanted to kiss you goodnight. He just chickened out and kissed your cheek instead!" Rhonda's voice was two levels too high as she said those words and Hannah blushed in embarrassment. Other people were looking their way again.

Hannah couldn't respond, so she just looked at Rhonda and smiled.

"I got some kissing action of my own!" Rhonda was gloating as Hannah responded, "Yes, I noticed that."

Ignoring Rhonda's incessant chatter, Hannah felt light and airy as she took a shower and got ready for bed. As she was getting into bed, the phone rang and it was Michael!

"I just wanted to talk to you again," he said in a low voice.

Hannah's heart leapt, and she did a little dance since he couldn't see her through the phone. She repeated what a great time she had that evening. They talked for another hour until both began to get sleepy.

At one point, Rhonda came out of the bathroom, and she said, "Is that Michael?" Of course, she asked loudly and made ridiculous kissy sounds, causing Hannah to cover the receiver of the phone until she passed by. They finally said good night and Hannah was smiling as she hung up the phone.

After hanging up, she commented, "Can you please not do that when I am on the phone with Michael?" Hannah didn't think her comment was offensive at all, but all of a sudden Rhonda whirled around with a crazed look on her face.

"What did you just say to me?" she snarled. She advanced toward Hannah in a threatening manner causing Hannah to cower in fear. Her brother had been physical with her in the past, which was why she detested him so much, but this was completely different!

"Rhonda, I didn't mean to upset you. I don't want you doing that when I am on the phone with Michael," Hannah tried to answer in a calm voice, but Rhonda's facial expression did not change.

Rhonda growled, "You stupid bitch, I can say and do anything that I want!" She took another threatening step toward Hannah.

With fear in her voice, Hannah said, "I need to go to the bathroom." She darted into the bathroom and locked the door as Rhonda pounded on it as she shouted at Hannah.

Hannah knocked on the adjoining door and Michelle opened it with a look of concern. "Hannah, what is going on?"

With tears in her eyes, Hannah said, "Can I sleep in here tonight? Rhonda got mad at me, and I was afraid she was going to hit me!"

Jackie ran to lock the door leading into the hallway as she heard Rhonda's shouts in the hallway. "Come over here," she said, guiding Hannah toward her bed.

"Fine! Just stay out!" Rhonda bellowed and they heard the hallway door shut and lock.

"What is wrong with her?" Michelle criticized.

"I don't know," Hannah whispered. "I asked her not to make comments while I was on the phone with Michael, and she became enraged after I said that! I thought she was going to hit me!"

"That seems like a valid request. You're staying in here tonight, that's for sure," Michelle said. "I'm starting to think that she is a little crazy!"

With frustration in her voice, Hannah said, "I've tried to be nice and get to know her, but she just snapped."

Jackie shook her head and said, "It seems like she has a Jekyll and Hyde personality!"

"I wish I could get my pillow and blanket, but I'm afraid to go back in there! I can sleep on your floor!" Hannah said the words in a shaky voice.

"Hannah, you are not sleeping on the floor!" Jackie said.

"Come over here and you can share with me," Michelle commented. She scooted against the wall to make room for Hannah. It was a snug fit, but she drew comfort from Michelle being right next to her at the moment.

The three girls talked for a couple more hours until Hannah's heart rate slowed, and she began to get drowsy. Jackie switched off her lamp and they fell asleep. In spite of the horrible incident with Rhonda, Hannah fell asleep smiling as she thought about her time with Michael.

***

After calling Hannah, Michael hung up the phone, smiling to himself. He was beginning to think that she was amazing, and he found himself wanting to go out again, which is why he asked her out the next night. When he kissed her cheek, he was amazed at her soft skin. He lost his mind a little when she moved her cheek like she wanted him to kiss her on the lips. His last girlfriend was a selfish human being and he hated kissing her.

He swiftly pushed down guilty feelings of what his mother would say to him.

Chapter 5

The next morning, Hannah was surprised that she had slept so well after the incident with Rhonda. Thankfully, it was Saturday and regular classes began on Monday. Next Friday was a dance in celebration of becoming true college freshmen.

"Oh, my God!" Rhonda shouted from next door. "How long does it take to finish taking a shower?" She banged again and shouted. "You better not have used all of the hot water!"

Jackie was in there at the moment. Hannah knew that eventually she needed to go next door so that she could also get ready. She didn't exactly know when that would happen.

The bathroom door slammed open. "Here you go!" said Jackie in a sarcastic voice. "So sorry that I took so much time. Although, it was only a few minutes." After letting Rhonda in, she made sure to lock her entrance to their room just in case she was still angry at Hannah. Their bathroom doors had locks on both sides, which was a convenience.

"Thanks," said Rhonda in a voice that belied her attitude just minutes before. It was also as if the threatening stance toward Hannah the night before had never happened.

It made Hannah wonder if it was safe for her to go back in there. She voiced it and Michelle suggested, "Maybe you should wait and just hang out here for a while. You can borrow some of my clothes so we can go to breakfast."

"What if Rhonda wants to eat with us?" Hannah asked.

"Hmm..." Jackie answered. "Maybe we need to go out for breakfast."

Comforted by her friends, Hannah said, "That's great, but somehow I need to get my purse from there before we go."

"You can pay us back," Michelle said.

The three girls drove to a diner in the small town and they enjoyed the kind of breakfast that Hannah's mom made every Saturday morning which added comfort.

***

The rest of the morning, Hannah, Jackie and Michelle were laying around and listening to music. Hannah was telling them about her date with Michael, but actually she was afraid to go back to her room with Rhonda after last night. Rhonda had been out when they came back from breakfast, so Hannah dashed in there quickly to grab some things, her purse, her pillow, blanket and book, just in case she was locked out again. She also moved all of her toiletries and make-up items into the bathroom just in case.

"You and Michael seem to be getting quite close!" Jackie said in a teasing voice. "Are we going to have to start seeing unnecessary public displays?"

"I don't know what you are talking about!" Hannah replied in a saucy voice.

All of a sudden, Rhonda appeared and shouted, "Why are all of you in here? The least you could have done was tell me where you were instead of leaving me out!!"

"Okay, sorry" said Michelle in a tone lacking confidence. "We weren't trying to leave you out." As she spoke, her tone became more impatient. "You know," she said. "There is no need for you to speak to all of us so rudely! And to tell the truth, we are in here to avoid you! You were the one who locked Hannah out last night!"

Jackie and Hannah looked at each other in surprise. They were shocked that Michelle was standing up to Rhonda. Watching Rhonda's expression showed that she was not used to people talking to her in that manner either.

"What did you just say to me??" she asked in a deprecating tone. However, she did not advance toward Michelle as she had done to Hannah the night before.

"You heard me!" Michelle said, not backing down. Her body language and her tone said that she was not afraid of Rhonda, and she was not going to take her abuse lying down. "You tried to threaten Hannah last night, but you're not going to do it to me!"

After their comments on Rhonda's strange personality, she was off the charts.

Jackie tried speaking to her in a calm voice, "Why are you so angry with us and why were you so angry with Hannah? We would like for you to hang out with us but not if you're going to act like this."

Rhonda narrowed her eyes and said, "This is nothing but bullshit. I wouldn't hang out with you if I was paid a thousand dollars. You can take your attitudes and shove them! Come on, Hannah." she yelled as she went back to their room.

"Uh, I think I'm just going to stay here," Hannah told her as she was slightly nervous about going back into their room. "We were comparing our class schedules. I'll be back in a little while." Her insides were quivering as she was fearful of how Rhonda would react to her this time.

"If you want to hang out with these snobby bitches, be my guest! But just know that I see that you are truly not my friend!" yelled Rhonda and she slammed the bathroom door.

Hannah walked through to try and talk to Rhonda, but she had locked it. She said, "Rhonda, I know you've been mad at me, but you can't lock me out of my own room!"

"Go to hell!" bellowed Rhonda.

"You know, it's my room too!" yelled Hannah. She felt like she was trying to reason with a three-year-old and her low self-esteem made her wonder why Rhonda was so mad at her.

"Yeah well, you should have sided with me if you wanted back in," Rhonda called. "You're just like her."

"Like who?" Hannah yelled in a bewildered voice.

Rhonda broke down crying, and Hannah did not know what to do. She walked back into her friends' room.

After pulling her inside, Jackie locked their door. "You need to be careful with her," Jackie suggested. "She already looked like she might attack you last night. Who knows when she will do it again?"

Shaking all over from fear, Hannah said, "I know. How will I get back into my own room? Do I just keep staying with both of you? I need to get what I'm wearing for my date tonight!"

"Hey, we're here for you," said Michelle. "Leave it to us and we will turn you into a princess!"

"Are you sure? I don't want to put you out and I feel like I've invaded your space."

Michelle's voice was sarcastic when she said, "It's not like you can help it for the moment, but you're right that you do need to get back in at some point."

Quietly, they decided to call the supervisor of their dorm so that Hannah could get back into their room. Danah was the name of the dorm mom, and she didn't answer her phone.

***

Michelle was slightly shorter than Hannah, but her hair color and skin tone were similar. Jackie, on the other hand, was much taller than Hannah with bleached, blond hair who liked wearing a jersey and a baseball cap.

Michelle went to her closet and found a gorgeous pink top that Hannah could put on with her jeans. She handed her a towel so that Hannah could take a shower. Hannah showered quickly. Moving her toiletries into the bathroom was a smart move that morning and Michelle helped with her hair and makeup. Putting on the shared blouse, Hannah looked in the mirror. "Wow! This looks amazing!" she said. "Thanks, Michelle!!"

Pink definitely suited Hannah's coloring. Her eyes looked almost green from how it complimented her skin tone.

"No problem." replied Michelle. "Your hair and makeup look awesome, no thanks to yours truly!

"I can't thank you enough for all your help!" Hannah looked at her bare feet. "Now, for shoes. I can't go in my tennis shoes."

"Well, technically you could," Jackie argued. "But I guess you want to impress Michael." She went to her closet and pulled out a pair of black heels. "Here you can borrow these."

Hannah looked at the shoes in surprise and then she looked at her new friend.

"What!" said Jackie. "I have things to dress up in, but I just don't do it very often.

Hannah slipped them on her feet and she was surprised that they were only half a size larger. Jackie's height made her think that they would be too big.

"You look sensational!" Michelle pronounced as she looked at her handiwork in pride.

Hannah had called Michael from their room earlier that afternoon to tell him where she would be when he came to pick her up for their date, so she was not surprised when the phone rang.

"Go ahead and answer it," said Jackie in a joking manner. "We know it's your lover boy!!"

"You're crazy! And I mean that in a positive way!" laughed Hannah as she answered the phone.

"Have an amazing time!" Both girls told her.

"Thanks, I love you guys!" Hannah said as she left.

***

Hannah's heart fluttered at seeing Michael. He looked amazing in a navy, blue shirt and more acid-washed jeans. This time, he was wearing tennis shoes, but they looked brand new.

"Hey" he said as his eyes seized her from head to toe. It made Hannah feel all squishy inside the way he looked at her like that. She had never received much praise from a guy before. "You look amazing again! Are you ready?"

"Sure," said Hannah in a breathless voice, unable to stop the blush stealing over her face. "Where are we going?"

"Well, I thought we would get something to eat and then go see a movie. Does that sound okay?" he suggested.

"That sounds wonderful," Hannah gushed.

It took them about thirty minutes to drive to a town over to where there was a movie theater. The town with their university did not have one. Both Hannah and Michael talked easily about their day. Hannah even took the time to share the situation with Rhonda.

"She sounds really weird," Michael said. "I kind of got a strange vibe from her when you first introduced the two of you. It's why I didn't say anything to you originally because I thought the two of you were playing a joke on me."

"I would never do that to someone!" Hannah exclaimed as Michael glanced over at her and smiled, "I'm learning that about you. Then, he continued, "She sounds like she's got some problems."

"Yeah, I'm not sure what to do," Hannah replied. "I'm not sure she will even let me in my room and the supervisor wasn't there when we called earlier. I will have to call her again in the morning."

They pulled into the restaurant Michael had chosen. It was a pizza restaurant next to the movie theater.

"Does this sound good?" Michael questioned.

"I love pizza!" Hannah gushed. "Who doesn't?"

Michael walked over to her side of the car to open her door, and when he took her hand, he did not let go. They walked hand in hand into the restaurant and as they were walking inside, Hannah felt emotions she had never experienced before. Not having dated much in high school, there weren't opportunities for her to experience a deep relationship with a guy. She had observed friends in high school in similar relationships, but she never understood their feelings until this moment.

Supper was amazing again just like it had been the previous night. Hannah and Michael shared a pizza with breadsticks. Their conversation was just as natural as it was the previous night. Hannah could not believe how easily they were able to talk to one another. It was like she had known him all her life. They had similar interests in movies and music, their families had similar views in political and religious beliefs, and they both loved eighties music.

They left the restaurant and walked over to the theater since it was next to the restaurant. Michael paid for the movie and asked, "Do you want popcorn and a drink?"

"I would love some candy and a diet soda," said Hannah, unsure whether she should let him pay. "But I can buy my own."

"Nah, I have it," said Michael in a casual tone. He paid for their candy and drinks.

They walked into the theater and found a seat near the back.

As they got seated, Michael put his arm around Hannah and pulled her closer to him. Her heart went a little 'haywire' sitting so closely to him. She turned to look at him and found that he was gazing at her. Then, he leaned toward her and kissed her warmly on the lips. She was amazed at how soft his lips were, and if Hannah could read his mind, she would learn that he was thinking exactly the same thoughts about her lips. After he pulled back, she leaned against his side.

The movie was a comedy and Hannah enjoyed laughing with Michael.

After finishing their snacks, he leaned close and kissed her again and Hannah's insides turned to jelly as he lengthened the kiss, and he wrapped her closer with his arm. With his other hand, he reached up and caressed her cheek.

Finally, he pulled away and stared into her eyes. "Hannah Mathis" he whispered. "You are beautiful!"

"Thank you," Hannah said, and she felt her heart filling with an emotion that she couldn't identify. "And to think, I had to introduce myself to you first," she whispered back in a teasing voice.

"Boy, am I glad you did," Michael murmured as he continued rubbing his knuckles across her face.

The movie ended and he intertwined their hands, pulling her close as they left the theater. Opening the car door, he leaned in for one more kiss before allowing her to get in.

"I have an idea," he said. "Why don't you come and stay with me?"

"What?" Hannah exclaimed. Inappropriate thoughts immediately popped into her head, and she wasn't so sure about Michael after he asked that question.

"No, I'm serious! I live in an apartment across the street with Alex. You can come and sleep on the couch. I promise it's clean!" he said.

"I don't know..." said Hannah. "I don't have any clothes or any way of getting them unless Rhonda went out somewhere."

"Why don't we drive back to your dorm and you can see if she is there." Michael replied. "If she's not, grab some items and bring them to my place. And Hannah, it's only a place for you to sleep tonight. I promise not to do anything inappropriate. You can totally trust me!" In her heart, Hannah knew that she could.

"Okay, I guess we can go check," she answered. "I can tell Jackie and Michelle where I will be while I'm there."

Michael drove Hannah to her dorm. She walked inside and down the hall. Just as she had hoped, Rhonda was out somewhere. However, she had thrown some of Hannah's items on the floor in her rage.

Hannah's temper rose as she saw it, but fear filled her as well. Her temper won in the moment as she spoke to herself, "How dare she!

I didn't do anything wrong!" Pissed off, she quickly grabbed some things and packed a bag including her toothbrush and other toiletry items. As she was packing, she saw an open jar of peanut butter sitting on Rhonda's desk with crushed cracker crumbs.

Disgusted by the mess and feeling a bit rebellious, she grabbed the jar and threw it in the trash in the bathroom. She felt a bit better afterward, but she wondered if there would be repercussions from it. She made a note to herself to call the supervisor first thing in the morning before coming back.

When she was done, she knocked on the bathroom door.

"Well, you're back early!" Jackie exclaimed.

"I just came to pack some things. Michael asked me to spend the night at his apartment to give Rhonda and myself some space." Hannah said.

"Oh wow!" said Jackie, making weird expressions with her eyebrows.

"Oh stop!" said Hannah laughing and turning red. "It's not going to be like that! He's just letting me stay on the couch. By the way, let me grab my pillow and blanket."

Hannah ran back to their room and grabbed both items, stuffing them into her oversized bag.

"She left to go somewhere," Michelle replied, "and she yelled hateful words all the way down the hallway so that everyone could hear! I tell you, that girl is psycho! Thankfully, when we came back from eating in town, she was gone!"

"How about I call you in a little while with Michael's phone number?" asked Hannah. "That way you will know how to reach me."

"Sounds good," Michelle answered.

"And, have a great time," laughed Jackie, wagging her eyebrows up and down again.

Hannah left laughing at her friends.

***

Michael pulled up to his apartment and he pulled off the driveway to park to the side of the garage. Hannah noticed two other cars were there as well and she remembered him telling her that there was another apartment beside theirs. Hannah's heart fluttered for the millionth time as he walked around and opened her door. He also took her bag from the backseat and carried it inside for her.

Hannah was not sure what to expect, but she was surprised when she saw the inside, which consisted of a small kitchen, eating area and living room. Two bedrooms were down a short hallway along with a door that Hannah assumed was a bathroom. The room was sparsely furnished, with just a couch, a chair and a television stand, but it was extremely neat and in order. The kitchen counters were cleared off and the shelves to the side were neatly stacked with various food items.

"Come on in." Michael said as he shut the door behind them. "I try to keep things neat, but Alex does tend to leave some messes behind." The truth was that Michael was overly focused on having things clean because his house growing up was cluttered with things. His mom never got rid of anything and the junk drove him crazy!

"I love it," Hannah said as she smiled at him.

The walls were covered with posters from popular hair bands of the eighties. A VCR was below the TV. The shelf below was neatly lined with VHS tapes of Star Wars, and other various movies. It was definitely a guy's place!

"The bathroom is down the hall," said Michael. "Do you want to sit and watch another movie?"

"Sure," said Hannah. "But where is Alex? Will he be here soon?"

"He went out, but I'm not sure what he is doing or when he will be back. Go ahead and pick a movie that you want to watch."

Hannah knew that Michael did not have movies like Dirty Dancing or Top Gun, but she looked and she chose Karate Kid.

Michael slipped it into the VCR. "Do you want something to drink?" he asked.

"No, I'm fine right now," Hannah answered.

They sat together on the couch. Hannah slipped her shoes off onto the floor and tucked her feet under her. Michael slipped his arm around the back of the couch as she got comfortable, and they got lost in the movie that they had both seen several times.

Hannah opened her eyes and realized that she had fallen asleep. It took her a minute to realize where she was. She was at Michael's apartment, and they had fallen asleep watching a movie. She had been leaning against him and his arm was still curved loosely around her. Not wanting to wake him, Hannah slowly got up and went down the hall to the bathroom. When she came out, he was sitting up and the movie had been stopped. He had some sports game on, but Hannah had no idea what it was.

"Hey," he smiled. "Guess we fell asleep."

"Yeah," said Hannah sitting down next to him.

He grabbed her hand and pulled her closer. Hannah was unsure of what to do, but Michael touched her face and leaned in to kiss her. It was a magical moment as their lips pressed together caressing each other. Hannah kissed him back with enthusiasm. He deepened the kiss, and they pressed closer to one another growing breathless as the kiss continued on for a few more seconds. Shivers ran down Hannah's spine as he kissed her forehead, her jaw and her cheeks. She couldn't help sighing softly as his hands caressed her back.

Hannah had been kissed before and she had regrets of intimate relations with other guys, but none of those experiences had been anything like this! This was intoxicating! She couldn't pull away and she wasn't sure that she wanted to. Every kiss was sweet and tender, showing Hannah that Michael respected her and cared about her.

As they were deepening another kiss, they heard a key in the door. They both sprang apart to sit with space in between them.

"Hey guys!" Alex said as he came in the door. He had a silly smirk on his face like he knew exactly what they had been doing.

"Hey," Michael and Hannah replied together. Michael placed his arm back around the back of the couch and he grinned at Alex. "We were just watching a movie." Hannah knew her face was beet red, but she was relieved to see that Michael's face was also red.

"Yeah, sure!" replied Alex with a chuckle.

"Where have you been?" Hannah asked in an effort to divert the conversation even though she knew her red face was giving away what they had been doing.

"I was hanging out with Rhonda. We went to get some burgers and wound up sitting and talking in my car when I took her back to the dorm. Why are you here?" Alex asked.

Hannah knew that he was starting to like Rhonda and she was torn with what to tell him about what happened. She tried being nonchalant and saying, "She and I had a disagreement earlier. Michael invited me to stay here on the couch to give us a little space."

"Oh, okay," Alex answered without giving it another thought. He walked into the kitchen and grabbed a soda from the refrigerator. He didn't say anything else, so neither did Hannah.

Michael glanced at her in understanding that she was trying not to overshare with Alex. She could tell that he knew what she was thinking, and it was amazing how well he knew her after only being on two dates!

"Well, I guess I will get myself ready for bed," said Hannah. It was after midnight already because they had fallen asleep earlier. "Do you mind if I use the bathroom?"

"Go ahead, No problem," both guys said at the same time.

In the bathroom, she tried feeling guilty about what she and Michael were just doing, but she couldn't. It was amazing how she was feeling about it and it felt so natural. When she was with him, she didn't constantly doubt herself and she wondered about that.

She put on pajama pants and a T-shirt, still in her bra since she was staying in an apartment with guys. She brushed her teeth and opened the door. When she walked back down the hall, Michael had set a blanket and pillow on the couch for her, and she was grateful even though she had brought her own with her.

"Well, good night!" he said and he leaned in and gave her another gentle kiss before going into the bathroom and turning on the shower.

Hannah lay down with a smile on her face and a dreamy expression. Alex was nowhere to be seen, but the other bedroom door was closed.

Hannah didn't think she would fall asleep so easily, but she drifted off with thoughts of Michael.

Chapter 6

The next morning, Hannah woke up completely disoriented. Then, it came to her that she had spent the night at Michael's apartment. She was off-track because it was Sunday, and she usually went to church with her family. She stretched and turned onto her back, and she heard the shower running down the hall. The other bedroom door opened and Michael walked out in a T-shirt and sweatpants. He looked wonderful even though he had just woken up and her heart rate went into double-time.

"Good morning" he smiled as he walked to the couch and sat beside her.

"Morning," Hannah replied as she smiled back.

Michael reached over and kissed her sweetly. "Are you hungry?" he asked. "We have some cereal here, or we can walk to the dining hall for breakfast."

"Let's walk there," Hannah suggested. "I don't want to eat up your food. After that, I need to call Danah again."

"You can use our phone to call. Give me five minutes to get dressed," Michael said as he squeezed her arm standing up.

"Thanks! I'll change as soon as I can get into the bathroom," Hannah answered. Just as she spoke, the door opened. Alex quickly walked out and into his room.

"Perfect timing!" she said.

After getting ready, Hannah and Michael walked down the sidewalk and crossed the street. Once on campus, they walked quickly to the dining hall and got in line. Michael held her hand the entire time. They got their food and moved to a table to eat with Jackie and Michelle. Later, Michael saw Alex in line, and he called him over to eat with them. "Alex, over here!" he yelled.

Alex walked that way and as he was walking, Rhonda joined him. "Hey, guys!" he said. "Thanks for inviting us to eat with you!." He looked at her and asked, "Is this okay?" He was obviously ignorant of Rhonda and her mood swings. Hannah wondered how long it would take for her to go off on him.

"Sure" smiled Rhonda. It was amazing at how she looked like everything was normal.

Hannah, Jackie and Michelle looked at each other not sure what to do or think.

"No problem" Michael said as he glanced Hannah's way.

Alex pulled out a chair for Rhonda, and she smiled at him. "Thanks!" she told him. She turned toward the girls and said, "Hey y'all! Hannah, where were you last night?" She was acting as if none of the events the day before had happened.

"Umm..., I stayed at Michael's. I went and grabbed some things while you were out." She looked at Jackie and Michelle again as she said it.

"Oh, okay," said Rhonda. "Next time, leave me a note or something."

The group began talking about classes starting the next day, and the dance on Friday night. Hannah pondered Rhonda and her strange behavior. She had never met someone with wild mood swings like she had witnessed with Rhonda. It was clear that there was something off about her. She knew that she couldn't remain her roommate, but she wasn't sure how to go about changing it.

***

"Are you alright?" Michael asked as they walked away from the table.

"Yes, I'm fine. I'm not sure what to do about this situation. Rhonda got so upset and it's almost as if she doesn't remember! I've never met anyone like her." Hannah looked at Michael and she was so glad to see the understanding and caring in his eyes.

Michael suggested, "Maybe you should walk and see if she is there. We can go back and get your things later."

Smiling up at him, Hannah said, "Thanks. That's great advice."

"Sure, thing," Michael answered, reaching up to push her hair behind her ear. "But first..." He pulled her into a small part of the student center that was secluded. He reached for her face and cupped it before his lips touched hers. She felt complete satisfaction as he kissed her thoroughly. "I just couldn't wait any longer," he said, smiling down at her. "I needed another kiss."

"I'm certainly not complaining" she murmured as his lips touched hers again. It was hard for her to think straight when he kissed her because his lips were hypnotizing. As they pulled back, he hugged her close for a moment. They walked hand-in-hand to Hannah's dorm.

"Hey, ladies!" Hannah called as they noticed Jackie and Michelle going into the dorm. "I'm going to see if I can talk to Danah about Rhonda."

"We'll come with you. Too bad you can't just move in with us." Michelle replied. "If only we had one more bed!"

"That would be great," said Hannah. "I know that I can't keep living with her if she's going to freak and come after me for defending myself."

"You know that there are some rooms with three beds in them. It's definitely something to think about." Jackie piped in. "Like Michelle said, we would be fine if you moved in with us. And we will definitely vouch for you and be a witness to her craziness!"

The girls and Michael walked across the room to the supervisor's apartment. Unfortunately, with it being Sunday, Hannah was worried that she wouldn't be there.

"I'll wait for you over here," Michael said as he pointed to the couch and television.

"Thanks," Hannah waved and smiled at him. Jackie pinched her softly on her arm teasingly as she saw Hannah watching him as he walked away. Hannah pushed Jackie ahead of her as they went to knock on Danah's door, mouthing the word "stop" as her friends were laughing.

Fortunately, Danah was home, and she answered her door. Hannah wondered if it was because it was the first weekend after students moved in and she had to handle specific issues with their rooms.

Hannah, Jackie and Michelle talked with Danah for forty-five minutes. She suggested that the four of them sit down with Rhonda and communicate their feelings.

Hannah tried to explain that Rhonda acted as if nothing had happened, but Danah did not really listen to her. It also seemed like she wasn't taking her seriously. Danah talked about getting everyone together that evening and the girls agreed. As they walked out of her apartment, Hannah felt like it was still unresolved.

"Well, that didn't go like I hoped." commented Hannah.

"I think she's going to have to see Rhonda in the act of one of her "crazy spells" to understand what we are talking about." Jackie said. "Maybe she'll go nuts tonight."

They all moved over to the couches where Michael was watching a football game on the television.

"How did it go?" Michael asked.

"Not like we thought," Michelle answered for them. "Danah wants us all to sit down at seven tonight and talk out our feelings. We aren't sure if that will accomplish anything."

"Maybe Rhonda will be crazy with her." Michael answered.

"That's what we're hoping for!" Hannah said as she sat down beside him on the couch.

Jackie said, "We'll see the two of you later. I need to go call my parents and let them know that I'm still alive."

"I'm going to finish unpacking my last two boxes that I've tried to forget about," Michelle said. "See you later!"

Michael and Hannah waved at them, and he flipped the channel and found an old sit-com playing. Hannah moved closer beside him and lay back against the cushions as they watched the show. They weren't supposed to show public displays of affection in the girls' dorm, but Michael reached for her hand and moved it to where it couldn't be seen. Hannah's heart did flip flops when he did.

They sat and watched television together most of the afternoon, laughing and talking. The more that they talked, the more that they got to know one another.

Around five o'clock, Michael flipped off the television and he stood up. "I need to go back to my apartment to call my folks as well. After you meet with Danah, do you want to go and get an ice cream? I figured you might need to get away if it doesn't go well!"

Hannah smiled, "That sounds great." She couldn't stop herself from smiling when she talked to Michael. Sometimes she felt silly, but he made her feel complete. Underneath her happiness was the seed of doubt that she might mess things up in some way.

Michael looked behind them and he didn't see anyone or Danah. He leaned over and gave Hannah a soft kiss. "I'll see you later." And he left.

Hannah walked up to her room grinning. As she walked, she knew that she needed to call home as well. She hadn't spoken to her mom since before she left on Tuesday morning. Having to go back to work, her mother couldn't help her move in and Hannah knew that she was sad about it.

She opened her door, and she was relieved to have the room to herself. She dialed her parents' number and sat back to enjoy the conversation with them.

***

As Michael walked back, he thought about Hannah and how much he was coming to care for her. His plan of focusing on school was becoming less of a priority. As much as he liked Hannah, he wondered if it was the right thing for him to date her so much. Once school began, he would have to determine if going out with her would become too much of a distraction. In high school, he had tried to maintain a high grade point average and if he allowed that to slip, he felt like he would be letting his family down. Worrying that he would mess things up was a constant emotion he carried every day, and he didn't ever tell anyone the pressure he felt.

***

After dinner, Hannah, Jackie and Michelle walked back to their dorm to meet with Danah. Thankfully, they were able to relax and enjoy dinner with Michael and several other guys they met over the past week.

They knocked on Danah's door. When she opened it, they saw Rhonda sitting in her small living room.

Rhonda looked at them and she did not seem upset at all. "Hey guys!" she said. "Danah invited me to come and have a soda with her! What are you guys doing here?"

Hannah muttered, "Okay, great." Jackie and Michelle looked at each other, but they did not comment.

"Rhonda," Danah said, "Hannah, Jackie and Michelle have shared some concerns regarding some things that have happened in the past few days. They shared that you became very upset with them at one point and that you locked Hannah out of her room."

"Oh, my God!" Rhonda growled. "This again? Why can't you let this go?"

Danah spoke up for the others before they could comment. Her voice contained authority and firmness in what she said next. "Rhonda, I understand that there might be moments where you don't get along with the people living with you, but Hannah's parents are paying for her to stay in that room just as yours are paying for you. It's a part of her tuition. You can't lock her out again or I will have to inform your parents."

Rhonda had a seething look in her eyes, but she seemed to calm down when Danah mentioned contacting her parents.

"Okay, I'm sorry," she said to Hannah. "I was just mad, but I shouldn't have locked you out of your room."

Hannah smiled slightly and she said, "I want to say it's okay, but I really need to know why you got so mad at me telling you not to yell when I was having a phone conversation." Her saying those words to Rhonda startled her because it was completely out of character for her.

"I don't know," Rhonda replied. "Sometimes, when I get angry, it's hard for me to listen to what people are saying. I promise it won't happen again."

Hannah, Jackie and Michelle looked at each other and then at Rhonda, wondering if she was being truthful or if she was just saying it to please Danah.

She looked at them again before she addressed Rhonda, "Maybe we can start again. You and I seemed to do better when we were getting to know one another. Would you like to continue that? We could include Jackie and Michelle as well."

"That would be great!" Rhonda replied in a bubbly voice.

"It sounds like you are going to work this out!" Danah said.

Nodding their heads, all of them stood up and walked out of Danah's apartment.

After thanking Danah, Rhonda turned to Hannah, Jackie and Michelle. "Hey guys, Alex and I are going to get some ice cream. Do y'all want to come with us?"

All three girls nodded. They walked to their rooms to get money and Hannah called Michael to let him know that they were all going out as a group.

It turned out to be a nice time as Rhonda and Alex kept them laughing with their jokes and crazy antics. With the way she was acting now, it was almost as if she had two different personalities.

They had brought three cars,Hannah and Michael, Alex and Rhonda and the third car was Jackie, Michelle, and Danny. As they were getting ready to leave, Michael opened the car door for Hannah. His thoughtfulness overwhelmed her.

All of a sudden, they heard Rhonda yelling at Alex.

"Hey!" she shouted. "Why don't you open the door for me just like Michael did for Hannah? Or, are you just going to be a jerk?"

"Sorry, I was coming," Alex said in an uncertain tone as he moved around to open the door for her. "I didn't mean to offend you," he said as he opened her door. Rhonda slapped him on the upper arm, growling about how selfish he was.

With a shocked look on his face, Alex shut it and moved around to the other side of the car keeping his eyes downcast.

Once they were in the car, Michael spoke up with a comment. "Now I see what you are talking about! That girl is certifiable!"

"I know, right?" asked Hannah. "We need to warn Alex to stop seeing her!"

Michael reached for her hand as he was driving down the street back to the campus. "Do you want to wait to go back for a little while?" he asked. "We can go back to my place and watch another movie, or we can go and get some coffee or something."

"We need to find Alex first and talk to him and then I would love to come back with you," said Hannah. The truth was, she was beginning to not want their time together to end.

"Maybe he will be back in a little while and we can talk to him then." Michael commented.

***

Michael pulled into his driveway, but his car was the only one.

Hannah asked about the other cars in the driveway. Michael answered saying, "Danny and another guy live in the apartment beside us." He was holding her hand as they walked up to the door. He opened it and ushered her inside.

As soon as he shut the door and leaned against it, he said, "Come here," in a soft voice. He pulled her close to him and he touched her cheek, pulling her close for another amazing kiss. Hannah was beginning to feel captivated by his kisses!

She kissed him back, twining her hands up around his neck. The kiss became stronger and more intoxicating as they both opened their mouths to deepen the kiss. She inhaled a delighted breath as his tongue touched hers and his hands caressed up and down her back.

Michael pulled back and tugged her over to the couch. Cradling her face, he kissed her deeply again and his hands found their way up under her shirt.

His hands paused as he asked, "Is this okay?" She was affected deeply by how he treated her.

"Yes," she breathed, and he marveled at the silkiness of Hannah's skin as his hands rubbed her back and he kissed down her neck. Completely lost in each other, they kissed for a few more minutes and Hannah's hands went under Michael's shirt. The ringing of the phone brought Hannah back from the bliss of Michael's kisses.

"Michael, the phone is ringing." Her words were wispy as they came out because his hands moved around to her stomach, stopping below her bra.

"What?" he asked as he did not stop immediately.

"The phone. It's ringing," Hannah repeated.

He sat up and realized what she was saying. Giving her a final kiss, he adjusted his shirt to walk to the table where the cordless phone sat.

She heard him say, "Oh, hi Mom!"

Hannah immediately sat up and rearranged her top. He grinned at her wanting to laugh, but he restrained himself since it was his mom on the phone. She walked over to him, and she purposely drew her fingers down the front of his shirt, dipping underneath it, causing him to twitch.

Hannah laughed as she walked into the kitchen to get some water. She walked back to the sofa to sit down as she drank.

By the time he finished talking to his mom, it had gotten rather late.

"I guess I need to get back," Hannah said. "I need to make sure everything is ready for my first class tomorrow. It's going to be a busy week with the dance on Friday night."

Michael reached and kissed her again as he said, "Speaking of... do you want me to come and get you? We can go together."

Hannah smiled at him and said, "I'd like that!" As she stood to go, the door was unlocking. Alex walked in smiling broadly.

"Hey, guys," he said with a silly grin on his face. "Life is so great!"

Hannah was actually surprised considering how Rhonda had assaulted him earlier.

"What makes it so great?" Michael quipped at him.

"Rhonda agreed to be my date on Friday night," Alex replied, grinning broadly.

Hannah was gentle in saying. "Alex, I want to warn you to be careful with Rhonda. She threatened me the other day in my room and that's why I stayed here on the couch last night. And, she slapped you today!"

Shaking his head, Alex said, "She apologized. She said that she didn't mean to slap me and that she won't do it again."

"Please be careful with her," Michael warned. "She's gotten rough with you and Hannah. Personally, I don't trust her!"

"I think it will be fine," Alex said. "But if you are so worried, why don't the two of you double with us?"

Michael and Hannah nodded their heads, but they both had worried looks on their faces.

***

Michael drove Hannah back to the dorm. Her insides were quivering because she was scared to go back into her room. He came around to help her out of the passenger side and he took her hand to lead her around to the side of the porch. He took her hand and he noticed her trembling.

"Hannah, are you okay?" Concern for her filled his eyes and he squeezed her hand in a comforting manner.

With a shaky smile, Hannah said, "I'm a little nervous, but Jackie and Michelle are right next door. Maybe I will just sleep over there for now!"

Michael reached down to kiss Hannah gently. "Call me if you need me and you can come back over here again." He pulled back and continued by saying, "Hannah, I want to let you know that I don't usually kiss a girl this much when I go out on dates. But I feel a connection with you that I haven't felt before." He touched her cheek softly.

Looking into his eyes, Hannah said, "Michael, I've been amazed at how quickly you and I have bonded and I'm glad that you feel the same way."

"I hope you have a wonderful night. Remember to call if you need me!" he said, squeezing her hand.

"Thank you. I hope you do, too." Hannah replied. She turned to go, but he pulled her back for another soft kiss. Then, he said, "Good night, beautiful!"

Unable to control her blush, Hannah had to make herself tell him good night because she was speechless from his calling her that word. Never in her few years of dating did anyone call her beautiful. Her mind was in a daze as she walked inside.

Rhonda was hanging up the phone when she walked into their room.

"Hey!" Rhonda said. "Alex just called and said we were double dating with you and Michael to the dance on Friday night! That's totally awesome!"

"Yeah, it will be fun." Hannah said to her as she gathered her items to go into the bathroom and shower. She wanted some time to herself to reflect on what Michael just said to her without Rhonda's constant jabbering. Plus, she was also apprehensive about staying in the room with her.

However, everything went smoothly for the rest of the night as they prepared for bed and went to sleep.

Chapter 7

The first full week of classes began, and Hannah settled into a routine with Michael and her friends. Nothing happened with Rhonda that week.

Hannah had a very hard time sitting through her classes on Friday because she was elated about going to the dance with Michael. They had not seen each other much because their different majors were on different parts of the campus. Hannah spent the day in the English building while Michael was in the music building.

On Friday, she rushed from her last class back to her room. As she did, she could hear Rhonda yelling at the top of her lungs, but she could not make out the words. Afraid of what she was walking into, she knocked on her neighbors' door.

Jackie opened the door with a look on her face.

"What is happening?" Hannah asked in a soft voice. Although, it would not have mattered with how loudly Rhonda was screaming at someone.

"She's on the phone with someone. I think it's her mom or something." Michelle replied as she came out of the bathroom. She had just finished taking a shower.

"I need to get in there to get my dress and things to get ready," Hannah said with trepidation.

"I don't think she will notice right now. Just go through the bathroom and bring everything over here. You can get ready with us," Jackie said.

"Okay," Hannah replied. She quietly opened the door and walked to her closet. Rhonda was yelling and crying at this point.

"I hate you!" she cried. "I'm so glad that I am out of that house and not living with you anymore!" And she slammed the phone down. She flopped onto the bed as Hannah gathered everything she needed to take next door. She was trying to slip out unobtrusively.

"Where are you going?" Rhonda cried.

"Hey," Hannah said. "I was just going to get ready next door to give you some space since you seem to be upset."

"Oh, of course!" she yelled. "Go hang out with them and leave me out again."

Hannah didn't say anything as she walked across the room.

"Why don't you answer me?" Rhonda growled as she stood in the way of Hannah and the door.

Here we go again, Hannah thought. Quivering with a fear she had never experienced before, Hannah found herself trapped with Rhonda's eyes full of rage.

She knew she needed to do something in self-defense. With fire that she didn't feel, Hannah turned around and put her hand up between them. "You better not come any closer!" she yelled in a firm voice. "I understand you are upset over something, but you better not touch me! I am sorry for what you are going through, but you will NOT take it out on me!" Hannah was normally non-confrontational, and she was surprised at herself for being so assertive. It must have come from being picked on by her brother for many years.

She stood there, trembling, unsure of what Rhonda would do to her. She was proud of herself for taking a stand, but deep down, Hannah knew she was still a scared little girl and she had to push down the tears that wanted to come into her eyes.

Hearing her yelling, Jackie and Michelle stepped into the room. Feeling stronger from her friends being in there with her, Hannah pushed past Rhonda to stand next to them.

"Calm down!" said Michelle. "Hannah is coming in with us, so you need to back off and leave her alone. It's apparent that you need some space." With her arm around Hannah, Michelle walked the two of them into their bedroom.

"Fine, just stay over there!" Rhonda cried and she shut the bedroom door locking Hannah out just as she had done before. Then, with a whiney voice, she wailed, "Poor little Hannah!"

Throwing up her hands and rolling her eyes, Hannah said, "Oh my gosh, not again!! I am done rooming with her!"

With a gentle voice, Michelle hugged her and said, "Let's focus on getting ready. We can deal with her after the dance is over."

Hannah nodded, but she couldn't control the tears that sprang into her eyes. She allowed Michelle to lead her into the bathroom and wet a warm rag to wash her face. "We're here for you, friend. You don't have to deal with her alone," Michelle said in a sympathetic voice.

As Michelle helped her wash her face, they continued to hear Rhonda repeating, "Poor little Hannah! You think everything is about you!" Then, she cried, "I hate you!"

"What am I going to do?" Hannah asked as her eyes widened. "Michael and I are going with her and Alex to the dance."

Jackie replied, "Based on how quickly she gets over her rants from the times before, she might be fine by then."

As Rhonda continued to chant, Hannah said, "It doesn't sound like she's getting over this one." She tried to push it from her mind and focus on getting ready. She had brought a beautiful blue dress for the dance. Her mom had taken her shopping before she moved to college, and she was so excited to wear it.

After Hannah got herself together, she said, "I need to get my pillow and blanket because I'm not staying in there tonight!"

"You're not going in there alone," Jackie said.

She gently knocked on the bathroom door leading to their room. "Rhonda, I need to get something else."

There wasn't an answer. Knocking again, Hannah said, "Danah said you can't lock me out again, so I need you to open the door."

She heard the door unlock. Without saying a word, she and Jackie walked in and saw Rhonda face-down on her bed. Hannah didn't dare try speaking to her. She grabbed her pajamas and clothes to change into along with her pillow and blanket.

***

Jackie and Michelle left before Hannah but she walked down to the lobby with them. She helped take pictures with their dates, James and Danny. Hannah also decided to wait in the lobby because she was terrified to be next door by herself because she didn't know what Rhonda might do if she knew Hannah was in there alone.

Five minutes later, Michael walked in wearing a black suit with a dark blue tie. Hannah had told him what she was wearing, and his blue tie was the same color as her dress. Feeling faint from how wonderful he looked, she had to take a couple of deep breaths to calm her racing heart.

"Wow!" he breathed as he took her hands and he looked up and down her body. "You take my breath away, Hannah Mathis!"

He twirled her around in a circle to get a good look at her dress as it dipped in the back and showed off her slim waist. The dress flared out down past her knees but Michael was able to see her gorgeous calves in the silvery hose she had pulled over them.

He bent to give her a quick kiss on the lips and she could tell that he had a hard time pulling away from her.

"Thank you," Hannah said, unable to stop her blush. "You look amazing yourself!"

Michael had to restrain himself because she was so gorgeous. The bodice of her dress dipped slightly, and he was almost jealous that other guys would see that tiny bit of cleavage. Her hair was curled, framing her face as it fell past her shoulders. Her eyes were covered with a smoky, blue color on the lids. He pulled her closer, feeling possessive, when what he really wanted to do was to find a quiet place to make out with her again. Because of his errant thoughts, he didn't notice the anxiety in Hannah's eyes.

Alex walked in and whistled at Hannah. Michael tightened his hold, feeling jealous from Alex's whistle. Hannah smiled at them both, but it was as if she was making herself smile and her heart wasn't really into it. Michael noticed the worry in her eyes.

"Are you alright?" he asked softly with concern.

Hannah sighed and answered in soft words so that Alex would not overhear, "Rhonda was upset earlier with her mom. When I tried to leave and go next door, she blocked me like she was going to attack me again. Thankfully, Jackie and Michelle were there to help me get out of there but she locked me out again." Her eyes started filling as she told him what had happened. A sob came out as she explained the things Rhonda said behind the locked door.

An protectiveness Michael couldn't understand filled him and he pulled her close into a hug. The only other person he ever felt this way about was his younger sister, Jenny. His gut burned with rage at the thought of Hannah getting hurt by that crazy girl!

"Hey," Michael said against her ear, as he held her tight. "I'm sorry. Do you want to go by ourselves?"

Hannah relished his strong embrace. "Do you mind?" she asked as pulled back to look into his eyes. "I'm afraid to be alone with her anymore."

"Do I mind having you all to myself?" Michael smiled at Hannah. He leaned down in her ear and whispered, "I would rather the two of us go somewhere where I can properly kiss you and not get in trouble with chaperones!"

Hannah blushed because she had improper thoughts about him from how he looked. His mouth next to her ear was doing crazy things to her pulse and she shivered from the sensation. She leaned back and laughed, but the laugh was breathless with what Michael's close proximity was doing to her!

Looking down, she was fearful as she asked, "Is it possible for me to sleep on your couch again? I don't feel safe there anymore." Hannah worried about coming across as forward when she asked.

Tilting her chin up, Michael said, "I was just about to suggest that, so it won't be a problem. Let me go tell Alex," Michael said as he gave Hannah a kiss on the forehead and then he walked over to talk to Alex. Hannah watched him walk and she admired his strong back and legs.

From what Hannah could see, Alex didn't seem to mind. He was smiling and she could see that he was in an upbeat mood. She worried about him going with Rhonda, but she knew he wouldn't listen if she tried to stop him.

Michael walked back over to her and put his hand on her back. Then, they walked out the door to his car. "Alex said that they would take Rhonda's car, but I'm a bit nervous that he's going to be alone with her!"

Hannah nodded her head. "I don't want her going crazy on him, either. We will have to watch out for him when they get there. If she goes into her 'attack mode,' he can ride back with us."

"Sounds like a plan," Michael murmured as he opened Hannah's door for her. Once he climbed in, he said, "Thank goodness," as he reached over and gave Hannah a deep kiss. "I've been wanting to do that since I saw you!" he said as he ran his thumb down her cheek.

Hannah giggled, and she kissed him back. "I am not complaining one bit." She couldn't help but shiver in anticipation of the evening.

***

A few minutes later, they walked into the campus ballroom where the dance was being held. The lights were low and there was loud music playing. Michael had his arm around Hannah's waist as they walked to the table where Jackie, Michelle and their dates were sitting. "Can we sit with y'all?" he asked. They motioned to the other chairs. "We saved them for the two of you," Michelle answered for the group.

They sat and talked for a few minutes until the dean of students came to the podium to announce that dinner was ready. They walked to the buffet line, enjoying their time together. Alex and Rhonda entered the room, and Michael pulled Hannah protectively in front of him, with his chest against her back, as they waited. His arms were around her waist, and she appreciated the feeling of his strong arms. Still concerned for Alex, he watched them.

Alex and Rhonda sat with another group of friends at the table next to them. They walked and joined the line a few people behind Michael and Hannah. Rhonda was laughing and flirting with Alex and she no longer seemed upset.

Dinner was delicious as Hannah's table enjoyed the meal. As soon as she put her spoon back onto her plate, Michael reached for her hand to pull her out onto the dance floor. The band was playing an upbeat song at the moment, so they laughed and enjoyed the dance near Jackie, Michelle and their dates. A slight frown came over Michael's face as he saw Alex and Rhonda dancing nearby.

The band moved into a slower ballad. Michael pulled Hannah against him, and she slid her arms around his neck. He rested his head on top of hers as she put her head on his chest. He was right at six feet, so she was able to hear his heart beating as they swayed to the music together. She felt completely safe with him, which is why she was not afraid of the thought of becoming more intimate with him.

Michael continued holding Hannah close and he was amazed at how deep his feelings were for her in just a week and the thought terrified him. He had never been in love or told another girl that he loved her. He told himself not to say anything yet, but he loved how she snuggled up to him every time that they embraced. He was not a *"macho"* kind of guy, but he enjoyed how she made him feel like a man.

Swaying together for a few moments, he pulled back and rubbed his hands up her back. He reached down and kissed her softly but quickly, mindful of the chaperones who might not want to see public displays of affection. Hannah melted against him, and he was amazed at how she reacted to him.

He lifted his head and gazed deeply into her eyes. "Hannah Mathis," he murmured. "I know we have just started going out, but I think

I am falling in love with you." He surprised himself by saying that so soon and he couldn't believe that he allowed the words to come out of his mouth after he just told himself not to tell her.

"Michael..." Hannah breathed. "I can't believe how much I am coming to care for you, too. I've never felt this way about anyone!"

Her words terrified him, but he didn't think about it as he looked around before he leaned in again to kiss her slowly and leisurely. By the time he pulled away, both of them were breathless. The song changed to another slow ballad. Michael and Hannah did not even notice as they were so caught up with each other. She laid her head against his chest comforted by his warmth. He kissed the top of her head and moved one hand to the back of her neck under her soft hair as they continued moving to the music.

The song ended and they walked back to their table. As they did, they noticed shouting and a commotion nearby. It was Rhonda and Alex. Alex was looking mortified along with a confused look as she was yelling at him.

"I don't understand you!" Rhonda shouted. "All I wanted was for you to go and get me some punch like a gentleman! What is wrong with you??"

"I'm sorry," Alex said, looking around in embarrassment. "I asked you a little while ago and you didn't want any. I didn't realize that you had changed your mind, but I will get you some now." He started walking away.

Rhonda growled much like she did the time that Hannah tried to wake her up from taking a nap. "Just forget it. You're such a jerk!!" she said, as she slapped his face and then she pushed him away from her. Several chaperones were walking in their direction. With a shocked expression, Alex looked around at everyone staring at him and he walked out the door to escape.

Michael squeezed Hannah's arm and said, "Give me a minute to see if he's okay."

"Sure," Hannah replied, looking at Jackie and Michelle. "Go talk to him, it's fine!" She felt bad for Alex, and she knew that Rhonda had humiliated him.

"Well, the crazy is starting to come out more and more!" commented Michelle. "At least others are seeing it now."

The chaperones had pulled Rhonda to the side and were talking to her. Apparently, she was being kicked out of the dance because she was yelling at them as they escorted her to the door.

Hannah didn't dare go anywhere near her, but she saw the wild expression as Rhonda's eyes landed on her. Hair stood up on her arms as she saw complete hatred as Rhonda glared at her. As sheltered as Hannah had been in her life, she had never met any type of person like Rhonda. All she knew was safety and security, but that had changed since meeting this roommate of hers. Part of her wondered if she made a stupid mistake by rooming with her in the first place and that this was her fault.

She saw Alex walk back in and the chaperones pulled him aside to question him about what had happened. Hannah was afraid he would be kicked out as well and she was happy to see Michael standing beside him in support. After Michael also spoke to the adults, both of them walked back to their table. Alex had his hands stuffed in his pockets and his shoulders were hunched as he sat down beside Danny and James. Hannah could see a welt on his face from where Rhonda had slapped him. Michael said something to him, and he nodded his head with a grateful expression toward his roommate.

Hannah smiled at him as he sat down. "How's Alex?" she whispered.

"He was very confused. I finally told him what has been happening with you, Jackie and Michelle." Michael's eyes were filled with concern for his friend and Hannah also saw anger in them.

"I'm so sorry that she treated him so hatefully." Hannah commented, but she refrained from telling Michael about the look Rhonda gave her a minute ago. She was continuing to question herself wondering if she brought this on all of them by befriending Rhonda.

A song came on and Danny said, "Hey, let's go dance!"

Alex, Michael and Hannah didn't really want to, but their friends persuaded them to join them. It was a nice diversion from the altercation that had just occurred and they wound up enjoying it.

Much later, Hannah, Michael, and Alex walked outside after the dance ended. Michael said, "Alex, Hannah is coming over to stay again tonight because Rhonda also cornered her in their room earlier."

With a dejected walk, Alex said, "Sure, no problem." They walked to Michael's car, and he opened Hannah's side for her before driving the three of them back to their place.

Wanting to ease the rejection he felt, Hannah said, "Alex, I am so sorry for what Rhonda did to you tonight. I'm sorry I didn't try to convince you sooner that she is crazy!"

"You did try," Alex said. "But I didn't want to hear it because I really liked her." Shaking his head, he moaned, "Man, was I stupid!"

Michael said, "Quit beating yourself up! Sometimes it's hard for us to see someone's true nature."

Alex gave a small smile and said, "I know. I just need some time to process it. If you don't mind, I'm going home to stay with my mom for the night. The drive will give me some time to think."

Both Hannah and Michael nodded their heads and Hannah said, "Let us know if we can do anything to help."

"Thanks, Hannah," Alex said as he walked into his room. Ten minutes later he came out wearing jeans and a T-shirt while carrying an overnight bag. He said, "See you guys on Monday!" Then he walked to his car and drove off.

Michael took Hannah's hand entwining their fingers and they walked to the couch.

Chapter 8

"**I** hope he will be okay." Michael commented softly.

"Me too," Hannah said as she looked at Michael. Her nerves were on edge, but he pulled her against him in a comforting hug which eased her nervousness. She felt his voice vibrate in his chest as he said, "Just letting you know that I'm kind of nervous with you right now."

Breathing out in relief, Hannah pulled back and looked up at his face, "I was just feeling the same way."

"Do you want to just sit together and watch a movie?" Michael asked.

"Yes," Hannah replied as relief swept over her. "But, do you mind if I change clothes?" She had brought a bag of clothes to change into because she wasn't sure what they were going to be doing after the dance was over.

"Hmmm..." teased Michael as he smiled down at her. "You look so hot in that dress that I'm not sure if I want you changing out of it!"

Hannah laughed as she walked to the bathroom. Changing into some sweat-pants and a T-shirt, she opened the bathroom door and his bedroom door opened at the same time.

"Fancy seeing you here!" he joked as he walked with her into the living room. He had changed clothes as well. "I must say that you look pretty hot in sweatpants, too!"

Hannah laughed and wiggled her eyebrows up and down, "You do, too!" Chuckling, Michael put a movie into the video cassette player, and he went into the kitchen to grab them a couple of drinks before he joined Hannah on the couch. Sitting close to her, he pulled her into his embrace. However, it was loose and relaxed. Hannah leaned back against his chest enjoying his arms around her as the movie started. Halfway through, she turned so that she could look up at Michael's face.

He was already looking at her and his face became serious as he gazed into her eyes. He reached down and softly touched his lips to hers. She leaned up to kiss him back, sighing softly as his kiss grew deeper and more intense. She twisted her body and her head to get a better angle to kiss him. It was hard not to notice that she was practically lying in his lap. He turned them both to where they were laying side by side, facing each other. As he moved, he continued caressing her lips and the kiss deepened. The movie continued, but they were too caught up in their kissing.

Finally, he pulled back and looked in Hannah's eyes. He said, "I don't want to pressure you into anything. I know I told you I was nervous earlier and you said the same. Are you okay with this or are we moving too fast?"

"I want to be with you, too." Hannah murmured softly. "But, I do feel a little nervous to tell you the truth. I don't have a lot of experience with this."

Michael rubbed his hands up and down her arms as he kissed her again. "How about we go as far as you are comfortable with going?"

Hannah reached up and caressed his face as she looked at him and said, "Thank you for thinking about my feelings. You are always such a gentleman with me!"

"Hannah, you can count on me to take care of you." Surprised at his own comment, Michael was starting to realize how special Hannah was becoming to him.

Hannah knew that he was not just saying a line to get her to sleep with him. She noticed that his eyes were cobalt blue as they were filled with sincerity, and she felt cherished in the way he was holding her and looking deeply into her eyes.

"Do you want to go into my room or are you more comfortable out here?" Michael asked. As he questioned her, he was giving her soft kisses down the side of her face. He softly nibbled on her ear as his mouth moved to the sensitive part of her neck and she shivered.

"Yes," Hannah mumbled as she was experiencing sensations that she had not ever felt before.

Michael sat up and then he stood. Surprising her, he carefully lifted Hannah into his arms, causing her to yelp and say, "What are you doing?" Then, he carried her into his room, shut the door and turned the lock. "Wait just a minute," he said, putting her on his bed in order to walk over to his dresser. He lifted a box of condoms out of his drawer and set them on the table beside his bed. "I have these in case we want to go all the way."

Michael's bed was a double, and Hannah was not surprised that it was made neatly. She was amazed at how neat and tidy Michael was compared to her brother (and even her sister).

He walked over to her and cradled her face as he leaned to kiss her again. When her mouth opened, his tongue dipped inside as one hand continued down her neck to the bottom of her shirt. He leaned back one more time and asked if she was comfortable with what they were doing. Her answer was to reach up his shirt to rub his back.

Smiling against her mouth, he reached and pulled her shirt over her head. He breathed deeply at seeing the beautiful satin bra that Hannah had on. It was the same color as the dress she wore. He touched the smooth feeling of the material and gazed into her gorgeous, hazel eyes. His hand rubbed the cup of her bra over her breast causing her nipple to harden. He dipped his hand into the cup of the bra and felt her soft breast which caused her to inhale sharply. "You're so beautiful," he breathed as his lips found hers again.

She immediately began kissing him harder and faster in response to his soft touches on her breast. Hannah surprised herself as she pulled his shirt over his head. She also unclasped her bra and let it fall to the floor.

Looking up at Michael's eyes, she leaned against him and her breasts rubbed against his chest. His breath caught at the sensation of her against him. "Hannah" he said as he moved his hands up over her breasts causing her nipples to harden even more. She gasped at the sensation with half-closed eyes.

Before they continued, Michael looked at Hannah and said, "We can stop if you are uncomfortable. I don't want to do anything else until I know you are ready."

Hannah gazed at him and said, "I like what we are doing now, but I'm still unsure about the next part. Are you okay with that?"

"Hannah, I want you to feel safe with me. You don't have to worry about me pushing you too hard in order to pressure you into something that you don't want." Michael had nothing but honesty on his face as Hannah gazed into his eyes. She took his hands and placed them back on her breasts. Then, her hands grazed up and down his chest.

Michael pulled them down side by side and kissed her passionately as his hands stroked over her breasts and down to her stomach. His hands drifted to her soft, silky back and around again. He couldn't get enough of her, and he wanted to touch her all over. Hannah moved her hands up his chest again and around to his back as they were both gasping with pleasure.

Michael kissed her cheeks, her lips and moved down to her neck. Finally, his mouth moved onto one of her breasts causing her to sigh in a glorious way. Michael was enthralled by the sounds she was making. He was mesmerized by her feminine manners and the protective feelings from earlier cascaded back through him.

Hannah surprised him by putting her hands into his pants and rubbing his butt as she kissed his neck and down his chest.

After they touched a while longer, Michael looked at her and said, "Hannah, I love you."

Her eyes welled up with tears and she breathed, "I love you, too" in response to him.

His eyes grew concerned at her tears and he brushed them away saying, "I didn't mean to make you cry."

"I'm crying because I am happy," Hannah said, smiling at him. "I came to school expecting to make friends and focus on my classes. But meeting you was a complete surprise. I've never had anyone treat me as wonderfully as you do and we've only known each other for two weeks."

Michael smiled back as he rubbed his hand down the soft skin of her back. "I feel as if I have known you forever. This caught me off-guard too but, I'm thankful that I found you."

Hannah buried her face in his neck as he pulled her close. He still smelled wonderful from the deodorant and after-shave he wore to the dance.

They lay together kissing for a while longer. Michael said, "I know you don't want to go all the way, but since you are staying over tonight, do you want to sleep in here instead of on the couch?"

Smiling into his eyes, Hannah said, "I would like that."

***

After preparing for bed, Michael pulled her against him again. It wasn't long before he heard Hannah's breathing change and he knew that she was asleep.

Michael knew he struggled with wanting everything to be perfect. He wanted everything to be clean and he always picked up everything so that it could go back into its proper place. He had even turned back his bed covers neatly before he climbed in each night. It came from growing up in a cluttered home where stuff was everywhere. As much as he loved and tried to obey his mother, she loved too much junk and it was all over the house. He knew it drove his dad crazy which is why Bill Davis spent most of his time in his well-organized garage.

This situation with Rhonda and her actions toward Alex and Hannah made him feel a little out of control. He wished he could quickly fix it, but he had no idea what to do because he had never met someone like her. His mother was controlling in her own way, and she did not allow him or his sister to go far from their house because she was always paranoid that something bad could happen to them. She also controlled how he spent time with his friends. He was allowed to go over to the houses of friends who only went to church with him. Therefore, Michael had never been exposed to people unlike him or his family. He wanted the situation with Rhonda resolved for the protection of his friends, but he didn't know how. As he thought about all of it while Hannah slept against him, it took him a while to fall asleep as he worried about her safety.

***

The next morning, Rhonda woke up remembering where she was and the events of the night before. The idiot chaperones had kicked her out of the dance. She wandered around the campus burning with rage at the unfairness from being made to leave. It wasn't her fault! The complete fault lay at the feet of one human being, Hannah Mathis. Nobody rejected Rhonda and got away with it.

After being escorted to the door, Rhonda continued wandering around until she saw people leaving the dance. The entire time, she thought about revenge on her roommate and how she could make her pay. Not paying attention to where she was going, she happened to glance across the street and she noticed something. Michael was helping Hannah out of the car and he led her inside a building. "Must be where he stays," she whispered to herself. Part of her wished she could march over there and tear Hannah's face off, but she restrained herself. A half hour later, she found herself back at the dorm with a plan in place. If Hannah thought she could get away with rejecting her, she had another thing coming! Smirking to herself, Rhonda couldn't wait until she could corner her roommate again.

***

Opening her eyes, Hannah woke up to an empty bed and she had to remind herself that she was at Michael's apartment. She walked into the kitchen to see Michael at the table drinking orange juice and studying.

Leaning against the doorjamb, Hannah said, "Good morning."

Looking up, Michael's face broke out into a smile. "Good morning!" he said. "How did you sleep?"

"Your bed is extremely comfortable," Hannah commented as she sat down across from him at the small table.

Continuing to smile at her, Michael said, "Can I take you out for breakfast?"

"We don't have to," Hannah commented in a moment of indecision which was something she did often. "We can just walk to the student center for breakfast."

Michael reached over and touched Hannah's cheek. "I thought it might be good for you to stay away in case Rhonda is in there. We can go to that little diner down the road."

Hannah said, "Okay, but I insist on paying for my own breakfast."

With a gentle look on his face, Michael said, "Please Hannah, let me pay for it. I can't do a whole lot to help with your situation with Rhonda, but I can pay for your breakfast."

With her eyes showing acceptance, Hannah said, "Give me a minute to change and clean up."

Once at the restaurant, Michael sat across from Hannah for a split second and then he commented, "This is silly." Hannah didn't quite follow what he meant as he stood and moved to her side. "Scoot over." Sitting beside her, he gave her a soft kiss, with his arm around her, and said, "This is much better."

Overwhelmed with what he just did, Hannah was speechless as she looked at the menu. She knew her face was beet red, and she kept her gaze down. Thankfully, the server came and took their order. Michael kept his arm around her during the entire time they ate, which Hannah wondered if it was difficult to eat with one hand. He kissed her head and her cheek a couple of times during their meal. Even though she was not familiar with such loving attention, the conversation was natural and she couldn't get enough of spending time with him. Her swooning went to a deeper level this morning.

As he was driving back, he commented, "So, what's your plan with Rhonda?"

"I need to try and find Danah to talk to her about what happened yesterday afternoon." She hadn't commented on Rhonda's evil look yet, but she knew that she couldn't hold it in any longer as terror was running through her. Looking down at her hands, she said, "I didn't mention that Rhonda looked at me in a threatening way as the chaperones made her leave last night."

"What do you mean, *a threatening way*?" Michael's voice grew hard as he asked. He touched Hannah's arm. "Hannah, why didn't you say this last night?" Anger filled him and he wished he could get in Rhonda's face and give her a piece of his mind! Thankfully, they were at the dorm, so he pulled into a parking space and parked before turning toward Hannah.

"I don't know," she said in a despondent tone. "I just wonder why she is so hateful to me and if I did anything to cause her to be so angry. Maybe this is all my fault." She honestly didn't mean to say those words out loud, but Michael brought out an honesty in her that made her want to bare her soul to him.

"Hannah, look at me," Michael urged and her gaze was pained as she looked up at him. "There is nothing you have done to cause her to become so angry. There's nothing Alex did, either. She has some problems that go beyond both of you. I think after talking to Danah, you need to stay with me at least another night. Alex won't be back until tomorrow, so please stay."

With her gaze lowered again, Hannah nodded her head and said, "I guess so if it won't put you out. I don't want to get in the way."

"Hannah, look at me," Michael repeated as he touched her face. "I don't know how to stop Rhonda because I've never met someone like her. As much as I want to defend you, being physical is probably not the best course of action. But, I can help you to stay safe. I want you to stay with me. It will put my mind at ease." Caressing her cheek, he continued by saying, "Do you really think I would think that you are in the way?" Gently smiling at her, he leaned and kissed her softly.

With a grateful expression, Hannah said, "Thank you. I appreciate all of your help."

They got out of the car and Michael walked with Hannah inside. "Give me a minute to find Jackie and Michelle."

"Please be careful," Michael said. "In case you run into her."

"I will," Hannah said. "I need to tell them that I'm staying with you again tonight in case my parents call."

Hannah walked inside and knocked on her friends' door. She wanted to get an idea of where Rhonda was at the moment before she let herself into her room.

Jackie opened the door. "Welcome back!" she said with sarcasm. "How was your night with your lover boy?"

Laughing, Hannah said, "We really did go to sleep and that was all." She wasn't going to share about their heavy kissing scene. It wasn't something Hannah wanted to talk about with anyone.

"The two of you make a cute couple," Michelle chimed in as she walked in from the bathroom. "I'm glad things are going so well for you both."

"Thanks. So...," Hannah asked in a questioning manner. "Have you heard from Rhonda? Alex left to go to his mom's to get away for the weekend."

"We heard her yelling as she went in last night," Jackie answered. "But, we heard the door open and close a little while ago, so she went somewhere."

"If she's out, I can get a shower and pack some more of my things. Then, I'm going to talk to Danah about moving out," Hannah commented. Her brow dipped with worry as she looked at her friends before saying, "Can I move some things in here? It would be temporary until I can move somewhere else."

"I was about to suggest that," Michelle said. "We can go with you to talk to Danah. Jackie and I would love it if we could get a room for three people. Would you be interested?"

"Yes," Hannah breathed. "As long as it's far away from her! Give me ten minutes to shower and move most of my things out of there. I don't want my stuff in your way, so I will put it over there." She pointed to the corner near one of the closets.

"Hannah, you will not be in our way! We want to room with you, and we'll help you with whatever you need," Jackie said.

Fearful of Rhonda's return, Hannah moved her things into her friends' room as quickly as she could, and she locked the bathroom door before taking her shower. Not knowing if she would come back, Hannah knew that a homecoming with Rhonda would become even more threatening than it already had after her hateful look last night. Chills ran over her with fear of what Rhonda might try to do.

Before they went with her, Hannah mentioned the look Rhonda gave her at the dance the night before. She wanted them to be aware of the threat Rhonda now was.

"What?!" Jackie and Michelle yelped the word at the same time.

"That bitch!" Michelle breathed. With rage in her eyes, she said, "You can't be alone with her ever again! Why don't you go ahead and move everything in here before we talk to Danah. Like Jackie said, we will help."

It took a few more minutes to empty out Hannah's drawers and closet. Hannah found a basket to hold her extra towels, sheets and comforter. She didn't care how she placed her things in baskets and tubs in her haste to get out before Rhonda returned. Once her side of the room was completely empty, Jackie made sure to lock their door and she even moved a chair in front of it. "We don't know what she might try next," she said. Chills ran over Hannah's spine again at the thought of what might happen once she found out they were gone. Deep down, she knew that the problem was not over and that Rhonda would threaten her again.

Walking out to the lobby, Hannah saw Michael and she held up her bag, "Can I put this into your car before we go and find Danah? Michelle called her while I was taking a shower and she's expecting us."

"I'll take care of it. You go on and talk to her." Michael took her overnight bag to walk it out to his car.

"Hey, it may take a while," Hannah said, detaining him. "If she lets us move out, we will do that as soon as we can. You can go back, and I can call you when we are finished."

"No problem," Michael said. "Just call and let me know." He hugged her before taking her bag out to his car.

***

Thankfully, Danah had been informed of Rhonda's behavior the night before. She had already had a face-to-face meeting with Rhonda and she called her parents. Hannah explained new information of what happened at the dance and she requested to move out of the room.

"I think that's a good idea," Danah agreed. "But I think I need to call your parents and tell them as well, especially if Rhonda is a threat to you at the moment."

Gritting her teeth at the thought and restraining herself from rolling her eyes, Hannah nodded reluctantly. "I understand," she said.

"There is a three bedroom on the opposite hallway from where both of your rooms are," Danah said. "You girls can move while I speak to your parents, Hannah. They will probably want to talk to you when we are finished, so don't go anywhere after you have moved everything."

"Yes," "We are interested," "Please show us," all three girls answered Danah at the same time.

Danah walked them to the room and gave them keys. Hannah, Michelle and Jackie went and began moving their things out. Thankfully, several girls in other rooms helped them get everything moved. It took about an hour and a half with the extra help. After seeing Rhonda's behavior the night before, the others in their hallway were happy to help get Hannah and her friends away from her. Most of them talked about their plan to steer clear of her in the future.

In a small way, Hannah wished she could be a fly on the wall when Rhonda found out that she was all by herself. However, she didn't want to risk getting anywhere near her ever again. The chill on her spine was becoming a constant emotion.

***

Rhonda was seething with rage! All three of them had moved out and away from her. Pushing down her own self-doubt and anxiety (stemming from constant rejection from her parents), she allowed her anger to grow. When she had come back into the room, she noticed

Hannah's belongings were missing. She felt as if steam was leaking out of her ears when Danah informed her of Hannah's move, and more than anything, she wanted to growl and argue with her dorm mom. Knowing that her mom was informed, she restrained herself. *I will find her,* Rhonda thought. *And, I will make her pay for rejecting me!*

***

After everything was moved into their new room, Hannah called Michael to tell him and to give him her new room number.

"Will you still come and stay with me tonight?" Michael asked.

Smiling, Hannah said, "I would like that. Honestly, I don't know if Rhonda will try to find where we moved. Danah said she called her parents, but I don't know if it will do anything to stop her threats."

Michael responded, "Then, it's settled for sure. For your safety, you will stay here one more night! Hannah, please be careful!"

Comforted by his care for her, she said, "I will."

Michael continued by saying, "I also wanted to ask if you would like to go to church with me tomorrow. I promised my mom that I would visit churches and start going."

"I told my parents the same thing. Yes, I would like to go with you," Hannah replied. Then she continued, "I hate that Danah called them because they are going to drive me crazy now!"

"Maybe it won't be too bad," Michael commented but he understood Hannah's complaints because his mother would be the same way. "My mom would be on her way up here if it was happening to me!"

His comment worried Hannah that she was exposing Michael to this threat. Would his mother hate her because of that?

"I have to call them before coming over there," she said. "They are old-fashioned and wouldn't approve of my staying with you. I will be there around five."

"My mom wouldn't approve either, so you come over when you can," Michael said in a comforting voice. "How about I order pizza and we watch another movie?"

"Sounds wonderful," Hannah answered, and Michael could hear the smile in her voice. "See you in a couple of hours."

***

"Where are they?" Hannah, Michelle and Jackie heard screaming down the hall and they knew it was Rhonda. They didn't dare open their door. "How dare they think they can leave me like that? Hannah Mathis, I hope you can hear me because this is not over!!"

Hannah had just finished telling her parents that everything would be fine and that they didn't need to come here to see her. She told them that Rhonda was not a problem anymore and that she was far away from her. Her dad said he would call the school tomorrow and lodge a formal complaint so that proper authorities knew that he was concerned about his daughter's safety. From the screaming in the hallway, she wasn't so sure anymore. She was thankful that her dad was calling, and she hoped that it would help solve this matter.

Jackie said, "We can't go anywhere until we know she's gone." Then, she picked up the phone to call Danah's room to alert her.

"Let me call Michael and tell him it will be a little later," Hannah said.

Michael's response was, "I'm coming back over to pick you up."

"Michael, I can drive myself," Hannah protested.

"Hannah, I know you can, but I don't want you in the parking lot by yourself in case she is somewhere around there." Michael's voice was filled with worry.

"Okay, I will call you, but can Jackie and Michelle come over as well? I don't want Rhonda doing anything to them, either." Hannah said. Michael agreed. Deep down, Hannah was also afraid that

Michael was being put in Rhonda's crosshairs and she wondered if they should even go over there.

***

An hour later, Hannah called Michael because it seemed like Rhonda was long gone. He said he was on the way and that he would call them when he was out front.

A knock was on the door and Michelle opened it to see Danah.

"I wanted to let all of you know that I am having Rhonda transferred to another dorm immediately. On Monday, I will speak to authorities about possibly kicking her out of school if her behavior continues to escalate. A couple of my resident assistants are staying with Rhonda to make sure that she is packing and they will also escort her out of the building. She seems to understand that her behavior will not be tolerated and I'm hoping this will help ease the situation. I understand your dad is calling the school, but I'm going to inform the police as well if anything else happens," Danah took a breath and Hannah saw slight fear in her eyes. "I just wanted to let you know. I've not ever had experience with someone like Rhonda and I hope we can all be safe now."

"Thank you," they each commented. However, Hannah could not shake the feeling that all was not well. She had a niggling feeling that it was not over yet, but she kept quiet. She looked at her two friends and she said, "Why don't the two of you pack your bags and come stay with me at Michael's. I know it will be fine for you to stay there. We can even go buy some snacks so that we don't eat all of his food."

Jackie and Michelle looked like they wanted to protest, but Hannah saw fear in their eyes as well. They nodded and went to pack.

Michael called as soon as Danah left, and they walked out to the front. Jackie and Michelle decided to follow in their own car so that they could go pick up some snacks. Hannah chipped in some of her money to help.

Once they got back, Michael ordered pizza and they distracted themselves by watching a movie. None of them said anything, but the underlying fear was still there.

***

How dare they make her leave her own room? The injustice of how Rhonda had been treated filled her and now her mother was on the way. With hands trembling from her wrath, she made herself take a breath. Now that the authorities of the school and her mother were involved, Rhonda knew she couldn't unleash her original plan on Hannah.

Two hours later, her mother's car pulled into the parking lot of the dorm. Rhonda had been sitting in the lobby waiting for her and contemplating a new way to destroy Hannah and her stupid friends.

Walking out, she pasted a fake smile on her face as her mother got out of her car. "Hey mom," she called.

Fury was in her mother's eyes and she said, "Don't think this is a social visit! How could you be so stupid and get kicked out of a dance as well as your dorm?"

Rhonda's constant feelings of guilt and not measuring up overcame her as her mother continued to berate her for her poor decisions.

Coming to stand in front of her with her hands clenched, Brenda James (used to be Stillman until her Dad divorced her) growled at her saying, "Look at me and explain what you were thinking!"

Shame washed over Rhonda and she didn't dare argue with her mother. Rhonda had grown up all of her life enduring her mother's rants and tantrums. Most of her ire had been taken out on Rhonda. The few times she tried to fight against the emotional abuse, her mother unleashed physical anger. It was the reason her father had left them.

As he walked out for the last time, he said, "You are crazy and I'm not putting up with it anymore." As a young girl, Rhonda didn't understand his leaving and she wondered what was wrong with her that he didn't take her with him to wherever he moved.

Coming back to the present, Rhonda was meek as she said, "I'm really sorry, Mom. I guess I got carried away."

"I have never been so embarrassed than when I was called by your dorm mom and other school authorities to tell me that my daughter was behaving this way! Now, I have to go and deal with it. And to top it off, your father was called." Her mother's voice turned from yelling to a wail as she began a pity party for herself.

Glancing around in embarrassment, Rhonda said, "Let's go in my room, Mom."

She led the way as her mother made crying sounds behind her.

Chapter 9

True to his word, Hannah's dad called the school to file a complaint about Rhonda's threatening behavior. Hannah heard that Rhonda's mother had been called to meet with school authorities and that Rhonda was on probation. If she harassed anyone else, Rhonda would be kicked out of school and the police would be contacted.

Sunday evening, Hannah, Jackie and Michelle went back to their room because they knew they couldn't stay at Michael's forever. The four of them had gone to church Sunday morning which helped take their minds off of the situation. Alex came back while they were still hanging out at the apartment, and they filled him in on what had happened. Disbelief filled his face and he looked at them and said, "I will vouch for all of you if something else happens. I had a long talk with my mentor this morning and I can see that I am not at fault for her actions and neither are any of you."

***

Rhonda's mother left the following day after meeting with Danah and other school authorities to apologize profusely for her daughter's behavior. She came across as a doting and caring parent but Rhonda knew she would face more outrage after this meeting.

Rhonda sat meekly by her mother's side when the dean of students asked, "Rhonda, do you have anything to say for yourself?"

Playing her own role in this false charade, she made her face look repentant as she said, "I am really sorry for my actions. I got angry and I didn't handle it very well. I promise it won't happen ever again!"

"I expect you to apologize to your roommate, suitemates, and the boy you slapped at the dance. And, if anything more happens, I will have no choice than to expel you from attending this university. Do you understand?" The dean's face was stern and direct as he awaited her response.

"Yes, sir. I will apologize and I won't ever do anything like that again." Rhonda repeated her apology.

The dean's face softened slightly as he said, "It's fine to get angry at times, but maybe you need help in how to handle it. I am going to assign you to a counselor in our free counseling center. They will give you the help that you need to learn anger management."

Rhonda's mother glared at her, then she looked at the dean and said, "She will be at every session, I can promise you that!"

An hour later, Brenda James looked at Rhonda and said, "This better not ever happen again, do you understand me?"

"Yes ma'am," Rhonda replied meekly, but she wanted to roll her eyes at the possibility of counseling. Having been in it much of her life, she knew how to fake her way through sessions.

Her mother looked at her and said, "One day you will thank me for being so hard on you. I will call you later this week." Then, she got into her car and drove away.

Breathing a sigh of relief at her departure, Rhonda muttered, "Sure, I will." As she walked back to her room, she knew she needed to stay under the radar with the school and her mother. However, a new idea came to mind on how to torture Hannah and her little friends.

***

The next few days were busy as Hannah, Jackie and Michelle settled into their new room. Their days were busy with packing and going to class. Thankfully, they all got along beautifully. The month of August flew by quickly and they were into September.

Hannah had not seen Michael much lately. He called that evening asking if she wanted to go and get an ice cream. She couldn't believe how much she missed him in just a few days!

Around six o'clock, he came and picked her up and they drove to a fast-food place in town.

After they had settled into a booth with ice cream and drinks, Michael said, "I have something I want to ask you."

"Sure," Hannah said with a curious look in her gaze.

"My parents are coming to town this weekend and I wanted to see if you'd want to come and eat lunch with us on Saturday?" Michael asked her.

"Sure. I want to meet your parents," Hannah replied to him as he squeezed their clasped fingers.

"Thanks. My mom really wants to meet you. How about we go see a movie on Friday night? Just you and I?" he asked. Michael didn't mention that his mom wanted to meet her to see why she was such a distraction to his focusing on school.

"Spending time with you on both Friday and Saturday...how am I so lucky?" Hannah teased reaching up to run her fingers through the hair at the back of his neck. He insisted they sit together on the same side of the booth just as he had done at breakfast a week ago. It made Hannah feel loved and cherished at how much he wanted to be close to her and she was learning every day how affectionate he could be. It was something she had never experienced and she was falling harder and harder every day for him.

Michael leaned in to kiss her and murmured, "No, I'm the lucky one."

After finishing their ice cream, Michael drove her back to her dorm. They sat on the front porch swing for a few more minutes together. Thankfully, there hadn't been any sign of Rhonda. Although Hannah still had a nagging fear that it was not over yet.

When Michael said he needed to get back, he asked her to walk him to his car. It was parked to the side of the dorms and out of sight of any people who might be loitering around. Michael pulled Hannah close and kissed her passionately. Hannah lost all idea of where she was while he was putting his mouth on hers and deepening their kiss, placing one hand on the back of her neck. She had a very hard time restraining herself after their time together after the dance and she knew she was ready for all of it with Michael. They kissed for a few more minutes before Michael reluctantly pulled away. "See you tomorrow morning," he said because they met up each morning to eat breakfast before class.

"Bye," she whispered softly, watching him walk back to his car. He turned and looked at her, causing him to make an about-face to come back and kiss her soundly one more time.

"You are very hard to leave, Hannah Mathis," Michael murmured.

Hannah laughed softly as she hugged him closer and put her face in between his neck and shoulder. As she breathed in his scent, she finally pulled away and said, "Good night. I love you."

"I love you, too. Good night, beautiful!" he responded as he caressed her cheek one more time before walking to his car and driving away.

***

Friday afternoon, Hannah ran back to her room to get ready for her date with Michael. She was about to get into the shower when the phone rang.

She answered it hoping it was him. However, the line was silent. "Hello," she repeated. After saying it a third time, whoever it was hung up.

"Whatever," she muttered to herself. After her shower, it rang again. "Who is this?" Hannah asked without saying 'hello.'

"Hannah? What's going on?" Michael's voice was filled with confusion.

Breathing a sigh of relief, Hannah said, "Somebody has been calling and hanging up. I think it's a prank call."

"Okay," Michael said as he continued, "Do you want to come back to my place after the movie? I just wanted to ask to make sure that you were comfortable with it. You know that you can also stay the night if you want."

"You know I can't say no to that, but I'm not sure about staying the night," Hannah answered as she couldn't help smiling into the phone.

"Great!" said Michael. "My parents will be here by noon tomorrow, so that gives us plenty of time to get you back to your room if you wind up sleeping here with me."

"Yes, I definitely do not want your parents to catch me there with you!" Hannah answered. Both of them agreed that they did not want their parents to know they were thinking about sleeping together. Their parents were similar in the belief of waiting until you were married to have sex. As it was, Hannah was uneasy about meeting Michael's parents on Saturday.

"I'll be there to get you by five, so that we can eat before the movie," Michael said.

Hannah agreed and went to get ready. She couldn't get over the nerves she felt about meeting Michael's parents, especially his mom. She had met her over the phone a few nights ago, and she got the feeling that his mom wasn't pleased about them dating. However, Hannah never really knew if anyone liked her and her self-esteem would often get in the way.

***

Rhonda hung up the phone as she snickered to herself. It wasn't so bad having a room to herself. Danah felt that she didn't need another roommate after what happened with Hannah. If only Danah knew! She had just started the first phase of her new plan. It was one where she could fly under the radar and torture Hannah in a new way.

***

Hannah and Michael enjoyed dinner and the movie, especially sitting closely and making out in the dark theater. As he drove her back to his apartment, she couldn't help but worry a little about spending the night when his parents were coming tomorrow.

"I want to come over tonight, but I should get my car so that I can drive back to the dorm tonight instead of spending the night," she said looking at Michael.

He glanced her way and said, "Are you sure? Like I said, they won't be here until noon."

"I'm just not sure it's the best idea since I'm meeting them for the first time. Don't get me wrong, I definitely would like to stay, but I want your mom to like me." Hannah looked at him with an anxious look in her eyes.

"Hey, don't worry! My mom is going to love you! But I'm fine if you would rather go back tonight. However, I insist on following you back to make sure you will be safe since it will be late." Michael reached over to stroke Hannah's hair, pushing it behind her ear while pushing back his own doubts about his mother and Hannah.

"I'm sure I will be fine, but thank you," she replied, conceding to his following her back. Neither of them had spoken about it, but the threat of Rhonda was still there.

Michael took a detour, drove to the dorm and Hannah got into her car and followed him back to his place.

They pulled into Michael's driveway, and he opened her door even though she was in her own car. Butterflies fluttered in her stomach from the gesture. As he did, he leaned down and kissed her. Both of them had a hard time waiting to get inside the door before they were both kissing each other deeply and with great passion. Michael deepened the kiss, and she breathed in pleasure as her hands rubbed down his back and under his shirt.

"Let's go to my room," he murmured, having a hard time pulling back from kissing her. "I'm not sure when Alex will be back." Alex had gone out bowling with some other guys.

Michael pulled Hannah into his room, shutting the door and turning the lock. As he did, he began unbuttoning her blouse and pulling it off, leaving her standing in her bra and jeans.

"Finally," he whispered. "I've been thinking about being with you all week!"

Hannah melted as he kissed down her neck to her chest, then he kissed her breasts through her bra. She sighed with pleasure and she pulled his shirt over his head.

Hannah still could not believe how gentle Michael was in his treatment of her when they were together like this. It made her want to be with him even more.

Before going any further, he stopped and asked what she wanted to do. She responded by deepening their kiss.

He gently removed the rest of her clothes. At that point, he was standing in his jeans and without a shirt. He stood and looked at her rubbing his hand softly down her neck to her chest. "So beautiful," he murmured. His strokes on her breasts were light and feathery causing her to gasp as she leaned against him. He groaned when her breasts rubbed against his chest, and he went back to kissing her passionately.

Kissing Michael was magical, and it was as if they were made for this moment together. As he kissed her breasts and down her body, she urged him to remove the rest of his clothing. He complied and they laid on the bed together.

After a few more minutes of caressing each other, he reached for a condom and rolled it on before moving inside of her. Hannah exhaled sharply from the sensations washing through her.

"Hannah, oh my god!" Michael exclaimed as he was seated inside of her. It was better than he could have ever imagined.

Reveling in her own pleasure, she tilted her hips and they moved together learning what pleased the other. Hannah had experienced sex before, but they were mistakes that she now regretted. This time with Michael felt so right and it overwhelmed her.

Afterward, he held her in his arms and kissed her again softly. "I love you," he whispered in her ear.

She sighed in contentment and said, "I love you, too."

They lay together for a while before Hannah said, "I need to get back before it gets too late."

Michael said, "Okay, but I'm following you back. I want to make sure you are safe."

"Michael, I'm sure I will be fine," Hannah protested, but he silenced her with a gentle kiss.

"I won't take 'no' for an answer," Michael responded.

Nodding her head, they got dressed and Michael followed her back.

As he got out of his car to walk her to the door, she turned and smiled at him. "Thank you for a wonderful night. I will drive over to your apartment in the morning so that you don't have to worry about coming and getting me before your parents arrive."

"Are you sure you don't mind?" Michael asked her, reaching for her hand and interlacing their fingers together.

"No, it will be fine." Hannah squeezed his hand and turned to leave. However, Michael leaned close, kissing her one more time. Hannah couldn't help but shudder as desire fell over her again.

"Sleep well, beautiful!" he said as he released her. Hannah couldn't help but blush as she got out of the car and went inside.

***

The next morning, Hannah woke up and ate a quick breakfast in her room. She spent a couple of hours studying before getting ready to go to Michael's. He had called a few minutes ago to let her know that his parents got there earlier than planned. "Smart move," she said to herself as relief filled her that she came back last night. Getting caught with him would not have been a great way to meet them. Her roommates were both at the library doing research for papers they were writing.

Her hands were shaking as she pulled into Michael's driveway and turned off her car. As if in slow motion, she opened the car door and stepped out. She walked up to Michael's door and knocked, then clasped her hands together in hopes of easing the shaking.

Michael was quick to open it and he grabbed her hand to pull her inside. "Come in," he said as he squeezed her hand and Hannah wondered if he could feel it quivering.

However, as soon as she was inside the door, he released it as they walked into his small kitchen.

Michael's mother stood at the sink, washing the few dishes that were in there. "Michael, we need to get you some plastic mats to keep water from dripping on your floor," his mother said as she turned back around.

"Hi," Hannah said shyly with a small smile.

"Well, hello, Hannah," his mother said. "We finally get to meet you since Michael can't stop talking about you." Her smile did not quite reach her eyes as she studied her like a hawk studies its prey. Hannah averted her eyes as uneasiness spread over her.

"It's nice to meet you, too." Hannah answered as she looked over at Michael. He smiled encouragingly at her as he reached into the refrigerator to grab a drink.

"Do you want something?" he asked Hannah.

"No thanks," Hannah said, overcome with bashfulness.

With her gaze sharpened, Mrs. Davis asked, "Are you over here often with Michael? Does he share his drinks and food with you every time you are here? "

"No, ma'am," Hannah said looking at Michael as she began to think that Michael's mother did not like her. "I only drink water if I am here hanging out with Michael and Alex."

"Mom," Michael admonished. "We don't mind sharing drinks and snacks with Hannah. Alex has friends over, too."

"I know that, Michael," she said. "I know you have friends over, but I also know that you don't have a lot of extra money, so I want to make sure that you are taken care of."

She walked into the living room. Michael's dad was standing by the window.

"Dad," said Michael, putting his arm loosely around Hannah. "This is Hannah."

"It's nice to meet you, sir," Hannah said, smiling at both him and his mother.

"Well, Hannah!" his dad said jovially. "It's great to meet you, finally!" He continued by asking, "So, Hannah, Michael says that you are from Montgomery. Is that correct?"

"Yes sir," Hannah answered. "My family has lived there since I was three years old."

"What does your father do?" Michael's mother joined in the conversation.

"He is Vice President of a lumber company." Hannah said. "My mom teaches at the high school."

His mother smiled at Hannah a little, more sincerely than when they were in the kitchen.

"Michael, we need to get to the restaurant for lunch. We made a reservation for twelve thirty," Mrs. Davis said.

"Okay, we'll follow you over there," Michael said. His mother looked like she wanted to protest, but he said, "There isn't enough room in your car for Alex, too, and he's going to ride with us."

They walked out and once she was inside the vehicle, Hannah let out a breath. "I'm not sure your mom is very impressed with me," she said with a worried tone in her voice.

"Oh, she's like that with any girl that I date," Michael said smiling at her. "Just give her a chance. She will warm up to you, especially since I don't plan on dating any other girls."

"Oh, barf," Alex said. "Stop with the mushy talk!" He made a hilarious face causing Hannah and Michael to laugh. It was a great way to break up the tension and Hannah swallowed hard. She was happy to see Alex back to his normal self after the debacle with Rhonda.

Lunch was not a bad experience, but Hannah was able to see just how much Michael's mother adored her son. At one point when they were talking, Mrs. Davis reached over and laid her hand on his arm. Hannah realized that she was probably being over-protective of her "little boy." She relaxed a little more as his dad asked about growing up in Montgomery and she became more at ease when they asked her about her brother and sister, and where her family went to church.

Alex kept them entertained at lunch and again on the drive back to Michael's apartment. His parents were following behind them in their car and Hannah knew that they were going to do some shopping, so she planned to drive herself back to her dorm room to study.

Surprised when Michael's mother invited her to come to the mall with them, she didn't feel like she could refuse.

The drive was silent on the way with country music playing on the radio. As she sat next to Michael in the back seat, he reached over and put his hand on her leg. She knew it was meant to be reassuring, but it had the opposite effect. She pushed his hand off, but it came right back. She looked over at Michael and she saw his teasing grin. Behind the glance, she could see the desire in his eyes as well. She decided to play with him a little. She reached up and ran a finger down his forearm, causing his pulse to jump. She quietly laughed at his frustrated look. Her laughter stopped as his hand caressed the inside of her thigh and she gave a sharp inhale.

Shopping was very nice with Michael's parents. They stopped at the food court and bought all of them a snack even though Hannah tried to refuse and pay for her own. Michael reached and squeezed her hand under the table in reaction to how his mom was warming up to her.

Hannah couldn't help nodding off in the back seat on the drive back. Michael also leaned his head back to nap and before she realized it, they were back at his apartment. Not wanting to impose any longer, she said goodbye to Michael's parents and drove back to her room so that she could study and complete a couple of homework assignments.

Later that evening, her phone rang and Michael's voice came through the line.

"I just wanted to thank you for coming with me today. My mom really did like you." Michael's voice was filled with warmth.

"I had a great time, too," Hannah said, smiling into the phone. "Please tell your parents thank you for lunch and for inviting me to the mall with them."

"How about you come outside and take a walk with me?" Michael asked. "I'm standing in the lobby of your dorm."

"Where are your parents?" Hannah looked to the side as if she could see him.

"They went back to my grandparents' house in Carthage to spend the night." Michael replied. "I'm going to church with all of them tomorrow, so I won't be able to see you until later tomorrow evening. Come on out and we can take a walk for a little while."

When Hannah stepped into the lobby, Michael walked her outside and to the side of the dorm where he pulled her into his arms to kiss. "Hey, beautiful," he murmured in her ear.

"Hi," Hannah whispered softly, leaning her face between his neck and shoulder. It was becoming one of her favorite places to be.

They kissed for a while longer and their hands traveled up and down each other's backs. It did not take long before Hannah felt like jelly in his arms.

"Hannah," he exhaled deeply. "All of the teasing in the car earlier made me crazy with wanting you!"

Hannah's response was another whimper of contentment. Michael finally pulled back and took her hand to go for the promised walk. As they strolled, he said, "Thank you for coming with us today. My mom had some nice things to say about you when you left, and my dad couldn't stop complimenting you! He has never had anything positive to say about any girl I have ever dated in the past."

Hannah couldn't have been more surprised as she said, "Thank you for inviting me. I enjoyed meeting them and hearing about you growing up. Will you be up to meeting my parents? They are coming in a couple of weeks."

"I can't wait to meet them," Michael said, placing his arm around her shoulder as they strolled across the campus.

They came to a lovely bench in the middle of the campus green. They sat together and talked for another hour about their childhoods. Hannah had never felt so engrossed with someone that she had dated in the past. She always felt amazed at how deeply she felt about Michael after just a few, short months of knowing each other.

When Michael walked her back, he pulled her to a secluded area where they wouldn't be seen. His kiss became deeper as he kissed Hannah. Finally, he reluctantly pulled away.

"I love you, Hannah Mathis." Michael smiled into her eyes. "Seeing you with my parents only made me love you more. I hope you have the best sleep tonight."

"I love you too." Hannah reached up and kissed Michael's cheek.

"Good night, beautiful!" he said as he squeezed her hand before walking to his car.

***

Hannah walked in to see Michelle hanging up the phone with a bewildered expression.

"Is something wrong?" Hannah asked.

Michelle shook her head slightly as she said, "Someone just called and hung up. All I could hear was breathing."

"That happened to me yesterday," Hannah said. "They called twice and didn't say anything."

"I guess it's someone playing a prank, but I'm not sure who would do that," Michelle surmised.

A thought came to Hannah, but she did not voice it aloud. Doom spread over her as she wondered if Rhonda could possibly be behind these calls.

Trying to give an impassive gaze, she said, "I'm going to get ready for bed."

***

Two weeks later, Hannah's parents were calling her from the lobby to tell her that they had arrived. She was excited to see them because it had been a month since their last visit. She and Michael had gotten into a routine of attending classes, eating as many meals as they could together and going on dates on the weekends.

So far, the phone calls had been sporadic with one of them answering the phone each time. The threat from Rhonda seemed to be gone for the moment, yet Hannah couldn't help the nagging fear that all was not well as the phone calls continued. She had never thought of herself as someone having a sixth sense. Because she often doubted herself, she shook it off as silly and worried over nothing. Therefore, she didn't breathe a word about it to anyone.

She had told her parents that Michael was joining them, but she was a little nervous about their meeting. Her parents babied her in the past with boys that she dated, and she wasn't sure if they would accept that she and Michael were actually serious about each other.

She sat in the lobby with them, catching up with each other about her school schedule when Michael walked in the door. Keeping herself from swooning over how wonderful he looked, Hannah sprang to her feet and said, "Mom, Dad, I want you to meet Michael Davis."

Michael reached out his hand to shake hands with her parents. "It's so nice to meet you! Hannah has told me so much about you!"

"Well, Michael," said Hannah's mom. "It's wonderful to meet you. We were just about to take you kids out to lunch. Do you like Mexican food? We wanted to try the Mexican place here in town."

"Thank you, ma'am," Michael responded in a respectful voice. "Mexican sounds great and I appreciate you inviting me."

"Then, let's go," her father said. Hannah adored her father, but he was a man of few words. Her mother did most of the talking for the both of them.

Hannah and Michael trailed out behind her parents. Since they were not watching, he reached for her hand and squeezed it, whispering, "Good morning, beautiful."

Hannah blushed slightly and mouthed, "Good morning," back to Michael. He found himself thinking it was completely erotic as he gazed at her mouth.

Pulling his gaze back to her, he continued to hold her hand until they reached her parents' car. He respectfully let it go to open the back door for Hannah before walking around to the other side. Her mother raised her eyebrows in surprise at the manners he was showing to her daughter.

As soon as they were in the car and driving to the restaurant, Michael reached for Hannah's hand again, placing it on his leg as he entwined their fingers together. Hannah's heart skipped a little from the gesture.

"So, Michael," her mom said. "Hannah says you are from the Dallas area."

"Yes, ma'am," Michael answered. "We've lived there my entire life." Hannah tried pulling her hand away when her mother asked the question, but Michael refused to let it go as he glanced her way. Her heart couldn't help skipping again at the loving look he was giving her as he responded to her mom.

"What's your major?" her mom asked. She was doing her best to include Michael and to make him feel comfortable.

He answered that he wanted to be a music teacher in school. His desire was to be a choral director in a high school, working with teenagers to help them develop a talent for singing and performing.

The conversation continued on the drive to the restaurant and her mother seemed impressed with Michael's manners and his confident manner in speaking with her. Hannah's father did not add anything to the conversation, but Michael noticed him watching him through the rearview mirror since he was sitting behind the driver's seat. He wasn't sure what her father was thinking about him, but his perfectionist nature was determined to win him over and show him that he had honest intentions toward his daughter.

Lunch continued in the same manner. Her father was not much for talking, but he did ask Michael what his father did for work. Michael was kind in asking them about their home and family. Hannah could tell that her father was impressed with him as well.

At one point, Michael reached for Hannah's hand under the table. She was reluctant, but he refused to let go. Always surprised by it, she was unsure on how to react to his show of affection toward her. She was so glad that he seemed to be getting along with her parents so well after just meeting them.

After lunch, her mom insisted on stopping at a local store to restock some toiletries and other items for Hannah. She had told her parents about the situation with Rhonda, and they seemed relieved that she had moved out and wasn't rooming with her anymore. They thanked Michael for his help when she seemed to become threatening toward Hannah.

Michael piped in, "I didn't do a whole lot other than listen and provide Hannah a safe place to get away when Rhonda seemed to be a threat."

"Well, we appreciate that you gave Hannah a safe place to go," Hannah's mom said and her dad nodded his head toward Michael in the rearview mirror.

They had arrived back at the dorm. Hannah and her mom walked the purchases to her room while her Dad and Michael sat in the lobby watching a college football game. They seemed to be enjoying it together and Hannah was glad to observe them.

"Michael seems to be a nice, young man." Her mom said to her. "He has wonderful manners!"

Hannah couldn't help rolling her eyes, but contentment filled her at her mother's words. Manners were important to her mom, and she was glad that Michael made an impression on her.

"Yes, he does. He always holds the door for me and he opens the car door every time I am getting in," Hannah answered.

"Well, he wins points for that but I'm not sure about you staying over there when you did," her mom responded with a worried brow. Feeling some irritation, Hannah wondered if her mother would ever take her seriously and stop coddling her.

"Mom, it was completely innocent. I stayed on the couch, and nothing happened!" Hannah was glancing away hoping that her mother didn't see through the half-truth she was telling her. She also hoped her mother's naivety had a hand in that she would not ask about it anymore. However, Hannah's back straightened as she thought about how she was eighteen now and she could make her own choices.

Thankfully, her mother didn't say anything more other than, "Well, I'm glad that he helped keep you safe."

The thought made Hannah roll her eyes because of her mother's archaic view of the man being the stronger one in a relationship. "I did stand up to her," Hannah commented. "I put my hand between the two of us and told her to stop."

"Of course you did," was all her mother said. "We should go back out with your father."

They walked back out to the lobby and her father stood up saying that they needed to start their drive back home. Hannah gave both of them a hug and told them thank you for coming to visit her. The three of them stood in a close, family hug and Michael thanked them for lunch.

As soon as their car pulled away, Hannah pulled Michael around to the small porch to the side of the dorm. "Thank you!" she said as she looked in his eyes. "My parents loved you!"

Michael pulled her into his arms and said, "I had a wonderful time meeting them. You look very much like both of them and I loved learning more about your family."

She looked at him, blinking fiercely to wash away the tears that sprang into her eyes. Afraid he had hurt her, Michael grew concerned with seeing her about to cry, but she spoke up before he could say anything. "I love you, Michael Davis. You are the most wonderful guy that I have ever known and you were so charming with my Mom and Dad. "

"Hannah, I love you, too." Michael said, but Hannah missed the uncertainty in his eyes as he held her close.

They went back to kissing, and kissing, and kissing some more. Michael's embrace was gentle and thoughtful. Hannah almost wished that they could go back to his place, but she was not forward enough to invite herself. With a final kiss from him, they said goodbye and she walked to her room.

***

Rhonda watched Hannah walk out to the car with her parents and she smirked. 'It must be nice to have a perfect family,' she thought with envy as Hannah's parents surrounded her and they walked arm in arm to their car. Making sure she was behind some shrubs where she couldn't be seen, her plan was going well, following Hannah at times making sure not to be seen to put it into place. She hoped Hannah thought that she was leaving her alone and going on with her own life. Seeing Michael at times in the music building was also a plus since they were often together. She ducked as Hannah walked back out with Michael and they walked to the side closest to her and began kissing. Turning up her lips in disgust, Rhonda muttered, "Gross." She darted the other direction to walk to the other side of her dorm.

Chapter 10

Weeks went by and it was the month of October. Hannah and Michael went out or hung out with each other as much as their busy schedule would allow. They went out to eat, they ate out with friends, and they just enjoyed sitting and watching television shows together. They hadn't slept together again since that first time because Alex was usually there. Neither of them minded. They loved spending time together and they were slowly becoming best friends.

Michael was learning more about Hannah and he knew she was a people-pleaser. She often deferred her wishes to what he wanted. He tried not to take advantage of that because he loved her generous nature.

Fall Break was a week away. The university gave students Thursday and Friday off, and Hannah wanted to invite Michael to come and visit her hometown over the long weekend.

Friday night arrived and Michael and Hannah were going out with a group of their friends. Hannah, Jackie and Michelle had come up with an idea. Two nights ago, they had brainstormed what they could do.

"You know, there's a sports bar over the Louisiana state line that would be fun," Jackie commented.

"That does sound fun, but don't we need to be twenty-one to get in?" Hannah asked.

"If you are eighteen or older, they will let us in. We just can't buy any drinks," Jackie answered.

"That's perfect!" Michelle said and Hannah nodded her head.

They brought the idea up with everyone at breakfast yesterday and everyone agreed.

Hannah planned to ask Michael that evening to come home with her for Fall break, but she was slightly nervous about it.

As they got ready, Michelle insisted Hannah wear a black suede skirt in her closet with a slinky blouse. All of them were taking their time dressing, preparing their hair and makeup.

Michelle applied Hannah's makeup, and Hannah took the time to roll her hair, creating curls around her shoulders. Then, she did the same for Jackie and Michelle, helping them with their make-up and hair. She looked in the mirror knowing how her appearance would affect Michael once he saw her.

Danny borrowed a van from his parents (they lived one town over) so that they could all ride together to the bar. Hannah, Jackie and Michelle walked out to join them in the lobby.

She couldn't help but notice Michael's stunned look at seeing her in the skirt she borrowed from Michelle. The blouse dipped lower than anything else she had ever worn, showing quite a bit of cleavage. The skirt stopped just above her knees, giving him a view of her beautiful legs.

He didn't say anything because he knew it would embarrass her, but he winked at her with a smoldering gaze. She knew it was a promise of what would come later tonight, and she gave him a sultry look as she held out her hand to him. He coughed to cover a groan as he purposely pulled her back so that they could walk out last. He leaned down to whisper in her ear, "Do you have any idea what you are doing to me?"

"I have no idea what you are talking about," she whispered back, with a look of innocence. She shivered from his mouth so close to her ear and neck.

Without anyone seeing, his hand found its way under her shirt as he placed it on her back. One, soft stroke on her skin had her squealing and pulling away, causing Michael to chuckle with a glint in his eye. He also had a look of innocence on his face.

Everyone piled into the van. Danny turned up the music playing a popular song on the radio. The group sang the chorus in unison and the volume in the van was boisterous.

Alex had a date with him, a girl whom Hannah had seen in the dorm. She hadn't had a chance to get to know her yet. Her name was Suzanne and she was glad to see that Alex had moved on since getting hurt by Rhonda.

The thought made her stop and wonder about everything. The prank calls continued all week, but mostly when she was in the room. It was why she thought that Rhonda was behind them.

She and Suzanne enjoyed getting to know one another and found that they were both in the education program. Hannah changed her major last month once she realized that there wasn't much she could do with foreign languages. After making such great friends, she didn't want to transfer schools either.

Michael and Alex were laughing and joking together. Michael kept his hand on Hannah's knee as they talked, causing her to get goosebumps. This time, he wasn't doing it on purpose. She was learning that he just loved touching her and that displays of affection were important to him.

When they arrived at the restaurant, they piled out of the van. Alex had thought to call ahead to let them know that a large group was coming and there was a table ready for them.

Michael pulled out Hannah's chair for her, ensuring that it was pulled closer to his before seating her. He reached for her hand under the table and held it as they looked at the menu. Hannah insisted that they go dutch for this outing because she knew that Michael needed to save his money instead of always spending it on her.

Alex ordered pitchers of sodas for everyone to share, and it was decided that the group would also share wings and fries. As soon as they placed their order, Alex pulled Suzanne out onto the dance floor. Of course, Michael couldn't sit still, so he and Hannah moved out to dance with their friends until their food came.

As soon as they finished eating, the band began playing a slow tune. Michael pulled out Hannah's chair and he led her over to the other side of the dance floor.

Pulling her tightly into his embrace, he whispered, "Finally! I have you all to myself!" As he said the words, his lips were tickling the soft spot behind her ear causing more shivers to go down her spine.

Pulling back as much as he would allow, she looked up at him and said, "I want to ask you something."

Smiling at her, Michael answered her, "Baby, you can ask me any-thing."

Butterflies filled her stomach when he said that to her. Her dad called her mom that nickname all the time. Focusing back on him after being distracted, Hannah said, "I want to invite you to come home with me over Fall Break next weekend."

Michael's smile widened and he said, "I was thinking about inviting you home with me as well. I will come with you if you come with me the weekend after that."

Hannah's gut filled with relief as she said, "I would love to." Tightening her arms around his neck she said, "I love you, Michael."

"I love you too, baby," Michael said, pulling her close again. Then he began singing the chorus of the ballad in her ear, causing her to tremble even more. Shivering from him calling her "baby" again, she almost couldn't hold herself up in his arms. He didn't seem to mind as securely as he was holding her. His voice was mesmerizing as he crooned the words to her. Hannah hadn't heard him sing yet, but he had a wonderful voice.

Turning her face toward his, his lips touched hers and they were lost in their own world. They continued kissing deeply until the song ended. Thankfully, another slow song began, so they did not have to let go of each other.

Nearby, she saw Alex and Suzanne dancing closely. She was happy to see when he leaned in and gave her a kiss. She really liked Suzanne and she hoped that they would continue dating.

Alex was becoming one of her best friends and she loved seeing him so happy. Michelle was dancing with Danny and Jackie was dancing with another guy whom she did not know very well.

She had never been so happy as she was to be here tonight with Michael and their friends.

Michael leaned back and looked in her eyes, "Do you know that we will have been dating for two months next weekend?"

Hannah shook her head as she looked in his eyes. "I can't believe it," she said. "It feels like I have known you forever, Michael Davis!"

"All I know is that I want to keep getting to know you, Hannah Mathis." He leaned and touched his lips to hers after he said it.

Answering him with her lips against his, she said, "If you are trying to seduce me for later tonight, let me tell you that it's working! But, won't Alex be home tonight?"

"He will be, but he told me that it will be late. He wants to take Suzanne out for coffee. So, we will have the place to ourselves for a while before he is back." Michael was gazing deeply into Hannah's eyes as he said the words. She reached up and put her lips against his in response and they continued kissing softly.

A couple of hours later, the group drove back to the university campus. Michael told Danny that Hannah would take him back to his apartment, so he would get out with her. Hannah didn't miss the look Danny gave him, but at the moment she didn't care. She just wanted to be with him. They got into her car, and she drove to his place.

"Just a minute, pretty lady," he commented as he motioned for her to stay where she was. He unlocked the door and then he came back and opened the driver's side door, escorting her inside. As soon as she was in the kitchen, she looked at the table and saw a single red rose sitting in a vase in the middle of the table.

"Michael," she breathed. "What is this?"

"This is a gift for you. Do you like it?" Michael asked her.

Hannah moved into his arms saying, "It's so beautiful! Thank you!" She touched her lips to his before pulling back. Michael didn't want to let her go, but she reached down to smell the beautiful rose.

It didn't take long before she was in his embrace again. "I love you so much!" she whispered and then they kissed deeply. Since the intimacy from before, there wasn't any shyness at pulling off their clothes.

"I've wanted to do this all night after seeing you in that outfit!" Michael said as he kissed his way down her chest to her bra, unclasping it and letting it fall to the floor. Hannah sighed in satisfaction as his lips were on her breasts and she moaned. She was impatiently trying to raise his shirt. He stopped his kisses to pull it over his head.

He took her hand and led her to his bedroom. He closed it and locked it, saying, "Just in case." This time of making love was beautiful and full of passion. When they were finished, Hannah lay in Michael's arms. His hands were stroking her back, her hair, her neck. It was methodical and she found herself falling asleep.

She woke at one point and saw that it was two o'clock in the morning. At first, she worried about being there all night, but she was just too comfortable where she was in his arms. So, she closed her eyes and fell back asleep.

She woke up to Michael watching her. "Good morning," she said, covering her mouth knowing that she had 'morning breath.'

"You're beautiful, you know," he said softly as he was rubbing hair out of her face.

Hannah put her head against his chest in embarrassment. She had not ever had anyone say she was beautiful as much as Michael did. Sometimes, she didn't know what to do with the praise.

He pulled her up to look at him as he repeated it and his eyes were completely green. "You are. You're beautiful."

"Thank you," she murmured. "I didn't mean to fall asleep."

"It's nice having you with me this morning," Michael commented. "But, I guess we need to get you back before Alex wakes up."

They got dressed and Hannah walked out to her car. "Thank you for last night," she said, kissing him goodbye. She picked up the vase with the rose.

"It was my pleasure," Michael said, leaning in to kiss her once more. His hand cradled her face as he said, "I can't wait until next weekend!"

Leaning back, Hannah had a serious expression when she said, "You know that we can't do what we did last night, right?"

Chuckling at her, Michael said, "I wasn't planning on it. Your Dad will definitely not like me if I'm sleeping with his daughter under his roof! I'm happy to just be with you, Hannah."

Smiling, Hannah kissed him one more time with the vase in her hand. "Bye," she said, getting into her car and putting the vase on the passenger seat. Waving goodbye, Michael just stood there watching her drive away.

***

A week passed by, and it was time for Hannah and Michael to leave to go to her home. Hannah was so glad that they were leaving town because the prank calls had continued throughout the week at random times, but it was only when Hannah answered the phone. Again, she couldn't help but wonder if Rhonda was behind it since things had been so quiet since she moved to the other dorm.

The original plan was to leave right after class on Wednesday afternoon. Both Michael and Hannah had a full load of classes on Wednesdays, so they decided to wait and leave on Thursday. Being a holiday, Hannah wanted to sleep in for a little while before going. She finished packing her bag and drove to his apartment. She got out and knocked on his door. He opened it quickly saying, "Give me just a minute and I will be ready to go." He disappeared into his bedroom.

Stepping inside, Alex greeted her in the living room.

"Hey Alex," she replied. "What are your plans for the weekend?"

"I'm headed home to see my mom tomorrow morning," Alex answered her.

Michael walked back out of his bedroom with his bag in hand. "I'm ready now."

"See you, buddy!" Alex commented. "Y'all have a great time!"

As soon as they were in the car, Michael put his hand on Hannah's arm, and he leaned over the console to give her a kiss. "I didn't tell you hello, did I?" She smiled in response and kissed him back.

Then, she pulled back and said, "I'm so excited you're coming home with me!" The excitement was written all over Hannah as she bounced in the driver's seat.

Joy was in his gaze as Michael said, "If it's time with you, I'm excited, too." Hannah put the car into gear and pulled out of Michael's driveway.

She let Michael choose the music for the first part of the drive. Of course, he picked the Bon Jovi tape that he pulled out of the side of his overnight bag. They both sang "Living on a Prayer" at the top of their lungs when the song came on.

They stopped halfway in a small town to get gas and to buy snacks. Hannah let Michael take over driving the rest of the way to her house.Three hours later, with Hannah telling him directions, he pulled into her parents' driveway with a dazed expression. "Wow!" This is a great house!" he exclaimed. He gazed at the two story home in awe. His house was tiny, compared to this! His dad had a blue-collar job and his mom worked as a secretary at an elementary school. They did alright, but they definitely were not rich.

"Thanks," Hannah answered as she grabbed her bag out of the back seat. "Come on in!" She said to him as he followed her up the walkway.

Just as they got to the door, it opened and her Mom was in the doorway. "I'm so happy you're home!" she cried giving Hannah a big hug. She hugged Michael as well telling him that she was glad he could come for a visit. "Hannah, show Michael your brother's room. He can stay there."

"Okay, Mom," she said as she led the way up the stairs. She turned to the left and Michael saw a bedroom that looked like it belonged to a guy. The walls were covered with metal band posters and there was a deer head on the wall across from the bed. Across the hall was a bathroom with a shower.

"Here you go!" she said, motioning him to put his bag on the bed. After he did, she led the way to her bedroom, which was in the middle of the hall. Her room looked just as he imagined with white wallpaper decorated with pink and blue flowers. Under the window was a window seat and next to the bed was a white dresser with flowers on it as well. Along the wall near the closet were posters of famous heartbreak actors of that time period-John Schneider, Scott Baio, and John Stamos.

Hannah threw her bag on the floor near the closet and said, "Well, what do you think?"

"This looks like you!" Michael said, smiling at her as he studied her collection of books and cassette tapes on the shelves above her desk.

She smiled back as she flopped down on her bed. "Do you have anything you want to do? There's a park that is on the next block, and we can walk there if you feel like it."

Michael sat down beside her on the bed, and he just couldn't help himself. He leaned over and kissed Hannah, even though she said that they couldn't be physical at her parents' house. She didn't try to stop him as she kissed him back. However, it was short-lived because her mom was coming up the stairs. He stood up quickly, so as not to be caught sitting on her bed.

"Michael, I hope you will be comfortable in Hannah's brother's room this weekend. Please let me know if there's anything you need," she said as she came into the room.

"Thank you, Mrs. Mathis. I'm sure everything will be fine." Michael smiled at her in his easy manner.

Hannah was so proud to have him here with her! "Mom, we're going to walk over to the park for a little while if that's okay."

"Sure, that's fine. Your Dad will be home at six, so we will eat dinner at six-thirty. Michael, I hope you like spaghetti," her mom commented.

"Yes, ma'am, I do!" Michael answered.

"Let me freshen up in the bathroom and change and then we can go," Hannah told him.

"I will do the same," Michael said walking down the hallway.

It only took a few minutes for them to walk the two blocks to the park. He held her hand as they walked and pulled her so close that their arms brushed each other. They chatted easily about Hannah's growing up in this neighborhood.

Hannah and Michael each took several turns on the slide, then he pushed her in the swings for a few minutes before joining her. Then, they climbed to the top of monkey bars and sat closely together talking even more.

Michael was amazed that he and Hannah never ran out of things to tell each other. He was glad to come and see the place where she had grown up as a child. He knew he wouldn't meet her brother or her sister on this trip, but maybe he could meet them sometime in the near future. It was important to him to get to know everyone in her family because she was becoming so important to him. Again, he felt slight anxiety from how much he had grown to care about her, and it scared him. His heart skipped with worry that he shouldn't be so serious about someone since just beginning college. Deep down, he knew his mother would warn him not to be so involved with a girl.

At one point, they got into a "tickle-fest." Michael was quickly learning the spots where she was the most ticklish. However, Hannah gave back to him just as much as he dished out to her. They were bent over laughing at one point and he couldn't resist pulling her into his embrace from where he was sitting.

"Do I have your permission to kiss you right here since we aren't inside your house?" he teased, rubbing his nose against hers.

"Be my guest," she quipped as he moved in.

He kissed her tenderly, deepening it and she sighed softly. It was a sound that he was coming to love. He had learned ways that would elicit the sound from her and it brought him deep pleasure. She kissed him back and they made out on the monkey bars for a while longer before walking back to her house.

At one point she challenged him to a race which ended in him trying to tickle her again so that he could win. These were moments that both he and Hannah would look back on and remember from their early days of falling in love.

***

After dinner, Hannah's mother served a delicious chocolate dessert. Michael thanked her profusely for the amazing, home-cooked meal. He insisted on helping to clear the table and Hannah could see respect on her mother's face as a result of his willingness to help out.

After the dishes were done, Hannah told her mother that she and Michael were going to rent a movie that they could watch later.

"Okay," Hannah said as she pulled out of the driveway. "I'm going to take you on a tour of my small town. Tomorrow, I'm going to introduce you to my Nana. Are you ready?"

"I can't wait," Michael remarked as he reached for her hand and intertwined their fingers.

She drove him around all the important hangouts when she was in high school. They also drove by her elementary school, junior high school and high school. After driving him past the house where her family lived when they moved there, she drove to a video rental store. She and Michael both picked out a movie. She chose a romantic comedy and he chose a western with Kevin Costner. Her mom gave her money to pay for the movie rentals, and it took them a few minutes to check out.

Once they got back to her house, Hannah took the time to change to sweatpants and another T-shirt and it made her heart skip as she thought about the first time she wore the same kind of outfit at Michael's apartment. He came out of her brother's room wearing similar clothing and his eyes lit up at seeing her. The look that came into his eyes let her know that he remembered that as well. However, he was being respectful of her wishes to refrain from too much kissing and touching. He couldn't help himself from tickling her waist again as they walked down the stairs.

Her mom and dad had moved to their bedroom to relax and watch television. Michael let Hannah pick the first movie. Since her parents were in their room, she allowed him to pull her back against him on the couch. The romantic comedy had Tom Hanks in it, so they laughed together. Toward the end of the movie when there was a romantic scene, Michael nuzzled Hannah's neck, pulling her tighter into his embrace. She looked up at him and allowed him to touch his lips to hers. Even though it was a simple kiss, it was satisfyingly long.

In between movies, Hannah went into the kitchen to make some popcorn and pour drinks for them. He followed her in and looked at the pictures and mementos on the refrigerator. One picture had Hannah as a small girl, and he commented on how cute she was. Embarrassed, she groaned and led him back into the family room.

At one point, her parents came out to get glasses of water and to lock up before turning in for bed. Michael and Hannah both told them good night.

"You know that I want to see more pictures. I'm sure your mom has photo albums that she is willing to share." Michael said in a joking manner. "I promise that you can look at my humiliating photos when I take you home with me next weekend."

After persuading her to agree with him, Hannah walked over to the bookshelves on the opposite wall of the couch. She grabbed several photo albums and sat down so that they could look through them. Michael insisted that she move closer beside him. His excuse was so that he could see them, but she knew that he wanted her within reach because he loved touching her. An overwhelming sensation washed over her at how attractive he always made her feel.

Instead of watching the second movie, they looked through photo albums. The first one was when Hannah was a baby, all chubby and adorable.

Each album was a different phase of her life, but Michael was glad to see what her siblings looked like as he laughed at their seventies clothing.

Hannah shared how they were both adopted because her mom was told that she couldn't have children. They adopted her brother, and twelve months later she was born. Not able to stop himself, he kissed her after hearing it.

The time of looking through pictures led them sharing about their homes and growing up. They were learning that they had similar backgrounds in being raised to go to church on Sundays. Hannah couldn't remember ever sharing about her home and childhood as much as she did with Michael.

"You know when I tell you that you're beautiful that I mean it, so why do you not believe me?" Michael asked her, looking into her eyes as they were looking at pictures of her prom and graduation.

Hannah looked down, not sure how to respond. "I don't know." She replied. "I've never had someone tell me that I'm beautiful except for my dad. It's just hard to believe since I haven't heard it very much."

"Baby, look at me," Michael implored. His tone of voice was soft and gentle causing Hannah to meet his gaze. "You are gorgeous! I'm not the only one who thinks so! Several of the guys I play basketball with tell me how hot you are, and I sure wasn't happy hearing them say that!" He put the photo albums on the coffee table and took her face in his hands gazing into her eyes. "Please believe me when I say that you are so beautiful."

Tears sprang to Hannah's eyes as she said, "Thank you. I don't know why it's so hard for me to believe you. It's just difficult for me to imagine what you see."

Michael leaned down to get as close to her as he could without kissing her. "I want to help you come to the point where you believe that you take my breath away when I see you." He wiped a tear that had fallen down on her cheek, kissing it softly. It opened up the longing to kiss her and kiss her passionately, and he couldn't help himself. He leaned down and touched her lips urging her to deepen the kiss. She did and his tongue went inside touching hers. They kissed for several minutes, but they refrained from doing anything else.

When they pulled back, Hannah laid her head on his shoulder and said, "I love you."

"I love you, too," Michael said, kissing the top of her head. He held her against him. He didn't want to let her go and she seemed reluctant to move away, so they sat like that for a while.

Finally, they agreed to watch a syndicated television show that came on late at night. It was a comedy and Hannah leaned back against Michael again. The feeling of his arms around her as they snuggled was natural.

It was late when they decided to turn in for the night. Hannah was so tempted to invite Michael into her room with her. But he was a gentleman. He walked her to her door, kissed her goodnight before disappearing into the bathroom to get ready for bed.

Hannah went to bed looking forward to the next day because she was going to take him to her grandmother's house to introduce them. None of her friends were in town, but she was going to introduce him to leaders in her church on Sunday. Her brother, Peter, was out of town visiting a friend.

Her parents had plans with friends tomorrow night, so they were going to be able to go out together for dinner. Her parents wanted to grill steaks on Saturday evening, and then they had church the next day on Sunday before Hannah and Michael had to drive back to school.

***

Friday morning, Hannah was up at nine. She walked downstairs and found Michael already at the table. Satisfaction rolled over her heart at the sight of him and her mother together.

"Good morning, sweetie!" her mom said to her as she went into the kitchen asking if she was fine having toast and scrambled eggs for breakfast.

"Yes, that's great, Mom!" Hannah answered her as she walked to the refrigerator to get the orange juice. Pouring herself a glass, she sat at the table beside Michael.

Michael smiled at her and mouthed, "Good morning, beautiful,"

Even after their conversation last night, Hannah couldn't contain the blush that swept over her face. She was so thankful that she was sitting in the opposite direction of her mother.

Her mom was talking to her while she scrambled the eggs in the frying pan. "Do you want to come and put the toast into the toaster? You can also get out the butter and jelly."

"Yes, ma'am," Hannah answered as she walked back into the kitchen.

"Michael, will you eat some of these eggs?" her mom asked him.

"Yes, ma'am, that sounds delicious!" Michael said with a smile on his face. "Is there anything I can do to help?" He walked in and joined Hannah at the island where she was pulling out four pieces of bread to put into the toaster.

"No, I think Hannah and I have everything we need. I don't guess you drink coffee, do you? Hannah doesn't touch the stuff," her mom continued talking a mile a minute, which was typical for her. She dished the eggs into a bowl and walked it to the table.

Michael declined any coffee, but he did pull out butter and jelly from the refrigerator as Hannah brought the toast over to the table with three plates.

Breakfast was wonderful and relaxing as the three of them relished the meal and the conversation around the table.

After breakfast, Hannah and Michael went upstairs to get ready to go and see her grandmother. She was expecting them at eleven and she would serve them lunch. It was already after ten by the time they cleared the table and helped her mom clean the kitchen.

At one point, the phone rang and her mother called out, "Hannah, it's for you."

"Okay, Mom," she called back as she answered the phone in her room. After saying hello, all she heard was heavy breathing. "Who is this?" she demanded. They hung up after that and fear washed over her. Thankfully, Michael was in the bathroom taking a shower as Hannah pondered if it was the same person who had been calling at school.

Michael came out dressed and looking wonderful. He smiled as he saw her and said, "Ready?"

Shaking off her anxiety, Hannah smiled back and said, "Yes."

They left a few minutes later to go to Nana's house. Hannah had shared funny stories about her. Michael already felt like he knew her from the stories that both Hannah and her mother had told

Her grandmother lived in an old house that had been converted into a duplex. Hannah opened the front door, calling her name as they walked inside. The television was blaring with a daytime soap opera.

"Hey, Nana," Hannah called.

Nana appeared out of the kitchen, looking surprised. She was wearing a housedress and an apron. "Well, come in, honey! It's so good to see you!"

Hannah walked over and gave her grandmother a hug and a kiss on the cheek. "I'm so glad to see you, too!" She turned to Michael and introduced him.

"It's so nice to meet you, Michael!" her grandmother exclaimed. "Let me turn down the television. I didn't realize it was so loud."

"The Young and the Restless," Michael commented. "That's my grandmother's favorite soap opera as well!"

Her grandmother laughed and turned down the volume. She led them into her small living room, telling them that lunch would be ready in about fifteen minutes. "Now, tell me all about school!" she exclaimed.

Hannah and Michael both shared about how it was at college. Nana asked about Michael's family, which he updated her on.

Lunch was absolutely delicious! Her Nana had made homemade fried chicken, fresh green beans, sliced tomatoes and homemade biscuits. Michael couldn't say enough about it. He commented that he had not had a homemade meal in months. Her grandmother beamed at the compliments. Dessert was homemade pound cake even though Hannah and Michael were completely stuffed, but they each had a small piece.

When they got back to the house, her mom was gone. Hannah asked Michael what he wanted to do, and he suggested that they walk back to the park to walk off the huge lunch.

Hand-in-hand, they walked and talked, even though they had already shared so much. This time, Hannah insisted that she push Michael in the swings.

Racing to see who could get to the slide first caused another tickle fight. Michael teased Hannah about cheating when she won. Climbing on the jungle gym was the third task at the park since they never got over to it the day before. Sitting on the top with their legs dangling, they continued laughing and sharing about each other's lives growing up.

By the time they got back to the house, they were exhausted. Hannah's mom was still not home. She led the way upstairs to her room where they both lay down on her bed. Even though she told Michael that they couldn't be physical, she missed kissing him. Leaning over, she kissed him softly, surprising him.

"Hey! I thought you said 'no kissing!'" Michael joked.

"I know I said that, but my Mom isn't home right now. So, I'm saying it's okay." Hannah said in a teasing voice. "But, if you don't want to…" her voice trailed off.

"Far be it from me to argue with you," Michael quipped as he pulled her against him on the bed. They were laying side-by-side. Michael put his arm around her back and began caressing it as he leaned in to kiss her again. Hannah's whimper urged him to increase the pressure on the kiss.

Every time he kissed Hannah, he couldn't seem to get enough. Continuing to rub her back, his hand found its way under her shirt, and he rubbed the soft skin up and down on her lower back. Her hands also found their way under his shirt

Finally, he pulled back and said, "I won't be able to stop if we keep going, so tell me what you want to do." He was earnest in how he looked in her eyes and Hannah had never loved him as much as she did at that moment. He was more concerned with her well-being than getting sex.

"Can we just lay here together and hold each other?" she kissed his nose and snuggled up against him.

"I'm willing to do what makes you the most comfortable," he said, moving the hair out of her eyes.

At one point, both of them began to doze off holding hands and with arms wrapped around each other. An hour later, Hannah woke up to see that Michael was still sleeping, but his arm was relaxed and he had loosened the hold on their hands.

All of a sudden the door downstairs opened and closed. Her mother called out that she was home. The sound woke Michael and they fixed their clothing before they got up and went downstairs.

Chapter 11

Saturday, they hung around the house relaxing and watching television. Her mother invited them to go to the mall that they had in town to get them out of the house. Michael and Hannah walked hand in hand, stopping to browse in stores after her mom left to go to a specific department store. Finally, they stopped to get an ice cream, sitting in the food court enjoying being together.

At one point during the day, the phone rang and her mother answered it.

"Hannah, it's for you," she called into the den. Hannah and Michael were watching a show together.

Feeling anxiety, and predicting what would happen, she answered, Hannah said hello and there was breathing on the line. "Hello," Hannah said again. "Whoever this is needs to stop," she repeated. "First, you call me at school and now you are calling my house!" The other person immediately hung up.

When she walked back into the den, Michael looked at her and said, "Who was that?"

"It was nothing...just a wrong number," Hannah said with her gaze turned the other direction. But, trepidation filled her because the person had to be at school with her. And, they knew her home number!

"It didn't sound like 'nothing'." Michael commented. "You were yelling at them to stop. Then you yelled about them calling at school and now calling your house."

Her hands made a dismissal motion as she said, "Someone has been making stupid prank calls, that's all."

"What?!" Michael asked, sitting up straight. "How long has this been going on?"

Shrugging her shoulders, Hannah looked down as she said, "A couple of weeks,"

Taking her shoulders so that she would look at him, Michael repeated, "What? Hannah, why didn't you say something?"

"What can you do about it? It's probably nothing. Let's just forget about it." Shrugging out of his hold, Hannah took the remote control to change the channel. Michael wanted to talk about it further, but it was clear that she did not. At that moment, more seeds of doubt crept in and he wondered if he shouldn't be so focused on Hannah instead of his schoolwork. The persistent fear of failure was always in the back of his mind.

***

Both Hannah and Michael took a shower before going out to dinner. Hannah blow-dried her hair and put some curls in it with her curling iron. She took great consideration in applying her makeup so that she could look as nice as possible. She chose a red blouse with a black pencil skirt to wear to dinner. She put on black hose and heels.

Because he was trying to be a gentleman, Michael waited downstairs for her while she finished getting ready. Her mom and dad would be leaving in a few minutes, so they were all in the living room when she walked down.

"Well, don't you look pretty!" her dad commented as he came to give her a hug.

"Thanks, Dad," Hannah said softly as she reached up to kiss his cheek.

"Your blouse is lovely," her mom commented, coming over to straighten the back of it.

But, it was Michael's expression that drew her attention. He didn't say anything, but he had the same expression in his eyes as he did when they went to the sports bar with their friends. Her heart turned over from how he was gazing at her.

Her mom and dad gathered their things to go eat dinner with their friends. Hannah and Michael walked out with them so that her Dad could lock up.

As soon as they were walking toward the door, he commented softly in her ear, "You are absolutely gorgeous! I'm going to have a hard time following your rules tonight!"

Hannah smiled as his breath tickled her ear and his hand rested on the small of her back. She looked up at him and he leaned close to her as he pressed his lips onto her cheek. It didn't last long, but she could feel his desire.

Her mom was asking her if she had her house key for them to get back in the house. It took several seconds for her to answer, "Yes, I have it, Mom," with a breathy tone to her voice.

Turning back to Michael, she asked, "Are you ready to go?"

"Honestly, I would rather stay here with you," Michael commented as he walked behind her to the car, and he chuckled when he saw her blush.

Hannah was glad to let him drive them to the restaurant because she needed a moment to gain control of her senses. As soon as they parked, he walked around to open her door. Wearing a dark, red dress shirt with black slacks, he looked wonderful as well. His collar was open at the top making him look sexy.

As he opened her door, he pulled her into his arms and kissed her again. "See?" he said. "I'm having a very hard time keeping my hands off of you!"

Hannah wrapped her arms around his waist and returned his kiss. "You look amazing, too!"

They walked into the restaurant and were seated in a booth, Michael sitting on the same side as Hannah. He entwined their fingers while looking at the menu and it didn't take them long to order drinks, while deciding what they wanted for their meal. After ordering steaks, potatoes and salads, Michael wrapped his arm around Hannah as they continued talking. He asked if she had enjoyed this visit home to see her family.

"It's been wonderful because I've been able to show you off to them and my grandmother! I've told them so much about you on the phone, but I am glad that they have been able to see how wonderful you are." She looked deeply into his eyes as she told him those words.

"Your parents and your grandmother are great people. I'm glad to see that you've grown up in an amazing home!" Michael smiled into her eyes as he said the words.

As soon as he paid for dinner, Michael helped her out of the booth, and he pulled her close as they walked out to the car. As soon as his car door was shut, he pulled her to him and kissed her ardently like he wanted to do all evening! He caressed her lips, memorizing their touch and their taste. She sighed and opened her mouth for him. As he deepened the kiss, he groaned with pleasure.

Hannah pressed closer to him, as close as she could get with the console in the way. Michael kissed her neck and down her throat to the first button on her blouse. Breathing heavily, his hand found its way under her blouse and up to her satiny bra. Hannah's hands were caressing his chest on the outside of his shirt, but she was impatiently trying to pull it free from the waistband of his slacks. He helped pull it loose and her hands caressed his back, around to his stomach and up to his chest. Finally, Michael pulled back with as much restraint as he could get.

"Hannah, we need to stop." He cajoled her as her mouth was moving up and down his throat. He gently pushed her back away from him.

"Michael, why are you stopping? I want this with you." Hannah said with a dazed and confused expression.

"Baby, I have too much respect for you to pull you into the back seat of this car for us to have sex. I'm not going to do that to you." Michael ran his hand through his hair, trying to cool off.

"My parents aren't supposed to be back until late. We can go back to my house." She said, looking at him with an overly agreeable expression. Her lips were swollen from his kisses and he wanted nothing else than to press his lips to them again.

"I don't want to make you uncomfortable," he said looking into her eyes.

"Michael, I want this, and I want to be with you," she said in a convincing voice, but he worried that she was saying that to make him happy.

"I didn't bring any protection with me because I thought it would be off-limits," Michael commented thinking that would be the end of it.

"I haven't told you this before because it's kind of embarrassing, but I am on the pill because I have female issues. My time of the month is very painful, and my doctor put me on them to help ease the pressure and pain." Hannah looked quickly at him before gazing out the window.

"I'm glad you told me, but I don't want you to feel pressured that you have to do anything with me. I have loved being with you this weekend. I'm serious, Hannah!" Michael pulled her chin up to glimpse in her eyes again.

"I don't feel pressured, and I love being with you!" Hannah said.

"What time will your parents be home?" Michael asked.

"They said it would probably be around midnight because they are playing bridge at their friends' house," Hannah replied.

Michael looked at his watch to see that it was only a little after nine. He leaned over and kissed her again and he said, "Are you sure?"

Hannah kissed him again, slowly as her response to his question.

It took a few minutes to get back to the house. Michael came around to help her out of the car. Hannah unlocked the front door and led him upstairs to her room.

Their time of making love was just as wonderful as the past two times. Looking at the clock, it was only ten o'clock. Michael was rubbing her back, her arms and any other part of her body that he could reach as her hand was rubbing circles around his chest, causing the fire to spark in him once again.

She raised up and kissed his lips, causing him to see the cleavage in her breasts. He ran his finger between them, kissing her deeply.

Groaning, Michael moved away from Hannah. "How about we get dressed and go down and watch the other movie you rented? I don't want your parents coming home early and catching us up here," he said, reaching out and pushing her hair back over her shoulder and running his hand through it.

"That's probably a good idea," she said as she moved to get up, but Michael pulled her back down and kissed her thoroughly one more time before releasing her.

They cleaned up the clothing they had worn on their date and changed before going back downstairs. Hannah went to the kitchen to make them some drinks. As she was pouring sodas into glasses, Michael came up behind her and pulled her back against him. Pushing her hair to one side, he reached down and kissed the back of her neck.

"Umm," she sighed as she allowed herself to lean back further.

"I love you," he murmured as he pulled her into a tight hug against his chest.

"I love you, too," she whispered.

"Come on," he encouraged, pulling her into the living room. "I don't want your parents catching us making out in your kitchen! Your Dad might not like me anymore!"

Hannah couldn't resist teasing him as she went back for their drinks. "If he knew what we just did, I guarantee he wouldn't like you!" Laughing at the expression on his face, she set down the drinks. As she was settling into the couch, he grabbed her and began tickling her. Eventually, he stopped when they were both out of breath.

He stood up and put the video into the VCR and pressed play on the movie as Hannah used the remote to turn on the correct channel. Sitting behind her, he pulled her back into his embrace as they became engrossed in the movie. At one point, they were both completely relaxed and dozed off. The garage door opening startled them awake and Hannah moved to sit up beside Michael.

Her parents walked in and asked how their evening was.

"We had a great time!" Hannah said. "We ate at the steak place and then we came home and watched another movie." She prayed that her mother would not see right through what she just told her, but thankfully her mom seemed oblivious.

"I'm glad you had a good time," her mom said. As usual, Hannah's dad didn't have anything to say, but he came to stand behind Hannah's mom and smiled at both of them.

They moved around the kitchen getting water and making sure everything was locked up. They both said good night and disappeared into their bedroom.

Michael had paused the movie when her parents came in. He turned it back on for them to finish, pulling Hannah back against him once more.

The movie ended and before they got up, Hannah looked into his eyes. With shining eyes, she said, "Thank you again for coming with me this weekend. You said you wanted to prove that I was beautiful to you. I don't know that I will always believe it to be true, but I believe it tonight."

Michael kissed her forehead, her nose and finally her lips. "You know I would think you are beautiful even if you didn't sleep with me. Every time I see you walk in a room, I am overwhelmed by how gorgeous you are." He searched deep into her eyes hoping to find that she believed him, and he was pleased to see that she was trying to trust his words.

"Thank you," Hannah said. "I have never seen a guy with more beautiful eyes than you. The first time you kissed me, I was swept away with how soft your lips were. And I absolutely love you in basketball shorts!"

"I will make sure to wear them more often!" Michael teased and they both laughed. He stood and pulled her to a stand but the same worry he had been having at the back of his mind made him wonder if he should slow things down. He didn't want the night to end, but he knew they needed to go to bed so that they would be ready for church in the morning before driving back to school after lunch.

***

The church service with her parents was wonderful as well as lunch at the local Mexican restaurant.

Once they were back at the house, Hannah said, "We should change clothes and pack."

"Oh, you really have to go so soon?" her mom asked.

"Mom, it takes over three hours to drive there, and Michael and I both have early classes on Mondays." Hannah had to restrain herself from rolling her eyes at her mother's comment.

It only took a few minutes for them to change into jeans and t-shirts. Michael packed his duffel bag and walked downstairs to thank Hannah's parents for having him. He shook her dad's hand. "I can't thank you enough for everything, including the delicious meals and allowing me to see your charming town!"

Hannah's dad patted him on the back and said, "You are welcome back here anytime!" Her mom smiled and nodded her head in agreement as she commented, "It's evident that you make Hannah happy, and I appreciate that you were there to keep her safe when she needed it!" By that time, Hannah had come down with her overnight bag and she set it by the front door. Both parents moved in to hug her at the same time.

"Bye, sweetie," her mom said. "Call me to let me know you've made it there safely!"

"Goodbye, Hannah-bug," her dad murmured, kissing her cheek.

Hannah's mom hugged Michael and then they walked outside to wave goodbye as they drove away.

The drive back was uneventful. At one point, Michael began singing a song they were listening to very loudly and changing the lyrics to silly words. Thankful that he was the one driving, Hannah couldn't help doubling over with laughter. Holding hands with him, she smiled as he continued singing and she thought about how much she loved him. Thankfully, he didn't notice her studying him and thinking about their future.

Eventually, they were on the road back to the school. Michael pulled into the driveway of his apartment. After seeing him for four days, Hannah would miss seeing him every second of each day.

He set his bag on his porch and pulled her into his embrace. The look in his eyes let her know that he was thinking the same thing. He smiled into her eyes and said, "I'm going to miss you!"

"Me too," was all Hannah could say because she was afraid she would start crying which was silly as she berated herself that she would still see him every day.

His eyebrow dipped as he said, "Let me know if you get any more prank calls."

"Michael, it's probably nothing," she commented, pushing away the slight fear that came over her.

Michael continued, "I just want to make sure you're safe." After a slight pause, he said, "You know it's only a few days before you come home with me!"

Hannah smiled and said, "I can't wait."

Michael kissed her again and said, "I love you, baby!"

"I love you, too!" Hannah exclaimed before she turned to get back in her car.

"Don't forget to call your mom," he reminded her. "Good night, beautiful!"

Smiling, she started her car and drove off.

Chapter 12

The week flew by as Hannah and Michael were busy with papers and mid-term exams. Michael was preparing for his voice midterm which would involve him singing in front of his professor with a piece chosen precisely for his voice. He had spent many hours that week in the lab practicing. They both spent many hours at the library gathering research for term papers that were due as soon as they came back from his home.

All too soon, it was Thursday. The plan was to skip their classes on Friday and drive to his house on Thursday evening. Hannah was excited, but also nervous. His mom seemed very reserved, and Hannah still wasn't sure if she approved of her.

Hannah waited for him in the lobby after he called to tell her he was on the way.

He walked in and kissed her lightly before saying, "Hi," Smiling into her eyes, he asked, "Are you ready to go?"

Hannah nodded her head, saying, "Hello and yes."

He picked up her bag and took her hand again, walking her to the other side of the car. He opened the door, put her bag onto the back seat and helped her inside.

Walking around to the driver's side, he started the car and then took her hand in his. His eyes were bright green as he smiled at her again and said, "I'm so excited you're coming home with me!"

She chuckled and said, "Me too."

Halfway through the drive, a love song came on the cassette that he had slipped in before they left. As he held the steering wheel with one hand, he glanced at her while crooning the words. He sang the words with passion to show the depth of his love. He pulled her hand to his lips and kissed each finger, even while he was keeping his eyes on the road, as he sang. Averting his eyes back to the road was difficult because he couldn't help but get lost in Hannah's eyes. She was thankful he was focused on driving because her heartbeat was going nuts from how romantic this was!

An hour later, they pulled up into the driveway of an adorable house. Michael turned off the car and looked over at her. "Here we are. I told you that it's much smaller than your house."

"Michael, I don't care about that. I love this house and I'm sure the inside is great!" Hannah's response was encouraging. "Is your mom home?" she asked, looking at the house again.

"She doesn't get off work for a couple of hours and my dad works forty-five minutes from here. They will be home by five or so. So...we have the house to ourselves for a few hours if you are okay with that." Michael looked over at Hannah, wondering if she caught on to his inference.

The look in her eyes told him that she understood what he was saying. His actions on the drive went straight to her core and she was more than ready for what he was offering. "Well, give me the tour, first!" she said.

It made Michael happy that she wanted to be with him as he walked around the car and opened her door. Putting her bag on his other shoulder, he took both bags to the front porch and unlocked the door. "Wait a minute," he said as he stepped in and turned off the alarm code. "We had someone break in a few years ago, so my parents put in an alarm system."

"Wow!" Hannah breathed. "That's understandable!"

They walked into an adorable living room. It adjoined a dining room, and the kitchen was separated by a counter and a wall.

Eyes bright with joy, Hannah said, "I love your house!" He could read the sincerity in her gaze which made him love her more.

Michael led the way down the hall to the first bedroom. He turned on the light and placed Hannah's bag on the floor. "This is my sister's room. She's at a dance camp this weekend, so you can sleep in her bed."

"I love it!" Hannah said. Her room was pink, and it was decorated with a teddy bear theme. "I take it she loves bears."

"You have no idea!" Michael commented back. He took a couple of steps to the room beside the one where they were standing. He flipped on the light, and she saw posters all over the wall of rock bands and she knew this was Michael's room.

"I would've known this was your room, even if you weren't here to show me!" she teased him.

Michael grabbed her around the waist and began tickling her. "Oh, you think you would know?" He tickled her across the room and she fell onto the bed, where he immediately fell beside her. He pushed the hair back over her shoulder and kissed her softly. Hannah's hands immediately found their way under his shirt. He moaned softly as he kissed her. Deepening the kiss, he put his hands under her shirt and rubbed up and down her back.

She stopped and looked at him, "You're certain that your parents won't be home for a while, right?"

Against her mouth Michael murmured, "I promise that they have the same schedule every single day which results in them getting home around five. Trust me," He did pause as he said, "But, I don't want to pressure you."

Hannah hedged with fear of not pleasing him, but she finally said, "I don't think I'm comfortable going all the way with you in your childhood bedroom, but I am happy for us to kiss for a while."

"I understand," Michael said as he pulled Hannah down beside him on the bed.

They leaned toward each other at the same time, and they made out for a long while. A half hour later they woke up to realize they had fallen asleep. Michael was the first one to wake up and he pulled Hannah close and woke her up with another delicious kiss. Hannah snuggled closer to him as she inhaled from the pleasure of being woken up in such a lovely manner. Because they were young and in love, they couldn't contain themselves and they pulled off their shirts.

As soon as Michael saw Hannah in her bra, he breathed in sharply. Pulling down the cups to where they sprang free, his hands rubbed her breasts and her nipples hardened into peaks.

Leaning down to kiss one, he said, "You know, you're the only girl that I've ever brought home before. In fact, you're the only one who has been in my room with me." Hannah gasped at his mouth on her breast, but she pulled back and said, "Michael! I told you I'm not comfortable with this! I want your mom to still like me!" She tried getting up, but Michael wouldn't let her.

With his eyes filled with laughter, he pulled her back down beside him and he said, "Please don't worry about this. I want this to be an amazing weekend for you!"

After a few more minutes of kissing, they realized they were thirsty. They got dressed and went to get some drinks in the kitchen. Hannah observed out the back window while Michael called his mom to tell them that they had made it. She felt herself turning red at how he was calling her later than they actually arrived.

It was the beginning of a great weekend. There were a couple of times that Michael deserted her to go into the back of the house to talk with his mom, and Hannah didn't know what to do. Other than that, she did make Hannah feel at home.

Their family dynamics were quite different from her family's, especially at the dinner table where all of them got up to clean the kitchen while Hannah was not finished with her plate. Realizing that she was left sitting by herself, Michael dropped back into the chair beside her and murmured, "Sorry."

The first afternoon was their only opportunity to make out because they went to his mom's school on Friday and to meet his grandmother. Afterward, Michael drove her around just as she did. He showed her his different schools and where he and his friends liked to hang out. His best friend, another Michael, was home for the weekend, so he took her over to meet him on Friday evening. Hannah enjoyed getting to know him as well as hearing stories about their years growing up.

On Saturday, they went out shopping with his mom and on Saturday evening, Michael's parents grilled hamburgers, which were delicious. While eating, Hannah discovered that his mother had a passion for classic movies. She loved watching "Little Women" and "Gone with the Wind" with her mom, so she was able to talk about them. Michael's mother suggested that they watch the old version of "Father of the Bride" with Spencer Tracey and Elizabeth Taylor.

Excited, she agreed, and Michael had no choice but to go along with it. He wound up enjoying the movie and sat as close to Hannah as he could get away with (his mother sat in the chair across the room). He knew his mother would speak up if he pulled Hannah back to sit in his arms, which is what he wanted to do. She was even more old-fashioned than Hannah's parents when it came to displaying affection, especially considering Michael's age. At one point, she got up to go into the kitchen for a drink and Michael snuck a quick kiss and squeezed Hannah's knee, causing her to mouth, "*Stop.*"

His response was to move his hand a little further up her leg. Her expression caused him to muffle laughter as she turned beet red and pushed his hand away. He placed it back on her knee in rebellion, moving his hand to the inside of her thigh. He was proud to see her twitch with desire for him.

The minute his mother walked back into the room, he slid his hand behind Hannah's bottom. His fingers rubbed against her and Hannah had to cover her mouth to keep herself from yelping out loud.

Again, he was overcome with laughter as he looked at her innocently. He mouthed, "*What's the matter?*"

Her red face made him cover his mouth so that he would not laugh out loud, and she quickly closed the door to the bathroom.

His mother looked his way, so he averted his gaze. She had already asked him how serious he was about Hannah. He had honestly looked at his mother and said, "I love her, mom." She didn't say anything, but he wasn't sure if she was happy about it.

***

On Sunday, they went to church and then his parents took them out to lunch before they had to pack up to get ready to drive back to school.

Michael's mother slipped him some cash to help pay for his gas and she hugged him tight. Then, surprising Hannah, she turned and hugged her. Michael's dad hugged her good-bye as well. Hannah was surprised because he had stayed in the garage most of the weekend. Michael said that he tinkered with woodwork. He did come in for dinner each evening and asked Hannah questions about her home growing up.

As they drove home, Hannah stared out the window and pondered how much she was enjoying getting to know Michael these past couple of weeks. He reached over and brushed a thumb over her left cheek.

"Are you okay?" he asked, looking at her before looking back at the road.

Hannah looked at him and said, "I want you to know just how much I love you. Being with you these past two weeks have been some of the most wonderful days of my life. Thank you for inviting me home with you."

Once they got back to school, Hannah was reluctant to leave Michael again because their schedule would be crazy this next week with mid-terms and research papers that were due. They would see each other at meals and Hannah planned to go to Michael's game on Thursday evening.

He came around to open her side of the car and he set her bag on the ground. He pulled Hannah into his embrace and held her, rocking back and forth with her head against his chest.

Pulling back, he said, "I will miss you this week." Hannah's heart quickened as she realized he knew exactly what she was thinking.

"Let's plan something just for us on Thursday evening," Michael continued.

Nodding her head, Hannah said, "I will see you at your game on Tuesday."

"Thank you, baby." He kissed her tenderly as he reluctantly pulled back. "See you tomorrow morning. Good night, beautiful!"

Hannah pulled away and turned to go inside, waving as she walked away. Michael still stood there, and he winked at her, causing her heart to flutter. At this point in their relationship, it was beginning to feel more and more permanent.

Chapter 13

As Michael drove back to his apartment, he began feeling doubts about this relationship. As much as he had enjoyed these past two weeks with Hannah, he had the feeling that Hannah was wishing for this to be 'forever' and Michael wasn't sure if he was ready for that kind of commitment. Sure, he told his mother he loved her, but he had seen the doubt in her eyes.

"Michael, you're only eighteen and you've only been at college for three months," his mom commented.

Michael tried to protest and say, "I do love her, Mom."

His mother didn't say anything else, but he felt her disapproval and that bugged him more than anything. Remembering his desire to focus on school and getting his degree kept him from calling Hannah. Most nights he would call her before bed to tell her good night. Tonight, he took a shower and went straight to bed.

***

The next week was rather busy with school and assignments that were due, so Hannah and Michael did not have much time to spend together. They talked as much as they could on the phone. She attended his first game as promised. They even went out for a burger on Thursday evening. Hannah insisted that she pay for her own meal, especially after his mom's comment about Michael not having much spending money. She hoped she imagined it, but Michael seemed withdrawn and deep down she had feelings that she wasn't enough for him.

The prank calls continued sporadically with all three of the girls answering, but Hannah answered most of them. Michelle commented that perhaps they should report it, but with life being so busy, none of them did. As she walked to class and other places around the campus, Hannah couldn't shake the feeling that she was being watched by somebody. She constantly looked around, but she never saw anyone. She had struggled with paranoia as she grew up, so she shook it off as that silly habit from her younger days.

Since he had joined the intramural basketball league, Michael spent almost every evening practicing with his team. At that point, Hannah felt like he was definitely pulling back from her because his calls had become fewer and fewer. Before going home with him, he called her every night and he hadn't done it since they had been back. When they were together, it seemed like he was closed off from her. Wondering if she did something, Hannah overanalyzed what she had said and done at his house to cause him to draw away from her. She even went so far as to wonder if she should have slept with him that first time, or any of the other times.

Hannah, Jackie and Michelle went to watch one of their practices and she was amazed again at how good Michael looked in basketball shorts and a basketball jersey. He had sculpted calves that flexed as he ran up and down the basketball court. Hannah noticed some other girls on the other side of the bleachers also watching and cheering them on as they played. A sick feeling stole over her, and she felt like she was outside of her own body observing the downfall of their relationship.

"Those girls are acting a bit bold," Jackie said watching them ogle over Michael and several of the other guys on his team.

"Yeah, and Michael doesn't seem to mind," Hannah muttered, feeling rebuffed by him, especially since he hadn't acknowledged their presence.

Michelle stood up and cheered loudly while glaring at the other girls as they glanced their way. "Don't worry!" she said to Hannah. "We will get Michael's attention back on you!" She shouted his name saying, "Go Michael!" causing him to grin in their direction.

The practice ended thirty minutes later. Hannah, Michelle and Jackie hung around hoping that Michael would come over to Hannah. However, he stayed with his buddies who were busy flirting and talking to the other group of girls.

"Do you want to go over there?" Jackie asked, watching Hannah's expression.

"No, that's okay. Let's just go." As the typical wallflower, Hannah preferred one or two good friends. She didn't want to compete with so many people for Michael's attention.

As she, Jackie and Michelle stood to go, Michael did happen to look her way. Raising his hand to wave at her, Hannah reluctantly waved back. Her brain hurt because all she had done was think about everything and wonder what had changed. With a dejected heart, she trudged back to the dorm with heavy footsteps.

As she lay in her bed, she had a one-sided conversation with herself. *I must have done something to push Michael away because he has no desire for me.* Trying to close her eyes and fall asleep, she continued thinking, 'Once he has a few nights of sex from you, he must not be interested anymore. Maybe he was just pretending when your parents came." A few tears leaked out and Hannah continued laying there with conflicting thoughts. She had a hard time believing that Michael was so shallow because he had not acted that way with her at all during their time together. It was early morning when she finally drifted off to sleep.

***

The next day was busy, and Hannah did not hear from Michael at all, nor did she see him at breakfast and dinner, which had become a habit. It was almost like he was purposefully avoiding her and the ache in her heart grew as she realized that she wasn't good enough to hold onto him. Friday night had become a normal date night, but apparently it was not happening tonight. Her mom had asked about him the night before and she hedged and tried avoiding the subject.

Jackie and Michelle noticed that she was quiet and they were respectful of her need to think.

"Let's go get a milkshake," Michelle commented after they had finished dinner.

Hannah attempted a smile and she said, "That sounds wonderful."

The time with her friends was a nice diversion from her constant thoughts.

Jackie tried easing the tension by saying, "If Michael's being a jerk, just let me know and I will knock him upside the head."

"It is rather rude of him that he hasn't called you, especially since he was flirting with all of those heifers last night!" Michelle's comment actually brought a smile to Hannah's face, but she was too heartsick to laugh.

After getting ready for bed, the phone rang. Hannah's heart sang hoping it was Michael, but it was another prank call. Hannah's heart remained conflicted as she eventually fell asleep that night.

***

The next evening, Hannah was studying when her phone rang. Wishing for it to be Michael, her heart soared when she heard his voice. But she told herself not to get too excited.

"Hey, can you come out and go for a walk with me?" Michael asked her.

"Sure, I'll be out in a few minutes." Hannah did not put much enthusiasm into her response to him because she wasn't sure what was happening and why he was there all of a sudden after days of ghosting her. She told her friends that she was going out for a few minutes with him.

Jackie smiled at her encouragingly and said, "See, I knew he couldn't stay away from you! Go have fun."

Hannah didn't answer because she had a feeling that things weren't going to work out.

She walked to the lobby and saw him sitting on one of the couches. Her heart flipped over at seeing him. As he stood, she studied his face and saw that he did not seem overly excited to see her. He quietly came to her and said, "Hey."

"Hello," Hannah responded as she guarded her heart because she knew this was not going to be the conversation that she wished would happen.

Michael was polite in holding the door for her and they walked out the door across the campus to a lovely bench among the flowers. He didn't even reach for her hand as they walked, which is what he normally did.

After sitting down, he looked down at his feet and then he glanced at her. "Hannah," he said. "I feel that things have been going too fast for us and I think we need to cool things off and see other people."

Hannah's eyes welled with tears as she looked away, watching other couples walking hand-in-hand across the campus. Deep down, she knew that this was coming, but she couldn't help but respond with, "I don't understand. A week ago, you told me how much you loved me after meeting my parents."

"I know," Michael said, "But things seem to be moving faster than I am comfortable with and I just think we need a break from each other. How about if we hang out as friends for the time being?"

Hannah looked at Michael and said, "Okay, if that's what you want. But I don't think I can be friends with you right now. If you want a break, then I will give that to you. After the intensity that our relationship has taken, I won't feel comfortable with just hanging out with you. Please don't bother walking me back." Turning her face away from him, she stood up and walked away. Fat tears were rolling down her cheeks with every step she took.

Hearing Michael call her name, she ignored him. As she walked, her heart broke into a million pieces, and she couldn't stop the tears from flowing down her face. At that moment, she felt as if someone was watching her just as she had the other day. 'It's probably just Michael,' she thought to herself as she continued walking away from him.

***

Rhonda couldn't believe her luck and she cackled out loud. Following Hannah had become a habit and tonight, she watched Michael break up with her.

"Serves her right," she breathed to herself. "He must have realized what a bitch she could be."

Wondering if this was a chance to corner her alone again, Rhonda followed her as she began running around the perimeter of the school. Just as she was about to make herself known, Hannah walked into the student center and Tommy Anderson walked up to her and began talking.

"Shit," Rhonda breathed. He stayed with Hannah, even walking her back to the dorm. Burning inside, Rhonda cursed him silently for taking away her opportunity to approach Hannah. Dragging her feet in disappointment, she walked back to her dorm in hopes that she would be successful the next day.

Rhonda's plan involved making sure no one was around. At first, she planned to threaten her and then, she would unleash her revenge upon her.

***

Hannah was not ready to go back and see her friends, so she started jogging around the perimeter of the campus, feeling the burn in her thighs as she sped up to a faster pace. The briskness of the run seemed to help her release some of the pain that she was feeling.

She was dying of thirst after about an hour. She had put some cash into her shorts pockets in case they decided to go somewhere for food. Drying the tears on her cheeks, she walked into the student center to get water from the vending machine.

Turning around, she saw a guy named Tommy. She remembered meeting him when she and her mother came and stayed for the weekend last spring for incoming freshmen.

"Hey, Hannah," Tommy said. "How's it going?"

Hannah pasted a fake smile on her face and said, "It's great. I was just out for a run. You know, getting some exercise."

"Do you mind if I run with you?" Tommy asked.

"Sure, that would be great." Feeling rebellious, Hannah thought that if Michael actually wanted space, she would give it to him. Tommy was a really nice guy, and she enjoyed getting to know him back in the spring as they went to introductory sessions together learning about what college life would be like. She was distracted in realizing she also met Rhonda that weekend.

They ran for another thirty minutes and went back to the student center to cool down and get a drink from the snack bar. Tommy was kind in offering to buy her drink and they walked over to the couches near the ping pong tables. They sat down on the couch.

"I thought you and Michael Davis were together," he said looking at her. "You guys looked pretty involved at the dance."

"We decided to take a break," Hannah forced the words out, feeling her heart breaking. . She hung out with Tommy for a little while longer until she said that she needed to get back to her room to study.

"I'll walk you back," he said, standing and offering his hand to help her up

"Thanks," she said as she forced a smile. She noticed that she felt nothing when she placed her hand in his.

As they walked back, Tommy asked her more about herself. To be polite, Hannah inquired more about him as well.

"Would you want to eat breakfast with me tomorrow?" Tommy asked.

"Sure, if you're willing to join Jackie, Michelle, and me. We usually eat breakfast together each morning." Ignoring her wounded heart, Hannah tried not to think about how Michael usually joined them.

Tommy touched Hannah's arm and he said, "That will be great! See you tomorrow morning."

Jackie and Michelle saw her face as she came into the room, but Hannah was not ready to talk to them about what had happened.

They gave her space and after Hannah got a shower, they invited her to watch a sit-com episode with them. Surprised, Hannah found herself laughing as it helped take her mind off her pain for a little while.

A week later, Hannah, Jackie and Michelle walked to the dining hall to get breakfast since none of their classes started until ten o'clock that day. As they walked out of the food line, Michael was coming to get in line. Hannah saw him walking their way and she immediately turned the other way to avoid talking to him. Inwardly, she chided herself for allowing him to make her feel like this. Conflicting emotions had filled her insides for the entire week, missing him, hating him and being angry at him for hurting her, feeling like she wasn't good enough for anyone.

"Hey, Hannah," Michael called trying to get her attention. He missed her more than he realized that he would.

"Are you an idiot?" Michelle asked him in her blunt manner. "You break up with her and expect her to make small talk with you? Just leave her alone!"

Jackie stepped in between him and Hannah, keeping him from walking any closer to her. Instead of sitting at their regular table, Jackie and Michelle suggested that they sit at a table over by the windows. Hannah agreed and walked in that direction.

A few minutes later, Tommy walked over to their table with one of his friends. He sat down beside Hannah. She smiled at him to greet him and happened to look across the room at Michael's face. From his expression, she could tell he was not happy that Tommy was sitting beside her. *Too bad*, she thought to herself as she tried to forget about him.

She turned back to Tommy, ignoring Michael but she could feel him shooting daggers in her direction. At one point, Tommy reached and put his hand on top of hers. He had been joining their group of friends every day since she invited him the week before.

The only drawback was he liked when the other girls looked his way. He would smile and wave at them as they passed by.

Hannah glanced over at Michael's table and saw raw anger on his face as he saw Tommy's hand on top of hers.

The two guys who took Jackie and Michelle to the dance, James and Danny, also sat at their table. Hannah couldn't help but notice Danny's glances toward Michelle, but her friend seemed to be oblivious. Knowing Michelle's history, she understood that her friend didn't have much experience with guys. Michelle had an older brother who guarded her like a hawk. Anytime a guy showed interest in his sister, her brother would find out and stop them. Michelle loved her big brother, and she appreciated his protection, but it irritated her that she never had a chance to get to know any guy from their town. Hannah hoped that maybe she would get the chance to get to know Danny.

After breakfast, Jackie said, "Man, did you make Michael jealous!"

"I wasn't trying to," Hannah said. "But if he wants space, I'm trying to give it to him"

"I know you didn't, but I thought he was going to come over and punch Tommy!" Jackie said with a chuckle.

"Serves him right," Michelle joined into the conversation. "He deserves to suffer after he ended things so abruptly with you!"

Deep down, Hannah felt a small amount of satisfaction that she had made Michael jealous. It was how she felt when she saw him near that group of girls as they were flirting with him and his other teammates.

As she walked to class, she had a strange feeling again, that someone was watching her. Looking around, she didn't see anyone. Shaking off her paranoia, she walked to her class and sat down.

***

As Michael walked to his class, he couldn't stop thinking about Hannah and Tommy. He thought he had made the right choice to break up with her, but now he wasn't so sure. He hadn't talked to anyone but Alex about it.

Alex had looked at him and said, "You know you're crazy, right? She's a great girl and you had an amazing connection with her. I think you're making a mistake."

Deep down, Michael wondered the same thing. He missed her more than he could describe. He had mentioned on the phone with his mom that he had told Hannah that they needed a break.

"Michael, that's probably a good idea." his mom had commented. "You are both so young and you need to focus on your school-work. Hannah seems like a nice young lady, but her parents probably feel the same way."

Anger filled his gut at his mom's words, but he mumbled in agreement to her. Sometimes he felt like she had too much control over him even two hours away at college. They talked for a few more minutes before hanging up.

***

Hannah was coming into her room after her morning class when she heard her phone ringing. Wishing it to be Michael, she lifted it and said "hello."

It was another prank call as the breathing continued for a few more seconds as Hannah kept repeating hello. Then, whoever it was hung up as the phone rang again and she mindlessly answered it as she was typing the last few sentences of the term paper that was due on Wednesday.

Again, she was greeted with breathing on the other line. Whoever was behind them had not called this many times in a row until today.

"Who is this?" Hannah asked with annoyance in her voice, but a chill ran down her spine.

"Good grief," Hannah muttered as she hung up and pressed save on her word processor. She needed to go to the library in order to print it out so that it would be ready to turn in on Wednesday

A few hours later, she was returning from the library to her phone ringing again.

With a tremor in her hand, she picked it up and said, "Hello," in a terse tone of voice. Again, nothing but breathing. "Whoever this is, I'm calling the police if it continues."

The voice on the line whispered, "Bitch," before hanging up again. Hannah dropped the phone in shock as her roommates walked in.

Seeing Hannah's face and shaking hands, Michelle said, "Who was that?"

"Just a prank call," Hannah commented, averting her gaze.

"Okay, they've been happening for a while, but something is different with your face." Jackie said with concern in her own eyes.

Breathing out a huge sigh, Hannah talked about how they had increased that morning. Then, she mentioned the person whispering, 'bitch' that last time. She also told them that the person called her home during her visit over Fall Break.

"What?!" Jackie yelled. "Why haven't you told us!" Michelle exclaimed.

"Hannah, you need to report this, and you should probably call your Dad," Jackie said.

Michelle was studying Hannah's face and she said, "There's more that you're not telling us."

Sighing, Hannah looked at them and they could see raw terror in her eyes. "I'm just wondering if it could possibly be Rhonda. It seems that the problem with her is over, but I've been afraid that she might be trying to threaten me in a different way."

Looking at her intently, Michelle said, "What else, Hannah?"

Groaning, Hannah said, "You are getting to know me too well!" Michelle opened her mouth to speak, and Hannah held up her hands saying, "Okay, okay. I've had a strange feeling of being followed by someone. I used to be paranoid when I was younger over silly things, so I'm probably making this up."

"I don't think so if it's happened more than once, Hannah" Jackie commented.

Realization filled Jackie's gaze and she breathed out as she continued. "I wouldn't put it past Rhonda. She's crazy enough that stalking might be something she might do when she's angry and holding a grudge." Then, Jackie repeated her words from earlier, "You need to report this and call your Dad right now."

Groaning, Hannah said, "I don't want to call them because they will treat me like a little child once they hear this."

"Yeah, but Hannah," Michelle said, "This is stalking now. You might be in real danger."

"Who do I even call to report this?" Hannah asked bewildered at what to do.

Jackie thought for a minute and then she said, "Let's start by telling Danah. She can advise you on what to do."

Nodding her head, Hannah said, "I don't want the two of you to be involved in case it is Rhonda."

"No way, Hannah," Michelle insisted, shaking her head. "You aren't doing this alone! We will go with you!"

Faced with indecision, Hannah finally shook her head in agreement, relieved that she wasn't alone in this anymore. Maybe telling her parents wouldn't be so bad either.

They went to Danah's apartment, and she happened to be there. Hannah shared with her what had been happening. Danah wrote everything down and encouraged Hannah to tell her parents just as Jackie and Michelle had done. She also said that her boss was in the housing department of the school and that she would pass it on to them.

The three girls went to eat dinner before walking back to their room. Jackie and Michelle sat on their beds so that Hannah could have privacy to call her parents. Thankfully, her dad answered so she was thankful as she explained. He was much more logical and didn't usually overreact as much as her mother did. Hannah asked him to wait until she was off the phone to tell her mother because her anxiety would be off the charts with this news. He agreed as long as she promised to call and speak with her mom the next day. Begrudgingly, she agreed and hung up.

***

Three days later, Hannah was walking out of her dorm to go to the bookstore. She needed to buy supplies to complete a project for class. As she walked to the student center, she saw Michael coming from the music building across the campus.

She tried turning in the other direction to go into another door, but Michael spotted her. "Hannah," he called. "Wait up!" He jogged in her direction.

"Hey, Michael." Trying to avoid looking at him, Hannah said, "I've got to go and get something for class. So, I can't talk right now."

"Look, Hannah," Michael said, shuffling his feet as he looked down at them. "I know I hurt you, but I was hoping we could get together to talk about it."

Schooling her face, she said, "I don't know. You made it pretty clear that you wanted a break from me. I'm not sure there's anything else to say."

"Please, can we get together tonight? I really want us to sit down and talk," Michael pleaded with her as he looked at her.

"About what?" Hannah retorted with fire in her eyes. "Michael, please leave me alone. I'm not at a point where I can just be friends with you."

Shaking his head, he said, "I understand, but I want you to be careful with Tommy."

Eyes filled with bitterness, Hannah looked at him and said, "Why do you even care?"

"Because I still care about you, Hannah. Tommy is a player and he likes more than one girl. I don't want you to get hurt," Michael said.

"Why wouldn't he be willing to change? Is it so hard to believe that he might have actual feelings for me?" Hannah argued.

Looking down again, Michael said, "That's not what I'm saying. I've just seen him around campus with many different girls and I don't want him to do that to you."

"Michael, you lost the chance to have a say in what happens with me. I have to go." Hannah turned around and walked away as Michael hung his head. He knew now that he had made a huge mistake in letting her go because he still loved her.

As he walked back to his apartment, Michael took a moment to analyze this time apart from her. He had an exam in one of his classes that he did not score well on earlier in the week. His desire to focus on his studies didn't seem to be working. Light came into his eyes as it dawned on him that he actually did better when they were together. Could being with Hannah inspire him to do even better? It was definitely something to think about. *I will talk to Alex about it and see what he thinks.* Lost in thought, he didn't even realize he made it back to his apartment.

***

Rhonda relished the fear she saw in Hannah every day. Her constant calls and stalking were doing what she wanted. Whispering the word 'bitch' had brought her great delight as she heard Hannah drop the phone. She was nervous and Rhonda could see it in her as she followed her. Excitement filled her as she saw Hannah walking in her direction at that precise moment. "Time to up my game," she whispered to herself with delight at the torture she would finally unleash upon her ex-roommate.

Chapter 14

As Hannah left the bookstore, she took a shortcut back to the dorm (to avoid running into Michael) which was rather secluded. Distracted from their conversation, she wasn't paying attention to anything around her. She happened to look up and Rhonda was coming toward her.

"Hannah," Rhonda called as she strolled toward her.

"Hey, Rhonda. I'm in a hurry to get back to work on a project for class," Hannah said, as she tried to move around.

Rhonda wanted to shout with glee because she heard the fear in her voice. With a voice filled with syrup, Rhonda said, "I owe you an apology. I know I was horrible in how I treated you."

Her eyes were wide, and her mouth was pursed from anxiety as Hannah looked at Rhonda and she said, "It's over now, so don't worry about it."

"But that's the thing, I am worried about it. In fact, I think about it every day." Rhonda said with a look of regret in her eyes. Continuing with the false tone in her voice she said, "You and I were great friends and now we aren't. I feel terrible about it." She took another threatening step closer.

Terror filled her as Rhonda kept talking because she knew that she wasn't actually sorry. It was written all over her body. Hannah glanced around her, and she saw a friend of hers from one of her education classes a few yards away.

"Suzanne," she called. Suzanne turned and smiled when she saw Hannah. Hannah was so grateful that she stopped to wait for her.

"I need to go, Rhonda," Hannah said. "I have to talk to Suzanne about this project in class, so I will see you later. Everything is fine now."

Stepping even closer, Rhonda leaned in and mumbled, "I understand, go talk to your *friend*. You be careful, now. I wouldn't want anything happening to you." The smile she gave Hannah was petrifying.

Thankfully, Suzanne was a few steps away so Hannah said, "See you around, Rhonda."

"You sure will," Rhonda said and it almost sounded like a promise. Then she walked back in the other direction.

Suzanne looked at Hannah and said, "Isn't that the girl who went crazy at the dance with Alex?"

"Yes," Hannah commented as she began trembling all over her body.

"Hannah, are you alright?" Suzanne looked at her with worry.

Shaking off her fear, Hannah said, "I will be fine, but I wanted to talk to you about this project."

Diverting the conversation, they talked about the project and what Suzanne was doing for hers. As soon as she could, Hannah said goodbye to Suzanne and walked hurriedly back to the dorm. She didn't want any more chance encounters with her ex-roommate.

Almost at a jog, she wasn't paying attention again as she ran into someone.

Strong arms caught her, and Michael said, "Whoa, Hannah are you okay?"

Looking around, Hannah finally noticed her surroundings, "Sorry, Michael. I wasn't paying attention to where I was going."

Michael noticed that she wouldn't look at him and something about her seemed off. "Hannah, are you sure you're okay? What's wrong?"

"Nothing, Michael," With a wild look in her eyes, she finally looked at him. "I need to get back and work on my project."

Stepping in front of her, Michael studied her for a moment and then he said, "Hannah, I can tell that something's wrong. Is it Tommy?" His voice became hard as he asked. He was pissed at the thought of Tommy hurting her in some way.

With a shaky smile that didn't reach her eyes, Hannah said, "It's not Tommy. Everything is fine, but I need to go. Thanks, Michael."

Knowing that she wouldn't say anymore, Michael let her go. But a niggling thought stayed with him because he knew that she was troubled over something. He knew how mad her friends were with him, but he needed to talk to Jackie and Michelle. It was probable that they would tell him to go away, but he knew he wouldn't be able to rest until he at least asked them about it.

***

Later that afternoon, Michael counted his lucky stars at seeing Jackie in the student center by herself. Neither Michelle nor Hannah were anywhere around, so he took a chance by calling her name.

Her eyes filled with anger as she turned and walked in the other direction.

Jogging her way, Michael said, "Jackie, please wait! Look, I know you're mad and I get that. I appreciate what a great friend you are to Hannah, but I want you to know that I am sorry for hurting her."

"You totally ghosted her. The least you could have done was talk to her sooner about what you were feeling!" Jackie's words spewed out with frustration.

Putting up his hands, Michael said, "I know. I totally messed up how I handled everything. But I wanted to talk to you. I ran into her earlier and she looked stressed about something. I know I don't deserve to know anything about her, but it worried me. I've never seen her like that before."

Jackie studied him and he knew that she saw that he was genuinely concerned. "Okay, but I'm still loyal to her."

"I know that and I'm glad you are there for her. Jackie, is something wrong?" As he asked, he saw a look come over her face. "You know something, don't you?"

"Hannah would kill me if I told you. It took weeks for her to tell us," Jackie clapped her hand over her mouth as she realized what she just told him.

With suspicion in his eyes, Michael stepped closer as he asked, "What took weeks for her to tell you? Jackie, I was still with her at that point."

Moaning, Jackie said, "She's going to be so mad at me."

"Look, I know that I've hurt her, but I still care about her. I was a dumbass for breaking up with her. Does that make you feel better? I know I made a mistake." Sincerity was in his gaze. "I don't know if she will ever want to get back together with me, but I still want to be a friend. Please talk to me because I think I might know what you're going to say," Michael pleaded with Jackie.

Glancing around, she said, "Let's go sit over there." She motioned to the couches. "Hannah's working in the room so she shouldn't show up here anytime soon."

Once they were on the couches, Jackie looked at Michael and she said, "Hannah's been getting prank calls."

"Still?" Michael asked. "She got one when I was visiting her family."

"Yeah, they're coming more and more. The only reason we know is that we walked in on her terrified as she was hanging up the phone. The person whispered the word, 'bitch' that time and she was totally freaked out!" Jackie looked at Michael.

Michael's expression was filled with rage as he said, "What have you done about it? Do her parents know?"

Nodding, Jackie said, "We told Danah and she talked to her boss. Hannah did call her parents and her dad called the school. They've put a tap on the phone in our room, but so far we don't know anything." Jackie looked away with a guilty expression but Michael noticed.

"What else are you not saying?" Michael asked as more guilt crept onto her face.

"I'm so dead for telling you all of this, from Michelle too!" Pausing for a moment, Jackie took a deep breath.

"Jackie..." Michael prodded as he continued studying her.

"Okay, okay. Hannah thinks it might be Rhonda." She continued, "She also feels like someone has been following her and she tried to shake it off as being paranoid, but Michael it worries me!"

"Holy shit!" Michael exclaimed. "Why does she think that?"

Jackie actually looked relieved as she continued, "This whole time, Hannah had a feeling that everything with Rhonda wasn't settled. She was moved to another dorm, but Hannah had a sense that these calls could be from her. Truthfully, that girl is capable of anything!"

Michael was speechless as fear filled him. He knew Rhonda was troubled, but the fact that she could be stalking Hannah filled him with an emotion that he couldn't describe. Wishing he could move Hannah to his place, he knew it was futile and that she would refuse.

"I need to go," Jackie said. "They will both be furious with me once they know that I told you."

"I understand." Michael said. "I wish I could get you to convince Hannah to let me in at least as friends."

Jackie looked at him and said, "I know you said you're sorry, but you're going to have to grovel a lot more for that to be possible."

Michael nodded his head, and he was determined to get Hannah to forgive him. "I'm going to do all I can. I would love it if you would put a good word in for me."

"I can try," Jackie's tone was doubtful. "But I can't make any promises."

Smiling at her, Michael said, "Thanks. And please watch out for her with Tommy. The guy is a total jerk!"

With respect in her gaze, Jackie said, "I know. I've seen how he acts around other girls. I will try to warn her."

"Thanks, Jackie," Michael said as they stood. As he watched her walk away, he figured out a plan to gain Hannah's forgiveness.

***

The next day was Saturday, so Michael called home to talk to his mother. He was surprised when his dad answered the phone and told him that his mom was out running errands with his sister, Jenny.

"How are things with Hannah?" his dad asked.

Michael sighed as he said, "I told her a few weeks ago that we needed to see other people so it's over now."

"What?" his dad exclaimed. "Michael, why would you do that?"

"I don't know, Dad. I wanted to focus on my school and grades." As Michael said it, he realized it didn't make much sense.

"So, because you were dating Hannah, you didn't attend classes or complete any assignments?" Bill Davis was almost to the point of yelling. Michael had heard his dad yell many times, but he never imagined it would be over a girl he dated.

"We're young, Dad. I don't know that we were ready for any commitments yet," Michael argued.

"Michael, you need to go and stick your head in a cold shower! So what if you're young? Who says you have to make any commitments right away?" The volume in his Dad's voice increased.

"Why are you so stressed out about this, Dad?" Michael asked.

Calming slightly, his Dad continued, "That girl is the best thing that ever happened to you. I'm just saying that you don't need to let school and grades get in the way of dating her if that's what you want."

Overwhelmed by his dad's support, Michael knew he had messed up by breaking up with her. Talking to his dad was a wake-up call for him. He knew he needed to do whatever he could to get Hannah back and away from Tommy. He just hoped he wasn't too late!

Thanking his dad, he promised to call his mother the following day. His dad promised to tell her that he called.

Michael walked out and saw Alex lounging in front of their television. Sitting in the chair next to him, Michael said, "My dad just told me that I was crazy to break up with Hannah. He actually told me to 'stick my head in a cold shower!'"

Alex switched off the television and sat up to face his friend. "I agree with him," he said.

Shaking his head, Michael was still in shock from that conversation. "I was trying to do the right thing and focus on my schoolwork."

"Let me ask you something," Alex said. "Does Hannah distract you from focusing on your classes? Were you ever behind on assignments when the two of you were going out?"

Michael finally looked over at Alex and said, "No. If anything, she inspired me to do better than I ever have." Shaking his head again, he said, "Man, I screwed up! Now, she's dating Tommy, and I might have lost her forever." Leaning over he put his head in his hands moaning to himself.

"You know that Tommy will never be serious with her, right? The guy's nothing but a player. But you definitely need to go slow with her again. It's obvious that you hurt her when they stopped sitting near us at meals in the dining hall." Alex leaned closer to Michael, and he continued, "I believe you can think of a way to win her back!" He clapped Michael on the shoulder before standing up to walk to his room.

Turning around before closing his door, he said, "I'll be going out tonight and I just wanted you to know."

Michael focused on his friend and said, "Who are you going out with?"

"I asked Suzanne out and she said yes." Alex smiled as he said it.

Grinning at him, Michael said, "That's great! I'm happy for you, man!"

"I'm headed to the library in a few minutes, so see you later." Alex shut his door to get dressed, ending their conversation.

***

Hannah was studying on her bed when Jackie came over to her and sat down. There had been three more prank calls that afternoon, with the person whispering the word, 'bitch' the final time. Never having faced dangerous situations as a child, Hannah had no idea how to deal with these kinds of fears.

"I need to tell you something," Jackie said, pulling her out of her musings as her voice sounded meek.

Distracted from studying, Hannah said, "What's wrong?"

"I'm not sure anything is necessarily wrong, but I need to confess something to you. Michelle, you need to come over and hear this, too." Jackie looked over to their other friend sitting on her bed and Hannah was sure that Jackie actually looked guilty over something.

"Okay," Michelle said and she joined them on Hannah's bed.

Looking down, Jackie said, "Michael stopped me yesterday to ask if something was wrong with you, Hannah."

Hannah's voice deepened with horror as she said, "What did you tell him?"

More guilt filled Jackie's face and she admitted, "I told him everything about Rhonda." Holding up her hands as both of her friends were about to comment loudly, she continued, "He pretty much guessed it. Hannah, he remembered the prank call you got when he was at your house with you."

With a pained voice, Hannah said, "Yeah, he questioned me about it, but I didn't tell him what I really thought about it."

"Look, Hannah," Jackie said, "I know he was a jackass in breaking things off with you, but I think he still cares about you. He admitted that telling you to see other people was wrong."

Trying to guard her expression, Hannah couldn't stop the elated feeling that washed over her at Jackie's words. "What else did the two of you talk about?"

Looking over at Michelle, Jackie was quiet for a moment.

"Jackie, what did you talk about?" Hannah persisted.

Jackie's voice was filled with caution. "He's concerned about you seeing Tommy." Relief washed over Michelle's face when she said those words aloud.

"Why should he even care?" Hannah asked with bitterness in her voice.

Michelle put her hand over Hannah's, and she said, "Tommy is a real jerk. Even though he is all over you, we have seen him around campus with several other girls."

Momentary anger filled Hannah until she saw the expressions on her friends' faces. Her voice was resigned as she said, "I know. I saw him yesterday before my altercation with Rhonda."

"What altercation? What are you talking about?" Michelle and Jackie spoke at the same time.

Sighing, Hannah said, "She cornered me yesterday with an apology, but it sounded more like a threat."

"That bitch!" Michelle sat up. "Was she following you? Did she say anything else?"

Breath whooshed out of Hannah as she said in her own guilty voice, "She told me to be careful and that she didn't want anything to happen to me. I have to admit that it scared me, and I accidentally bumped into Michael right after that as I was running back here. I know he saw the fear in my face and that's probably why he questioned you, Jackie."

"You have to report it, Hannah," Jackie pleaded.

"What do I report? She said all the right words. Am I supposed to tell someone that I was scared of talking to her? They will think I'm crazy! We don't know if it's her behind the calls or the stalking." Hannah's voice was filled with desperation and her eyes filled with tears.

"I know we can't be with you every moment, but you can't be alone again if she is following you." Michelle's voice was insistent as she continued, "We need some way of checking in with each other so that Jackie and I know where you are at all times."

A tear ran down her cheek as she nodded her head at Michelle. "Okay," Hannah breathed. "How do we do that?"

Jackie piped in, "We can walk with one another as far as possible when going to class and we can have times to meet up with each other after our classes are finished."

"Let's get our schedules and write down a plan for what we should do," Michelle said as she walked over to her desk for her binder. Coming back, she hedged before saying, "Look, Hannah. I'm the first one to admit that Michael was a total jerk for what he did to you, but maybe you should at least be friends with him again. He can be someone else to help watch out for you when we can't be there."

Hannah nodded her head, but she wasn't sure if it would actually happen. She knew that she would not talk to Michael. He would have to come to her first. Deep down, she feared that he couldn't ever really love her. However, she brought her attention back to the present as she let her friends help her create a safety plan. Thankful was not a strong enough word for these girls and the wonderful friends that they had become!

***

A little while later, Hannah was back to studying. Jackie and Michelle also had textbooks in front of them and they studied in contented silence when the phone rang.

With eyes wide and her pupils dilated, Hannah whispered, "What if that's another prank call?" Now that her friends were working on her protection, the situation was more terrifying than when she was in denial.

"I'll get it," Jackie said as she walked and answered it. Hannah heard her say, "Hold on," as she put the receiver against her chest and looked at her. "It's Michael...he wants to talk to you. What should I tell him?"

Hannah didn't want to acknowledge the hope running through her and she wanted to tell Jackie to hang up. However, she stood up and came to take the phone.

Jackie walked away as she said, "Hello."

"Hey, Hannah," She struggled with holding the receiver steady because of all of the emotions running through her at the moment.

"Hi," was all she said in reply.

"Look, Hannah," Michael said as his next words rushed out. "I know I hurt you, but I was hoping we could get together to talk about it.

Schooling her expression even though Michael couldn't see her, she said, "I don't know. I'm not sure that it's a good idea."

"Please, can we get together tonight? I really want us to sit down and talk." Michael pleaded with her. "We can go to the diner a couple of blocks away and get something to eat. There are tables in the back where we can sit and talk privately."

Hannah wanted to say no, and deep down she knew that she needed to refuse. She knew her friends would support her with whatever she chose to do as indecision washed over her. Shoving her hands into the pockets of her jeans, she looked down, intent on saying no when, "Alright," came out instead. She continued saying, "But I need to finish studying for my midterm on Tuesday."

"How about I come pick you up at seven? Will that give you enough time?" Michael's voice was solicitous.

"Fine," Hannah said. "But I have to go now."

"Great, I will see you at seven." Michael said and the line went quiet like he wanted to say more, but he refrained as he said goodbye and hung up the phone.

With mixed emotions, Hannah hung up the phone. Why had she said yes when she wanted to say no?

Just that morning, Tommy had asked her to go out with him that evening and she told him that she would. It took her a few minutes to call him and cancel. It almost sounded as if Tommy was relieved, and it gave Hannah certainty that she needed to stop whatever they were doing. She didn't really feel anything for him, but she enjoyed his attention after the rejection from Michael. Making a mental note to call and end things the next day, she went back to studying.

Hannah studied for a couple more hours before putting on a casual top with the jeans she already was wearing. Jackie and Michelle hugged her and said they were there if she wanted to talk when she got back and she was thankful for that. She was putting her hair into a ponytail when her phone rang. Knowing it was him, she told him that she would be out in the lobby in a few minutes. Walking laps around the room, she decided to make him wait longer and she hoped the delay was making him sweat.

"What are you doing?" Michelle asked with a bewildered look on her face.

"Making him wait," Hannah retorted which caused both Jackie and Michelle to look at each other before they doubled over in laughter.

"If only he knew," Jackie laughed and she let Hannah wait as long as she wanted, going back to her own studying.

Ten minutes later, she walked out and saw him standing by the door. His face lit up as he saw her walking toward him. He raised his hand like he was going to hold her hand, but he reluctantly lowered it. Walking outside, he opened the car door for her in his polite manner before walking around to the driver's side.

The drive to the restaurant was quiet. Hannah looked out the window hoping she had made the right decision. She didn't want him thinking that he could string her along. Having gone through that in high school, she knew that Michael was not that type of guy.

Meanwhile, Michael was thinking about what he would say to her. He had missed her more than he realized these past few weeks. It took his dad yelling at him to make him realize how much he still loved her.

When he saw her with Tommy, jealousy burned inside of him as he thought about her enjoying another guy's attention. When they had walked out of the dining hall last week, Tommy had placed his hand on the small of Hannah's back. It took all of his restraint not to walk over and remove it. He wanted to tell Tommy to leave her alone. He wasn't sure if she would forgive him for being bone-headed, and he was terrified that he had lost her for good.

Chapter 15

Her plan was working! Rhonda was filled with glee as she remembered how scared Hannah was when she approached her the other day. More than anything, she wanted to backhand her, but she refrained, knowing that her revenge would be sweet in time. She would continue following Hannah and eventually she would be able to give her the same pain that Hannah had caused her by rejecting her. With irrational thoughts, Rhonda could no longer separate the pain and abuse from her mother with how Hannah treated her earlier in the semester. Everything was beginning to run together.

***

When they got to the restaurant, Hannah didn't let Michael open the car door for her this time. She opened it quickly and got out. "I was coming around," Michael protested as he caught up to her.

"I got it myself," Hannah said walking ahead of him into the restaurant. Michael almost had to run to keep up with her brisk pace.

After they were seated in a booth at the back of the restaurant, Michael asked her about the test she was studying for. Then the server came and took their order. Hannah ordered hot chocolate. She didn't have the stomach to eat anything. Michael ordered coffee and a slice of apple pie.

With anger burning inside of her gut, Hannah leveled him with a look, and she asked, "What are you doing, Michael? Am I supposed to make small talk with you?"

He looked down at his glass of water, twisting it around with his hand before looking at her and Hannah had not ever seen despair like what she was seeing in his expression. "Hannah, I made a mistake. I want to say that I am really sorry for screwing things up with you. I don't know what I was doing when I told you that we needed to see other people."

Hannah couldn't help feeling a spark of hope. However, she wanted to protect her heart from any more hurt. "Then, why did you tell me that?" she asked, looking into his eyes.

"I don't know," he said, shaking his head in anger at himself. "I guess I was scared. I've never dated someone like you, and I've never had these kinds of feelings before. It made me afraid of getting so close to someone in this way. I didn't mean to mess things up, but I really miss you."

Hannah couldn't stop the bitterness in her voice. "You said you wanted space, so I was trying to give that to you. But you couldn't expect me to sit around and not date anyone. Or is this because you've seen me with Tommy?"

"I didn't think you were going to start dating as soon as I broke things off! You sure didn't let any time pass!" Michael shot back at her in an angry tone. He had never spoken to her like that before. Feeling her eyes welling up with tears, she turned away so that he wouldn't see them as their server brought their beverages and Michael's dessert. However, he didn't touch it.

"I wasn't going to get serious with Tommy. He's a friend that I met at our freshman weekend back in April." Hannah retorted. "He was a diversion that helped me to stop thinking about you. And, it took me two weeks to even go on a date with him, Michael. It wasn't like it was the next day!"

"He took advantage by moving in on a weak moment with you!" Michael said in a sharp tone as his volume increased.

"What did you expect me to do? Did you want me to sit around and pine after you??" Hannah asked in a louder voice. Seeing people look their way, she lowered her voice and said, "I was trying to move on!"

"I know and I'm sorry," Michael said, cooling down and sounding contrite. "I know I messed up." Repeating his words from earlier, he said, "I've just never dated someone seriously before. If it makes you feel any better, my Dad told me to stick my head in a cold shower because he said I was crazy to let you go."

Hannah couldn't help smiling. "I knew I liked him," she said softly.

Michael laughed softly. "Yeah, he really drove home the point that I acted like a moron."

Hannah looked down at her place mat. "I just didn't understand where it came from. I thought we were on the same page with our relationship. We had just gotten back from visiting our families and our connection was so much stronger. I thought those other girls at basketball practice were what caused you to change your mind. I was afraid that you were regretting even going out with me and that I wasn't enough for you." Kicking herself for being so blunt, she spoke the words softly with her gaze still downward. She couldn't believe she let that slip, but Michael could hear the hurt in her voice.

He placed one hand on top of hers on the table. The movement caused Hannah to look up and he looked deeply into her eyes. "Hannah, that's absolutely not true! I don't want to date anyone else. Those girls were flirting with all of the guys on the team. I left right after practice and went back to my apartment. Nothing happened between me and them! Anyway, they are nothing but teases. I could tell they were just leading me on so that I would give them attention."

"This whole situation did make me stop and think about everything," Hannah said as she moved her gaze back down to the table. However, she was still allowing Michael to have his hand on top of hers. "I was awake most of that night when you broke up with me. Maybe we have gone too fast in our relationship and maybe we should slow down and see other people."

"No!" Michael exclaimed. "I don't want to see anyone else." He wanted to tell her that he didn't want her seeing anyone, especially Tommy, but he knew it would be too much. Reminding himself to be patient, he said, "Hannah, I know you think you are friends, but Tommy is a womanizer! He goes out with a different girl every weekend and I think he gets just about anything he wants from them. You don't need to be with him." He caressed the top of her hand, squeezing it as he looked into her gorgeous, hazel eyes. He wanted to say, 'You and I are supposed to be together and we were meant to find each other,' but he kept his mouth shut.

Hannah knew he was right, but she didn't tell him her plan to end things tomorrow. She wasn't ready for him to know. She continued by saying, "It hurt me so badly coming out of the blue like that. I'm not sure that I can trust that you won't do it again. I just don't know what you want from me now." When Hannah's eyes did fill with tears, Michael felt something break inside of him. He wanted to knock himself in his own head because he had hurt her so badly. Determination filled him as he thought that he would do whatever it took to get her back.

Looking at the table, he commented, "I know it will take a while for me to win back your trust, but I'm willing to try. I will wait for you, Hannah Mathis. I don't want to scare you off, but I think that you and I are forever and that we are supposed to be together," Michael's gaze was intent as he looked at her again.

Shuttering her gaze even though sparks raced through her at his words, she continued, "You said that your Dad was upset with you, but I bet your mom was happy. I don't think she ever liked me." As Hannah spoke the words, more bitterness rose in her voice.

Shocked at himself, Michael said, "Right now, I don't care what my mom thinks, but I believe she will come around eventually. Please give me another chance, Hannah," Michael took her hand in his and he rubbed the top of it softly. Hannah had to restrain herself from shivering from his touch. Despite how he hurt her, she still responded to him because he was right about them having a special connection. She was also shocked by his comment about his mom.

"Michael, I want to say yes, but I'm just not sure about whether you are truly committed. I'm willing to try to be friends and we can see where that leads us, but I'm not ready to date you again. Not yet." Michael's heart felt like it had been run over by a truck when he saw the doubt in Hannah's eyes, and he knew that he was responsible for it.

Disappointment filled him, but he knew he had to give her time. He said, "I understand. Like I said, I will wait for you. I know you need time to trust me again."

"So, where do we go from here?" Hannah asked, looking into his eyes. So often in her life, she had been hurt and trust was not something that came easily to her, especially when someone wounded her like Michael did.

"What do you want? I want to respect you and any boundaries that you set," Michael replied.

"Maybe we can start hanging out again, but only as friends," Hannah said.

"I'd like that," Michael responded. "I want to do what makes you comfortable. So, how about we go and see a movie on Friday?"

"That's fine, but I want to invite Jackie and Michelle. You can ask Alex if you want." She had a small smile on her face which gave him hope.

"That's fine with me," Michael said. "I will ask Alex if he wants to go with us."

Surprised at how authoritative she had just been with Michael, Hannah nodded her head before she said, "Maybe we can learn to be friends." Then, she looked at his dessert because she was still nervous about looking in his eyes and she pulled her hand away from his. "You know you haven't touched your pie."

Missing her touch, Michael glanced down at the table. "You're right. I forgot about it. Do you want to share it with me?" She nodded her head and reached for her fork. The pie was delicious and both Hannah and Michael used the time to talk. He knew he needed to make up for lost time.

He did make one more comment. "Hannah, will you please let me know if anything else happens with Rhonda?"

Nodding her head with her gaze downcast, Hannah said, "I will." Michael could tell she had more she wanted to say, and he forced himself to remain quiet to see if she would. Proud of himself, she did continue, "Jackie and Michelle have worked on a plan to know where I am at all times so that I don't get cornered again. They wanted me to ask you to help out as well."

Angry again with Rhonda's threatening behavior, Michael said, "Hannah, you can count on me to be there for you. Tell me what I can do."

His gaze was intent on her as she shared what they had planned. These two weeks apart caused him to realize that Hannah was the most precious person in his life, and it took almost losing her to recognize that. He would do anything to help keep her safe.

An hour later, Michael drove Hannah back to the dorm. She let him walk around and open her door. It was hard not to notice the spark of desire as he held out his hand to help her out of the car.

He wanted to hug her so badly, but he knew he needed to tread carefully with her. He kept her hand in a gentle grasp as he looked at her and he said, "Thanks for going out with me."

Hannah wanted to remove her hand from his. She told herself to do it, but the warmth of it filled her with joy. "You're welcome. I'm glad we were able to talk things out."

"Can I call you later? I really want to get back to talking on the phone in the evenings if that's okay with you?" Michael knew his voice was filled with desperation. Dipping his head to look her in the eye, he said, "Just as friends."

With a gentle smile, Hannah said, "I'd like that."

A smile broke over Michael's face and he squeezed her hand. "Thank you," he said with relief in his voice. Unable to contain himself, he leaned down and kissed Hannah on the cheek. "Goodbye..." he whispered. He wanted to end it with 'beautiful,' but he simply squeezed her hand again.

Not meaning to, her eyes slipped closed from his lips on her cheek. Opening them, she knew uncertainty was in her gaze as she said, "Bye."

Michael's heart was soaring as he drove back to his place. He took time himself to study and complete some homework. True to his word, he called Hannah before bed, and they talked for thirty minutes. He made sure the conversation was light and relaxing. That night, he fell asleep content because he knew in his heart that he would win her back. He could see in her eyes a while ago that she wanted it, but she was scared. He would honor her wishes and be a gentleman to show her that his heart was true for only her.

***

Sunday afternoon, Hannah called Tommy to see if he could come over so they could talk. She was trying to be kind and end things with him face to face.

"I have something planned," Tommy hedged and Hannah knew that it involved another girl. His tone cinched her decision, and she didn't care if it was over the phone.

"Look, Tommy," she said. "You are a great friend, but I don't want to go out with you anymore. I hope you understand. I need time for myself to figure some things out."

"Hannah, I really like you. But I understand. Is this because of Michael?" A slight jealous tone filled him as he asked.

Sighing, she said, "No, Tommy. He and I are friends, but I need this time for myself." Recognition came to her as she realized that she meant those words for herself as much as for Tommy.

They quickly ended the conversation and Tommy said he would see her around.

***

After she hung up, she sat at the desk for a while longer. She had never in her life said words like that out loud. She had never been exposed to any kind of counseling in her life with her family and she wondered if she would be a stronger person if they had explored it. Her parents seemed to think that church was the answer to all of their problems, but Hannah wasn't so sure. Remembering the counseling center available for students, she made a mental note to go and inquire about it when she had a break in her schedule this week. "Maybe it would be good to talk to a professional," she mused to herself.

***

The next morning, Hannah was surprised to see Michael waiting for her outside of the dining hall. He had asked her about her day last night, but she thought he was just inquiring. Michael hugged her from the side in a friendly manner. As they got their food, he surprised her as he carried her tray to where she wanted to sit. Jackie and Michelle had early classes and they ate in the room. However, because of their plan to keep Hannah safe, they had walked with her to the dining hall before heading in their own directions.

Michael couldn't help but notice that Tommy walked by their table, and he glanced their way before moving to another table with several girls.

After breakfast, Michael walked Hannah to her first class. As they walked, he touched the small of her back. "How did it go talking to Tommy?"

"It was okay," Hannah said. "He didn't seem too upset, probably because he can ask another girl to go out with him anytime. He seemed rather chummy with them this morning."

"I'm not surprised. I know that one of those girls at practice went out with him a couple of times in August." Michael said. He didn't comment that he had seen Tommy with her the past two weeks while they were supposedly going out.

"Well, I guess I better go inside so that I can get a decent seat," Hannah motioned to the building behind her.

"Can I see you after your last class today? We can take a walk or play some ping pong. I have a game tomorrow, but I would like for you to come watch, but only if you want." Michael looked at her intently as he asked.

"I'd like that," Hannah murmured as her brow dipped in uncertainty. "Thank you for walking me to class. You didn't have to do that, you know."

"I was happy to." Michael said and he reached over and gave Hannah a kiss on the cheek. "See you tonight!"

"Bye," Hannah said, and she knew the blush was filling her face as she turned to walk into her class. She had a conversation with herself to continue just as friends. But she wasn't sure that her heart was truly listening to what her brain was saying.

***

Michael was waiting for her at lunch again as she walked in with Jackie and Michelle. Both girls gave her pointed looks and then gave him looks of warning before walking ahead of them to get their lunch. Michael smiled to himself at their 'mama bear' protection over Hannah. It was a nice, relaxing time eating together and Hannah realized how much she had missed eating with Michael. Alex joined them and she realized she had missed his friendship. Hannah was happy to see her new friend, Suzanne, sitting next to him. She hoped they were getting together because she really liked her.

✳✳✳

Proud of herself for keeping her own promises, Hannah went that afternoon to the counseling center to see what was available. She had spoken to all three of them about where she was going and Michael walked with her before heading to his afternoon class. Jackie and Michelle had kept their promises of walking with Hannah to make sure that Rhonda couldn't get her alone again. Hannah had allowed Michelle to talk to Michael the night before when he called before bed. Michael agreed with Michelle's plan and Hannah knew she could count on him to help keep her safe. He had already proved that.

Even though the niggling fear of an attack from Rhonda was still there, she was thankful for people trying to look out for her. There hadn't been any sign of Rhonda anywhere. She knew that Michael probably saw her in the music building. However, she didn't want him to be in danger, so it was probably a good thing that they were just friends.

Hannah opened the door to the counseling center and walked inside. Doubts filled her and she almost turned back around to walk outside when she heard someone say, "Hello." Looking up, she saw kind eyes from an older gentleman as he said, "Can I help you?"

Indecision filled Hannah as she stood there awkwardly without saying anything.

The gentleman smiled and said, "It's okay. This happens all the time. Most people are nervous when they come in here."

Arguing with herself for being afraid, Hannah said, "I wanted to inquire of your services."

The man held out his hand and said, "My name is Mark Jones. I am the director of the counseling center." He gestured to the couch over to the side of the lobby. "How about we sit down, and I can tell you what we have to offer." Before joining her, he went to the desk and grabbed several pamphlets.

Seating herself on the edge of the couch with distance between them, Hannah blew out a breath before saying, "I'm Hannah Mathis and I've never done anything like this before."

With another gentle smile, Mark put Hannah at ease by saying, "Most people say the same thing. We don't have to do anything that you are not comfortable with doing. We can have someone available to talk to you and listen to anything you want to talk about. This is a free service provided in your tuition because college students are under tremendous pressures, both academically and socially."

Hearing that it didn't cost anything comforted Hannah because she didn't want her parents to know that she was coming here. "I'm not actually sure what I need. Are there females that I can talk with? I think I would be more comfortable with a girl."

"That's completely understandable and the choice is most certainly yours. Here are some of the services we offer and the names of counselors who work here. Many of them use this as an internship to help on their resumes for future employment." Mark's gaze remained open as he explained.

Knowing that there might be someone a female closer to her age gave Hannah more comfort. "Can I make an appointment to see someone?"

"Let's walk over to the calendar and see who might be available." Mark led the way as Hannah followed.

After making an appointment with a girl named Angela for the next day, Hannah thanked him before exiting the center. She knew that her friends all had class, so she made sure to look around to see if she spotted Rhonda. Thankfully, there were students walking the main pathway, and it was a short walk to where she attended her two o'clock class.

After class, Michael was waiting for her. Even though they had their backpacks with school-work, he convinced Hannah to go and play a game of ping pong. Setting their bags beside the table, Hannah found herself enjoying it just as she had before their breakup. Michael even gave her a high-five when she won a game against him. He wound up winning the next two games before she told him that she needed to get back to her room. She saw the disappointment in his gaze, and she was also sorry for their time to end, but she needed to begin a project that would be due at the end of the semester. Procrastinating saying goodbye, she invited Michael to the bookstore with her so that she could purchase them and he was happy to tag along.

As they walked back, she glanced at him and said, "Do you want to join us for dinner tonight?"

Undisguised joy filled Michael as he said, "Sure, if Alex can come again."

"Absolutely," Hannah said, unable to control her own smile.

They were at her dorm, so Michael told her he would see her later and he walked back toward his apartment. Walking to her room, Hannah warned herself to be careful. She didn't know if she could handle it if he hurt her a second time.

Chapter 16

The next day, Hannah had two morning classes and she scheduled a counseling meeting after lunch. She had spoken to Michael about it on the phone the night before when he called, and he offered to walk her there. Hannah was so thankful when he didn't question her about it. She wasn't ready to be that open with him, and she appreciated his understanding of her need to go slow with rebuilding their friendship.

Walking into the counseling center, Hannah saw a lady sitting at the desk.

Smiling over her nerves, she walked closer and said, "I'm Hannah Mathis. I have a meeting with Angela."

The lady stood and held out her hand. "I'm Angela Young. Hannah, it's nice to meet you. Let's walk back to the back office."

Hannah felt her knees quiver as she followed Angela to a room with soft lighting and sunlight shining through the windows. There was another sofa and a chair with a desk to the side of them.

Angela gestured to the couch saying, "Please have a seat while I grab my notepad." Once she had what she needed from the desk, she seated herself in the chair perpendicular to Hannah. "Let me start by telling you about myself. My major is counseling. I hope to become a psychologist and this internship gives me hours toward finishing my bachelor's degree. I will graduate in May."

Angela's easy-going demeanor calmed Hannah's anxiety. She explained that they would begin this session by getting Hannah's background. She also talked about how family history can have an effect on how people think and act. Angela openly shared about coming from a broken home and how her mom and dad were both still in her life. Compassion filled Hannah as Angela talked about how she always wondered if her parents' divorce was her fault. Then, she shared how counselors at this center helped her to work through her trauma.

She didn't think that she would share much, but Hannah found herself talking about her mom, dad, brother and sister. Angela's questions were for clarification so that she understood Hannah's background better. Shocking herself again, Hannah found herself talking about her brother. "He's eighteen months older than I and we were only a year apart in school." Tears came to her eyes as she said, "He and I do not get along. He treated me horribly growing up."

Angela put her hand on Hannah's arm as she said, "I can tell you have strong feelings regarding that."

"Yes," Hannah said. "I always wondered why he despised me so much. He never wanted to be around me except when we were little."

"Hannah, that's common among siblings. The two of you are so close in age and I believe given your background, he's adopted and you aren't, that he had strong jealousy toward you." Angela was gentle in her words.

"Why? He's older and he was much more popular than I was." Hannah argued.

Angela explained her thoughts on how her brother used his jealousy to create a wedge between them. He also used his confidence in making friends as a wall between himself and her. "Underneath, he is just as insecure as you are. He knows how to disguise his fears and unfortunately, he's allowed it to come out negatively toward you."

Wonder filled Hannah as she had never thought about it before.

Angela ended the session saying that she thought Hannah had enough to think about for one day. She gave Hannah an assignment before their next session to list positive things about herself and she gave her a notebook to write them down. "You may have to dig deep to find those good things, but they are there." Angela smiled at Hannah and Hannah immediately felt a connection with her.

"Can we meet again this week?" Hannah asked.

"We can meet as much as you are comfortable. However, I do need to check the calendar." Angela walked them to the front and consulted the calendar.

Hannah was so happy to set up another meeting on Thursday at the same time. As she walked out, she saw Jackie and Michelle sitting on the bench across from the counseling center. Thankfully, they didn't ask her anything because Hannah did not want to talk about it. However, she thought about all Angela said about her brother, Peter, and she was amazed at how talking about it had helped.

***

Rhonda couldn't believe her eyes! Thankfully, Hannah didn't see her standing off to the side. She caught sight of her leaving the counseling center. Following through on her promise for counseling, Rhonda gave false answers to appease the idiot who was trying to help her work on her anger problems. The counselor tried getting into her mind asking about her years of growing up. His nosiness frustrated her, and she refused to give him any personal information. She didn't realize it herself, but it was buried from many years of trying to escape her pain and trauma.

Wondering why Hannah was going there, she decided she didn't care. "She's crazy and probably needs help," she commented to herself. The girl had gotten smart, and her stupid friends were always with her now. Rhonda would have to find a way to get her away from them.

***

That night, Hannah went to watch Michael's basketball game. Before he went out onto the court, he walked over to her and pulled her into a hug. She allowed herself to melt in his arms.

"I'm glad you came," he murmured against the top of her head.

"Me too," she said softly. When she pulled away to go and sit by Jackie and Michelle, her friends gave her a pointed look.

"What?" she asked.

Rolling her eyes, Michelle said, "Nothing, nothing at all!" Jackie smirked at her as she looked over at Michael. "That seemed chummy for being 'just friends.'"

"Don't be ridiculous," Hannah said, shaking her head at them. "There wasn't anything to that hug."

Snorting loudly, both of her friends rolled their eyes this time.

Refusing to acknowledge any underlying message, Hannah ignored them and put her eyes on the basketball court where both teams were warming up. At that moment, Michael looked in her direction. When he caught her eye, he smiled and winked at her, and Hannah dropped her gaze. She knew her face was red, and she knew her friends saw the wink even though she refused to look at them.

"Yeah, yeah...just friends," Michelle muttered, and Jackie laughed as Hannah's blush turned beet red.

Michael's team won and all three girls got into the game, cheering as they played great defense.

Michael glanced in Hannah's direction many times, smiling at her. Confusion filled her because as much as she was beginning to care for him again, she was afraid to be more than friends. She just wished she could stop the somersaults her stomach did when she was with him.

Before they left, Hannah, Jackie and Michelle waited until Michael could get over to them to congratulate him on their win. Wiping his head with a towel, Michael thanked them, but his gaze focused more on Hannah than the other two girls.

As they walked away, Michael told Hannah he would call her later after he had a chance to shower.

"I look forward to it." Hannah said as she walked away, and her roommates rolled their eyes again.

***

Thursday afternoon, Hannah actually looked forward to another session with Angela. Michael walked her again since it was on the way to the music building. Despite her desire to keep her distance from him, Hannah found herself telling him Angela's thoughts regarding her relationship with her brother, Peter.

Once they were seated in the office, Angela said, "I enjoyed our time together on Tuesday."

"Me too," Hannah said with the notebook in her hands.

"I hope that's your homework," Angela commented.

Hannah found the page of her list in her spiral notebook ,and she handed it to Angela.

Reading it, Angela asked, "How much of this do you really believe about yourself?"

Hannah wondered if Angela could read minds and she wasn't going to admit it, but she found herself saying, "None of it."

Nodding her head, Angela continued, "What I want for us to do when we meet is to help you see the potential inside of you. You have so much to offer and you're going to be a great teacher." Angela smiled as she complimented Hannah.

"I want to believe that, but I just don't," Hannah said as she glanced down.

Angela's voice was firm in saying, "Hannah, look at me. Last time, I learned that you are the youngest in your family. I learned that your parents love you so much that they struggle with letting you be independent. I believe those are some reasons you doubt yourself so much."

With a bewildered expression, Hannah said, "I can't change that, so what do I do about it?"

"This list is a start," Angela commented. "I also want you to begin listening to some self-help tapes. They are designed to change how you think about yourself and others."

"Okay," Hannah said with a doubtful tone.

Looking at her, Angela said, "I also struggle with self-confidence, and they have helped me."

Startled, Hannah said, "I have a hard time believing that."

"Hannah, when I first started school, I was extremely shy, and I had a hard time even making friends. I knew that my background was why I wanted a counseling degree, but I have learned so much about myself and how I think as a result of my classes and this job." Nothing but honesty was on Angela's face.

Let's move on to something else for the rest of this session." Angela said and Hannah became anxious by the look on her face.

"Okay," she said with little to no expression.

"Let's focus on your relationship with your mother, first, and then your sister," Angela suggested.

Feeling herself tightening up, Hannah was reluctant to have this conversation. "What do you want to know?" she asked.

"Do you get along well with your mother?" she asked.

Sighing, Hannah said, "She can drive me crazy, and I get mad with her easily when she nags me about certain things."

"Do you feel like you have to live up to certain expectations?" Angela's voice became softer as she knew she was getting into sensitive territory.

Sighing again, Hannah said, "I try, but I don't live up to anything she expects of me. Sometimes I think she realizes that I can't live up to it either."

Angela nodded and jotted notes on her notepad. Then she asked, "What about your sister? Are you close to her?"

Hannah said, "We are closer than Peter and I are."

"How does she make you feel at times?" Angela inquired again in her soft voice.

"She cares about me, and she always hated when Peter was a jerk toward me," Hannah replied.

"Anything else? You compare yourself with her when you said she is extremely intelligent and that you aren't. How does that make you feel?" Angela asked.

With a downcast voice, Hannah said, "There's no way I can compete with her in any way."

"So, you don't feel like you are good enough for her?" Angela asked.

Shocked that Angela figured that out about her, Hannah looked at her and said, "No, I don't."

"So, you struggle with not thinking you can please your mom and that she doesn't believe in you. And you don't think you are good enough for your sister," Angela said before continuing. "Hannah, most of your struggles come from both of those things. Do you feel guilty with your mom at times?"

With a surprised voice, Hannah said, "Yes! All the time!"

"Again, Hannah, these are normal feelings that happen in families. More than you realize, actually." Angela said. "I am going to give you a tape to listen to and as you do, I want you to put all thoughts of your mom and your sister out of your mind. Even if they pop into your head while you listen, I want you to focus on what the tape is telling you without worrying about either of them. You need to learn to focus on you and who you want to become. It is okay for you to have these feelings, but you need to face them and work through them. Okay?"

Tears filled Hannah's eyes at the thought. With a shaky voice, she said, "Okay."

"Next time, we will continue this and talk about what you learned when you listened." Angela stood up to show their time was done for the day.

As her brow furrowed with disappointment, Hannah wished they had another hour together, even though some of what they talked about was difficult to hear. She thanked Angela and they set up a time for the following week.

Walking out, she saw Michael waiting for her outside. "What are you doing here?" she asked.

"My class ended early, so I decided to come and walk you back. Is that okay?" He stood as she walked closer.

An emotion came across Hannah, but she couldn't identify it. Her eyes were filled with confusion as she looked at Michael and said, "Yes, I'm glad you did."

Studying her for a moment, Michael smiled gently and he said, "How did the session go?"

Gazing off into the distance, Hannah said, "Better than I expected. I have a lot to think about." She didn't mention the self-help tape because she wasn't sure how helpful it would be, but she was so thankful for the two sessions with Angela.

"That's good," Michael said as he took her bag and put it on his shoulder. Hannah's heart flip-flopped at his thoughtful gesture.

The conversation turned lighter as they walked, and Hannah told him that she was looking forward to his game that night. "By the way," she said, "do you ever see Rhonda much in the music building?"

"Sometimes, but not very much," Michael answered. "I'm in music education and she has different classes than me because she wants to perform. Why do you ask?"

Hannah turned when they got to the front of the dorm and said, "I just wondered."

"She hasn't done anything else, has she?" Michael stepped closer as he asked.

Shaking her head, Hannah said, "No, and the phone calls have stopped. I'm wondering if it's because the authorities know about it now. But, how would she know that?" She was almost talking to herself as she continued.

"Maybe they contacted her parents again and they told Rhonda," Michael commented. "Hannah, please be careful. Even though nothing's happened lately, I don't trust her."

"I don't either," Hannah agreed. Then, she smiled at Michael and said, "I will see you tonight at your game." He didn't come to dinner on game nights.

Michael took Hannah's hand in his as he said, "I'm glad you are coming again."

He squeezed her hand as they said goodbye and he gave her a soft hug. Again, Hannah felt something inside of her that she couldn't put into words. Walking down the hallway to their room, she continued to ponder what it was.

***

That evening, Hannah and her friends were walking to the gym when she had the feeling of being watched again. It was becoming a daily habit and Hannah felt like she was going crazy with irrational fears.

They opened the door to the gym and walked inside. Jackie pointed to the spot where they sat for the last game as Michael waved and winked at Hannah (it was becoming a wonderful habit). With butter-flies fluttering within her, Hannah waved back hoping for the zillionth time that she was doing the right thing being friends with him again.

Rolling their eyes at her, Jackie and Michelle sat beside her on the bench. A movement at the door caught her attention. Rhonda was walking inside with another girl. The girl was someone Hannah knew to be rather wild, and she had a reputation for pushing the rules. Trying to look away, Rhonda leveled a stare at Hannah causing the hair to rise on her arms. Looking away from her sinister smile, Hannah put her eyes back on the guys warming up for the game.

Michelle noticed and she said, "I don't trust her being here since she hasn't bothered to come to any of the previous games."

"You don't go anywhere without us, Hannah," Jackie said, also watching Rhonda with suspicion.

"Alright," Hannah commented as Michael looked over at her with concern. She knew he saw Rhonda come in. She smiled and waved at him in assurance that all was well. He smiled back and moved to get in place for the tip-off.

Jackie, Hannah and Michelle were soon caught up in the competition of the game. Their opponents were strong and played excellent offense. The score was close, and Hannah felt herself shivering in fear of the other team gaining the lead. At one point, Hannah noticed that Rhonda was no longer sitting on the other side of the gym. Hoping she left, she soon forgot about her. When halftime came, the teams were tied.

Hannah looked at her friends and said, "I need to take a restroom break and then we can buy some snacks." Jackie and Michelle stood, and they made their way to the restroom. Neither of the other girls needed to go, but they were intent on coming in with Hannah.

"You can wait for me out here," Hannah reasoned. "I think Rhonda left because she wasn't sitting there anymore."

"Even so, we're trying to look out for you. We're coming in," Michelle said with all seriousness.

"Thank you," Hannah said, laughing at their constant protection. "But there's only one entrance and one exit, so I will be fine. It should only take a few minutes."

"We'll be right here," Jackie insisted, causing Hannah to shake her head at their overprotection as she walked into the bathroom.

What Hannah or her friends didn't know was that Rhonda had moved behind the three of them in order to stay out of sight. When she overheard Hannah say she needed to use the restroom, she slunk away and went into the restroom to wait until Hannah came inside.

The time for revenge had finally come, as thrill washed over her. The other girl, Vicki, had also been in trouble for various offenses with the school and with the local police since she began attending back in August. Rhonda met with her earlier and offered to pay her if she would cause a distraction with Jackie and Michelle so that she could corner Hannah in the bathroom. She explained to Vicki that she only wanted to talk to Hannah alone and that it was impossible with her roommates constantly with her.

Unsuspectingly, Hannah walked into the restroom. All of a sudden, arms came around her from behind and she felt herself being choked. She heard a chuckle as she gasped both in shock and in need of oxygen. She tried to shake her off as Rhonda held something metal to her side. Looking down, she saw it was a small knife.

With a sinister whisper, Rhonda uttered, "Didn't I warn you to watch out? Your friends can't be by your side all the time, little girl."

"What do you want?" Hannah asked with a quiver in her voice.

Chuckling again and putting her mouth next to Hannah's ear, Rhonda sneered, "What do I want? I want revenge! You and I are about to take a walk."

Repulsed from her bad breath, Hannah tried to pull away as she argued, "Jackie and Michelle are waiting for me outside and they will see you." However, she could feel the tip of the knife through her shirt.

Rhonda moved closer to Hannah's ear as she snarled, "They won't be a problem. I've created a small distraction for them."

Meanwhile as her friends were waiting for her, they heard screaming in the gym and someone yelled, "Help me! Rhonda's got me and she won't let me go!"

They ran into the gym without noticing Rhonda walking out of the bathroom with Hannah. Pushing the doors from the gym to the lobby shut with her feet, Rhonda still had the knife against Hannah's side, saying, "Don't move!" She moved an old chair in the lobby, and she propped it against the doors, creating a barrier. "Remember when you and your stupid friends tried to do this to me? Walk, now," she whispered. "Don't make a sound! And don't even think about running away. I've seen how slow you are and I will cut you open before you can get a hundred yards!"

Feeling terror as never before, Hannah had no choice but to do as she asked. Her fear was making her clumsy as she stumbled over the door jam. When they had opened the bathroom door, she felt her heart stop as she saw that her friends were no longer waiting for her just as Rhonda had promised. Wondering how long it would take them to find out she was gone, she continued walking as instructed.

Hannah chanced a look back at Rhonda and she saw the wild look in her eyes. Knowing that Rhonda truly wanted to hurt her scared her more than anything else in her life ever had, and she tried to think of a plan of escape.

With the knife at her side, they walked out into the darkening night and began walking across the gym parking lot to the softball field. Behind the field was a forest of trees and she knew that Rhonda was leading her to where people would not be able to witness anything.

A fleeting thought came to mind as she battled the tears in her eyes. She would never be able to tell Michael how she truly felt about him. This moment made her realize that she had never stopped loving him. It broke her heart that she couldn't tell her family she loved them, either. Why hadn't she asked her parents for more help? And, she had finally learned to try and help her struggles with herself! It was too late, now!

What Rhonda didn't notice was that Hannah was dropping items from her pockets hoping to leave a trail. Rhonda was too charged with energy to stop and notice.

***

"That was so strange," Michelle commented to Jackie as they turned back and saw the gym lobby doors closed.

"What the hell?" Jackie asked as she tried to push them open, but they wouldn't budge. Several other students pushed with them. They were finally able to force the doors open, knocking the chair bracing against it to fall and break. Once they opened, Michelle and Jackie rushed into the bathroom, but Hannah wasn't in any of the stalls.

"I have a bad feeling," Michelle commented as they ran back into the gym. The team was coming back out for their warm up before the second half began. Jackie and Michelle rushed out to the middle of the gym floor so that they could look in every corner to see if Hannah had come back into the gym. They didn't care that they were interrupting the warmup because they were frantically looking for their friend.

Michael had a ball in his hands, and he was practicing jump shots when he noticed them in the middle of the floor with crazed looks on their faces. A sick feeling washed over him, and he tossed the ball to his teammate before running in their direction.

"Jackie, Michelle ... .is something wrong? Where's Hannah?" Michael asked, but deep in his heart he knew something was terribly wrong.

Shocked to see the tears in Michelle's eyes, she wailed, "We just left her for a second so she could take a restroom break. But she vanished and we don't know where she is!"

Jackie's eyes were wild with fear as she continued spanning the entire room. Michael joined her as his gaze landed on the girl who had come in with Rhonda. Looking back at them, he asked, "Where's Rhonda?" The sick feeling became a vise on his gut.

Abandoning the game, several of his teammates called his name as he ran the opposite direction. Not caring, he ran with Jackie and Michelle to where she was sitting and asked, "Weren't you with Rhonda tonight?"

The girl had a guilty and defensive look on her face. "Yeah…so? Why do you ask?"

Trying to remain calm, Jackie said, "Our friend, Hannah, went to the restroom, but when we went to check on her, she was gone. Do you know if Rhonda was in there when Hannah was?"

Looking down, Vicki shrugged her shoulders defensively as she said, "Maybe, I don't know. I was at the concession stand getting some food."

Suddenly some other students approached them with curious expressions and said, "Weren't you that one that just yelled that Rhonda was hurting you? Where is she? You seem fine now."

"What??" Michael yelled. Looking at Vicki, he said, "What are they talking about?" He had been in the locker room with his teammates and had not heard the commotion.

Narrowing her eyes, Michelle said as she stepped closer, "It was you who yelled that, right? Did Rhonda put you up to it? Where on earth is Hannah? What has she done with her??"

With guilt on her face, the girl said, "I don't know where she is."

"Listen," Michael said, stepping close in a threatening manner. "You better start talking or I'm calling campus security." Panic rushed through him at the thought of where Hannah could be and what Rhonda was doing to her.

Vicki looked at him for a prolonged moment before she said, "Look. I don't know anything other than what Rhonda asked me to do. She paid me to create a distraction to get the two of you away from Hannah." She looked at Jackie and Michelle before continuing, "She said she wanted to talk to her alone." Raising her hands defensively, she said, "I swear I don't know anything else!"

Michael swore as he heard, "Oh my god" from Michelle with unrestrained terror in her eyes. Seeing his friend's worried expression, Alex joined them, and Michael explained what was happening. "Shit!" he exclaimed. "Let me go and explain to the coach what's happening, and I'll help."

"Let's see if we can use the phone in the snack bar to call the campus police," Jackie commented. Stepping toward Vicki, she took her arm as she said, "but you're coming with us so that you can tell them what you just told us!"

Not wanting to get in more trouble, Vicki knew that too many people were a part of this now. She nodded and they walked back into the lobby to use the phone. "I'll go check the bathroom one more time," Michelle said.

Soon, the game was postponed as more people realized that a young freshman girl was missing. Danny was also on the team and he spoke up, saying, "We'll go outside and look around," Danny said, catching Michelle's gaze and she thanked him with her eyes.

Jackie and Michelle called the police while Alex, Danny and their other teammates walked outside and around the perimeter of the gym looking for clues although the darkness made it difficult.

Chapter 17

Rhonda urged Hannah to keep walking across the baseball fields. At one point, she was pushing so hard that it caused Hannah to fall down onto her knees. She knew she bruised them on the packed dirt beneath it, but Rhonda cackled and said, "Get up!" As she pulled on Hannah's arm to make her stand up again, the tip of the knife skimmed across it. Hannah could feel the knife as it cut into her skin.

"Why are you so angry with me?" Hannah wanted to keep Rhonda talking in hopes of calming her down. She remembered the time when they sat and talked earlier in the semester. The conversation had a calming effect on Rhonda so she hoped it might work again.

Growling, Rhonda said, "You've caused me nothing but trouble since I got here. It's your fault that I have a record now and that I got kicked out of the dorm."

With a calm tone, Hannah said, "Rhonda, you know that's not true. You were angry with Alex at the dance, and you slapped him. That's how all of it started."

"I was still mad at you from earlier, so it's your fault that I slapped him!" Rhonda accused.

By this point, Hannah was exhausted from how fast Rhonda was pushing her. But she knew she needed to keep Rhonda talking.

"Rhonda, I'm sorry we quarreled earlier that evening. It was over something so silly. I should have stayed in the room with you instead of going next door with Jackie and Michelle." Schooling her voice to sound contrite, Hannah felt the knife slip a little to her side. However, when it did, the tip protruded slightly into her skin as it cut through her shirt.

"All I wanted was for us to be best friends," Rhonda's voice developed a whiny tone to it. "My plan was for us to do everything together and you ruined it!" As she finished that sentence, the hand not holding the knife slapped the back of Hannah's neck, causing her to wince in pain. But Hannah refused to cry out. They were almost to the woods and Hannah knew that Rhonda planned to assault her there, maybe even kill her.

***

The police arrived. Jackie and Michelle explained all that had happened from the beginning, not leaving out any details. There were two detectives, a man and a woman. The man was matter of fact in writing down the details. The female officer went over to question Vicki, having recognized her from earlier incidents of vandalism. She was also familiar with the tap that had been placed on their phone in their dorm room.

"Chances are Rhonda took her somewhere secluded. It sounds as if she is dealing with manic episodes of anger. We need to alert local police so we can widen the search for her." The female officer had kind eyes. She said, "We will do all that we can to find her."

Meanwhile, Michael, Danny, and Alex walked across the darkened parking lot where one lone street-lamp provided scarce light. Michael was out of his mind with worry as he was looking around and trying to find clues. He happened to glance down at his feet. Seeing something plastic on the ground, he couldn't tell in the little light what it might be. Picking it up, he realized that it was Hannah's ID card. "Look!" he exclaimed as his friends came over to him. "I bet she dropped this on purpose." His beautiful girl was trying to leave clues and he had never loved her more!

"Let's split up," Alex suggested. "I'll walk that way," he pointed to the parking lot leading to the street. "You go toward the baseball fields. Danny, you walk that way," Alex pointed at the other side of the gym closer to the rest of the campus even though it was doubtful that Rhonda took her that way because there would have been witnesses. Nodding his head, Michael's voice wasn't working at the moment.

Wishing it wasn't so dark, he wondered if they would see or notice anything else. The baseball fields had light for games, but the field was dark since it was the off season. Walking, he almost missed it, but he looked down again and saw something metal shining in the dark. Reaching down to pick it up, he realized it was a room key to a dorm room. Knowing it to be another clue from Hannah, he yelled at Alex, saying, "She went this way. I think this is her key!"

"Michael, we need to go tell the officers," Alex encouraged, but Michael shook his head.

"You can go tell them, but I have to keep going," Michael's voice shook as he continued walking across the fields. Squinting through the dark, he saw the shadows of trees in the background. "Rhonda's probably taking her to the woods," he whispered to himself as he increased his walk to a run. He heard yelling and knew Jackie and Michelle were running behind him. Alex must have told him the two clues he found, but Michael didn't slow down in his hope of finding Hannah before anything terrible happened. He knew they would eventually catch up.

***

Reaching the tree line, Hannah's heart began beating double-time because she knew that the woods would shield anyone from seeing what Rhonda was planning on doing.

With desperation in her voice, Hannah said, "Rhonda, you know that this is going to get you kicked out of school and you will be arrested." Hannah turned her head to glance at her.

Using her free hand, Rhonda backhanded Hannah in the face, saying, "Shut up!"

Wincing in pain, Hannah felt the tears to fall as she tasted blood in her mouth. Clutching her cheek, she pleaded, "Rhonda, please...don't do this! Your mom and Dad don't want you to go to prison!"

Squeezing Hannah's arm and twisting it painfully behind her, Rhonda said, "Don't you dare say a word about my mom and dad! I'm only doing what you deserve. What's surprising is that you haven't even cried once. I guess I need to inflict more pain!" She pushed Hannah, causing her to trip over a root on the ground and land on the side of her face that had already been hit. Then she kicked her in the back. "Are you in pain now? Come on, Hannah, let me hear you cry!" She continued kicking over and over again as Hannah curled up in a ball trying to shield from the abuse. She cried out at the continued blows on her lower back. Leaning down, Rhonda muttered, "That's much better! Now, get up again." She roughly yanked Hannah's arm, jabbing the knife harder against her side.

Even though she knew it would feed Rhonda's anger, Hannah waited a split second before jerking away and screaming, "Help, help me!" The tip of the knife sliced the skin next to Hannah's ribs and

Rhonda snarled, "Didn't I tell you not to make any noise. Shut up!" Unexpectedly, her other hand came up and the blow against the back of Hannah's head caused her to see stars as she let out another cry. She knew at that moment that Rhonda wanted to kill her. Frantic, she tried to think of a way to get free because at this point, they were deep enough in the woods that Hannah wasn't sure that she could find her way out. However, she was willing to put up a fight in hopes of getting away.

***

As Michael ran, he glanced down at the ground, and he saw another object. Catching his breath, he reached down and picked up Hannah's wallet knowing that she was actually trying to leave clues in hopes of being found. "Hannah, I'm on the way," he muttered as he heard a prolonged scream and a voice crying, "Help, help me!"

Turning around he yelled, "She's this way!" He wasn't sure who was behind him, but he didn't care as he began racing toward the screams. He was close enough to the treeline that he heard another cry of pain. Knowing it was Hannah, he wanted to yell that he was coming. However, it might incite Rhonda's anger even more if he did. Slowing to a walk, he began stepping carefully so as not to alert her. He heard yells behind him, and he was hopeful that the campus police were on the trail as he crept through the trees trying to listen for any more sounds. They were deep enough in the woods that it was hard to tell the way out, which was what Rhonda had probably planned.

***

Looking around her, Rhonda's mind was completely filled with her rage and revenge for Hannah. "This will work," she snarled, shoving Hannah down on the ground. Roughly grabbing Hannah's legs, she said, "Turn over, bitch. I want to watch your face as I put my knife through your heart!"

Knowing the knife was pointing the other direction as Rhonda tried manhandling her, Hannah took that moment to kick her feet with all her might. Flailing her legs in an effort to loosen Rhonda's hands, she began screaming. "Get off me! Help...!" The more Rhonda tried to grab a hold of her legs, the more Hannah began squirming in her grasp. Feeling pain on her cheek, her lip and head from Rhonda's blows, she continued screaming as she fought with strength that she didn't realize she had.

Within the scuffle, Hannah was relieved to hear the knife fall to the ground and she hoped the dark would keep her from finding it. However, she didn't see Rhonda's fist as it smashed into her face causing blood to spurt all over Rhonda's fist and Hannah's hands as she cried in pain and cradled her face. Knowing her nose was broken, she began sobbing as she heard Rhonda growling and rearing back for another blow. Hannah braced herself for it when she heard footsteps and someone yell, "Get the hell off of her, bitch."

Rhonda's growl increased as she turned to defend herself, but she wasn't fast enough before Michael's fist slammed into her face. She began screaming bloody murder from the pain as her face contorted in fury. But Michael was too quick for her to overpower him and his fist connected to her cheek a second time, knocking her out.

Rushing to Hannah's side, he said, "Oh my god, Hannah." He saw the blood all over her hands and he took off his shirt to press it gently against her nose. As soon as he did, he pulled her against his bare chest saying, "Baby, I'm so sorry! I'm here now." He didn't care that blood was all over him. He was relieved that he found her before it was too late, and he was determined not to ever let her go!

Hannah broke down into sobs against his chest as Alex, Jackie and Michelle caught up to them. The two officers pulled Rhonda off the ground as she was coming to and screaming, "They attacked me out of nowhere," A flashlight scanned the area as they recovered the knife with dried blood on it. Using a plastic bag to pick it up, the officers moved to both sides of Rhonda, saying, "And is this your blood? Let's run it for prints to see." Since they were campus security, they didn't have handcuffs, so they held tightly to her arms, one on each side, as they escorted her out of the woods. Danny followed behind them just in case. Sirens were blaring, alerting them that the police were almost there.

Jackie, Michelle and Alex caught up to Michael as he continued holding Hannah tightly against his chest. Her cries became uncontrollable sobs with hiccups in between them. He tightened his hold, rocking her back and forth as his own eyes filled with tears.

"Hannah, we are so sorry," Michelle sobbed as tears ran down her own face and her hand touched her uninjured arm. 'We've never been so scared when we realized you were gone!"

Jackie rubbed the part of her back she could reach, but she didn't say anything. With a pale face, constricted nostrils and dilated pupils, her face echoed Michelle's words. Tears sprang to her eyes as she heard Hannah's sobs.

Thankful for being rescued, Hannah began sobbing harder as relief filled her. Not wanting to think about what might have happened, she kept her face pressed against Michael, to prevent anyone from seeing her.

Michael kept murmuring soothing words as he lifted her into his arms. "Baby, I've got you. We're walking back so that the paramedics can take care of you." He began walking with her out of the woods and back to the gym where the sirens were louder. Irrationally, Hannah was thankful that his shirt was blocking her nose from bleeding all over his chest. Surrounded by calming words and hands rubbing her back, her friends stayed right beside her as Michael carried her.

Finally, she heard someone yell, "Bring her over here,"

"Hannah," Michael murmured softly as he kissed her hair. "An ambulance is here, and they need to check you out."

Nodding against him, she pulled away from Michael. Her friends gasped from the blood and bruises all over her face. One of her eyes was swollen shut. Hiccups were steadily escaping her, adding to her exhaustion, so they didn't say anything else. Michael sat her on the tailgate of the ambulance and he stepped back to allow them to work on her but keeping her within his line of sight. Alex brought him an extra shirt and he pulled it over his head while flexing his hand that had hit Rhonda. He only moved a few steps away, intent on not leaving her side. Alex squeezed his arm in understanding as he moved back with the others. He could hear sobs from Michelle, but he couldn't worry about her right now.

Michael had never been someone to fight other than roughhousing with his friends. When he came upon Rhonda putting her fist into Hannah's face, he had never experienced such anger. Moving on instinct, he plowed his own fist into Rhonda's face to stop her, ignoring her screams. Wanting to keep her down so that he could get to Hannah, he leveled a second blow to her knowing it would do the trick. Not an ounce of regret filled him as he watched with narrowed eyes and the corners of his mouth turned down as the paramedics worked on her. Taking his own deep breaths as the adrenaline wore off, his heart rate increased as he realized Rhonda's intent was to kill her.

Looking over his shoulder, he watched as the police handcuffed Rhonda and opened the back door of the police car for her to get inside. Continuing to cry and scream at the unfairness, the officers paid her no attention. Watching them leave the parking lot was a relief and he began shaking all over. A paramedic noticed and he had him sit with his head between his knees. Following directions, he made himself stop and remember that she was safe.

When the paramedics suggested they take Hannah to the hospital for an x-ray of her nose, he didn't hesitate as he stepped inside the ambulance, taking her hand in his. He could tell Jackie and Michelle also wanted to come, but there wasn't room. Alex waved at him, and he knew that his friend would also join them at the emergency room. "We'll meet you there," Jackie called as the ambulance door closed and pulled out of the parking lot.

***

Once the ambulance arrived at the hospital, the paramedics wheeled Hannah into the emergency room where a doctor immediately handed her an ice pack, wrapped in a cloth, to place on her nose. Then, she was wheeled to get the x-ray.

One of the paramedics walked over to Michael and said, "You can wait right over there. She won't be in there long and the doctor will come out and talk to you."

Nodding his head in thanks, Michael walked to a chair and sat as tears filled his own eyes for the second time. The hospital doors opened as Jackie, Michelle and Alex rushed inside. Seeing him, they walked over and asked how she was.

Breathing through his tears, Michael muttered, "They're taking her to get an x-ray of her nose because they think it's broken."

"I can't believe that stupid bitch did that to her!" Michelle wailed as she was in shock and continued to cry over her friend. "We shouldn't have left her!" She collapsed in a chair with her hands over her face.

"She had it planned." Eyes filled with fury, Michael continued, "Vicki testified to that, so you couldn't have known."

Shaking her head in anger at herself, Jackie said, "Yeah, but we should have gone into the bathroom with her! Why didn't we insist on it?"

The only calm one among them, Alex said, "She probably would have attacked and injured you as well before taking Hannah anyway. Or she would have found another time to get her alone. Like Michael said, this was a planned act."

A few more minutes passed before Michelle gasped, saying, "We need to call her parents!" Rubbing the tears on her face with shaking hands, she said, "I don't have their number. It's in the room." She looked at Jackie who shrugged her shoulders.

Coming down from his adrenaline high, Michael shook his head and said, "I have her wallet." Pulling it out of his pocket, he looked through the slots for her driver's license. He looked underneath it and saw a card with Hannah's emergency contact numbers, and he breathed out a sigh of relief. "Here we go."

Seeing Michelle overwrought with tears, he asked Jackie, "Do you want to call or should I?"

Jackie looked at him and said, "You should call." Michael felt her approval in hopes of his and Hannah getting back together. In his mind, he would do whatever he could to get her back. What had happened tonight made him realize that he didn't want to go one more second without knowing that Hannah was his. His plan of moving slowly had been revised and he would tell her his true feelings as soon as he could.

Getting directions from the emergency room desk, he found a pay phone. Once Hannah's mother answered, he explained what had happened. Hearing her cry out, Michael felt terrible as Hannah's mom began sobbing for her husband who took the phone. Michael explained the entire situation and they were on the way as soon as he hung up. He apologized as Hannah's dad said, "Michael, this wasn't your fault. Thank you for calling to let us know. We should be there in a few hours."

Speaking before he hung up, Michael said, "Sir, they may release her soon. Do I have your permission to bring her back to my apartment until you can get here? I have a double bed that Hannah can sleep in while I stay on the couch."

"That will be fine, Michael. Thank you again for taking care of her." Bill Mathis' voice was filled with gratitude for his daughter's safety.

After telling him his address, he hung up and walked back to the lobby

As he was walking back, he saw a doctor walk out. "I'm looking for the people who were with Hannah Mathis tonight."

All of them stood as Michael caught up to them, anxious to hear an update. "We were with her," Michael answered.

The doctor looked tired, but his eyes were kind as he said, "Your friend suffered a broken nose, but other than that her injuries were minor. Can someone tell me what happened?"

After telling the doctor of Hannah's abduction and assault, the doctor said, "What about her parents? Have they been contacted?"

Michael was the one who confirmed that they were on the way.

"I would prefer to tell her parents, but since you were all with her, I will talk to you as well. Like I said, her nose is broken. The good news is that it was broken in place, so surgery will not be necessary." The doctor took a breath before continuing. "That being said, Hannah will be in some pain for a few days. Both of her eyes are already blackening, and we stitched two cuts on her eye and above her eyebrow along with the one on her arm. She also has bruises on her lower back near her kidneys but we were able to rule out internal bleeding. She was a lucky girl."

Running a hand over his face with the agony of her injuries, Michael let out a breath as Michelle began sobbing again.

"Can we see her?" Jackie asked in a shaky voice.

"Yes, but only one at a time. I think she's been through enough trauma for one evening. She should be alright after getting some rest. Her heart rate has been elevated, so we want to monitor it for a while longer. She should be able to leave after it is stable again. She will need a week's rest for the bruises on her face and her kidneys to heal." The doctor nodded with another tired smile before leaving for another emergency.

"I can't wait any longer. If you don't mind, I would like to see her first," Michael requested with a pained expression. "I won't be long so that you can see her as well."

"Take your time," Alex said with a gentle smile to his friend. Jackie was still in a state of shock and did not say anything. Michelle continued to sob with her hands on her face once more.

***

Michael walked back to the small cubicle where Hannah was in the emergency room. Peeking around the curtain, he said, "Hey, can I come in?"

One eye was swollen shut, the other one was turning black, and her nose was severely swollen. Wincing from the cut on her lip, Hannah said, "Sure, come on in." Exhaustion was all over her face.

One hand had a tube in it which hooked it up to the machine pumping fluids and medicines into her system. Michael noticed a chair to the side and he pulled it up beside her taking her other hand in his. Looking around, he noticed the heart monitor on the other side. He couldn't stop the tears from coming to his eyes as he said, "I called your parents, and they are on the way." Swallowing convulsively, he kissed her fingers as he continued, "Hannah, I am so sorry!"

"Michael, you had no way of knowing this would happen. It's not your fault." Hannah squeezed his hand as she attempted a smile, wincing in pain as she reached up to gently touch her swollen nose.

Looking into her one good eye, he admitted, "I've never been so scared in my life! I'm so thankful you left clues for us to find you. Otherwise..." His eyes turned a darker blue, and his voice drifted off as more tears came and a few spilled over.

Hannah's own eyes welled up and she winced in pain. "I know. I was so scared! Thank you for finding me! I was afraid I wouldn't see you or my family ever again!"

She was crying softly as he pulled her hand to his lips in an effort to comfort her, wishing he could hold her without hurting her. His voice was filled with conviction as he said, "I would have gone to the ends of the earth for you! Hannah, I need you to know that I love you."

Tears leaked out of Hannah's eyes, and she tried to smile again, but it hurt too much. Gazing into his eyes, she said, "When Rhonda had me, I realized that I never stopped loving you. I love you so much!"

Wanting to kiss her, he pulled her hand back up to his mouth. Michael kissed the back of it gently and placed it beside his cheek before saying, "Does this mean that you will give us another chance?"

"Yes," Hannah breathed. "I only want to be with you. But I don't want to scare you again if we get too serious." Uncertainty joined the pain in her eyes.

Michael adamantly shook his head and said, "I only want to be with you! I promise you, Hannah, that I won't be stupid again!" Looking deeply into her eyes, he put her hand against his chest and continued, "You are the one! We're supposed to be together forever!"

More sobs came out of Hannah as she grimaced in pain. Her lower back and kidneys ached from Rhonda's kicks. Michael was sick at watching her pain and he said, "Baby, don't try to speak anymore. I wanted to tell you how I feel, but you need to rest now."

Nodding her head, her eyes became drowsy. "They gave me something for the pain and I think it's finally starting to work."

Michael stood and reached down to kiss her forehead. "Jackie and Michelle want to come in to see you, but the doctor told us we can only come one at a time. Once they are done, I will be back."

With a sleepy voice Hannah opened her eyes and tried to argue, "You don't have to stay."

With another violent shake of his head, Michael took her hand and kissed her fingertips, "I'm not leaving you. Your dad gave me permission to bring you back to my place when they release you. They will meet us there."

Gratefulness crossed Hannah's face as she mumbled, "Thank you."

Chapter 18

B oth Jackie and Michelle took their turn with Hannah. Michelle openly sobbed as she apologized profusely for not following her into the bathroom. Jackie's face was filled with guilt, and she couldn't stop apologizing, either.

Having a hard time keeping her eyes open, Hannah said to both of them. "It's not your fault. I'm the one who insisted you wait outside. I thought Rhonda had left."

Neither of them stayed long, but they promised to do whatever Hannah needed. Michelle commented, "Michael told us you are going to his house, so we will go and pack a bag to bring over."

"Don't worry about me," Hannah mumbled. "You both need to go to bed and get some rest."

Both of them knew it would be a while before they could fall asleep, but they didn't argue with Hannah because they didn't want to add to her pain.

***

Once Jackie and Michelle had their turn seeing Hannah, they rode back to the dorm with Alex. Alex said he would come back and wait with Michael until Hannah was released so that he could drive them back.

Walking back into the cubicle, Michael saw Hannah sleeping peacefully from the pain medicine that the nurse had given her. Sitting beside her, he took her hand again and stroked the hair back on her forehead. He was content to sit there, hold her hand, and watch her, grateful that she was going to be okay.

Alex briefly appeared to let Michael know he was back. As he was walking out, the doctor came in and told them that they were releasing her.

The doctor said, "I'm sending a prescription with you of pain medicine for Hannah to take over the next few days. Remind her to take it as prescribed because she will be extremely sore," Michael held out his hand for the doctor as he thanked him.

Thirty minutes later, Hannah was being wheeled out to Alex's car, her head drooping from the medication and exhaustion. Not able to stand seeing her like that, Michael reached down and lifted her into his arms once they were outside. Gently, he placed her into the backseat of Alex's car before walking around to the other side. Climbing in, he gently moved her to where she was leaning against him and her arms immediately wrapped around his waist seeking his comfort. His heart melted as he gathered her as close as he could without causing her any more pain. As Alex started the car, Michael couldn't take his eyes off Hannah as he gently stroked her hair. He hadn't noticed it before, but he saw stitches on her arm where Rhonda's knife had sliced it and he remembered the doctor talking about it. It broke his heart to see so many injuries on her beautiful face and body.

A few minutes later, Alex pulled into their driveway. Walking around to her side, Michael lifted her again and she tried to say she could walk. "Absolutely not," he answered, refusing to put her down.

Alex unlocked their door and Michael carried her into his room. He heard knocking as he was placing her on the bed. Michelle and Jackie walked in with a bag of Hannah's clothes, and he stepped out as they helped her out of the bloody clothing she had been wearing. When they came out, his eyes closed when he saw her torn and bloody clothes. He went in to turn back his covers so that she could climb in and sleep. Tenderly, he kissed her forehead again as his heart ached seeing the bruises on her cheek. Tears filled his eyes again as he whispered, "I will be right outside if you need me. I love you."

With her eyes closed, Hannah nodded her head, wincing as she burrowed deeper under the covers. Turning off the light, Michael stepped out into the living room.

Alex looked at him and said, "Why don't you take a shower now? You can borrow some of my clothes, so you don't have to go in and disturb her again." Michelle and Jackie were on the couch with dazed looks not having left yet.

Glancing down, Michael saw the dried blood on his hands and arms, along with smears on his shirt. Knowing it was on his chest, he nodded his head in agreement. Alex brought him some clothes and he went into the bathroom.

Feeling better after his shower, he walked out and told the girls, "You don't have to stay if you want to go back and rest."

Jackie said, "I won't be able to sleep for a while, so we want to stay." Michelle nodded her head in agreement.

Michael didn't argue with them as he walked into the kitchen. Alex was pouring a glass of water for him and Michael noticed the prescription sitting on the table. "Thanks, man," he said, taking the water glass and gulping it down. "I forgot to bring it inside to give to her parents."

"No problem," Alex said as he also drank deeply. After he finished, he filled up two more glasses to share with Jackie and Michelle before refilling the pitcher to put it back in the refrigerator.

Then, Michael poured another glass over some ice cubes and quietly opened his door to set it beside his bed for when Hannah woke up. She hadn't moved, but he adjusted the covers anyway. Needing to touch her, he kissed the top of her head again. Grabbing his extra pillow, he walked out to the living room as Alex was also coming out with an extra pillow and blanket.

Kindly, Alex asked the girls, "Do you want to lay down in my room?"

They both shook their heads, so Alex put the pillow and blanket beside them on the couch. "I think I have one more pillow," he commented. Finding it, he set it beside the other things before going and taking his own shower.

***

Two hours later, Hannah's parents arrived. Michael had checked on her constantly (he couldn't stop himself) and she was still sleeping soundly. He hated to wake her, but he knew they wanted to see her. Opening his door for them, Anita Mathis began tearing up with her hand over her mouth as she saw the bruises and swelling all over her daughter's face. Mr. Mathis walked over beside the bed and lightly touched her forehead as if he was checking to make sure she was still breathing. Michael gave them privacy to have a few moments alone with their daughter.

Grimacing in pain, Hannah lifted her head slightly and squinted at her parents. "Mom, Dad, thank you for coming."

Feeling protective, her mother said, "Don't move around too much. Stay where you are and rest. Baby, we are so sorry this happened to you." She masked her tears for Hannah's sake.

Bill Mathis sat gently beside Hannah on the bed and continued stroking her hair. When he spoke, his voice was soft as he said, "How are you Hannah-bear?"

Shifting slightly, Hannah moved to sit up as she answered, "I'm alright."

Holding up a hand, her mother said, "No, don't get up for us, sweetie. We just needed to see that you're okay. Go back to sleep."

Wincing as Hannah moved to the uninjured side of her face, she muttered, "I'll be okay. I love you."

A silent tear slipped down her mom's face and she moved to the other side of the bed, saying, "We love you, too."

Her dad reached down to kiss the top of her head and with thickness in his own voice, he also said, "We love you, baby girl. Sleep well. We have a hotel room, so we'll be back in the morning."

Almost asleep again, Hannah nodded her head.

When Hannah's parents walked back out into the small living room, Jackie and Michelle rushed to them. Introducing themselves, they continued apologizing as they had been doing all night since the attack.

Hannah's mom touched Michelle's cheek as she addressed both of them. "This isn't your fault. That girl is crazy, and you had no idea what she was capable of doing! Thank you for being such good friends and working so hard to find her."

Bill Mathis nodded in agreement before turning to Michael. "Michael, we cannot thank you enough for helping to rescue her."

Looking him in his eyes, Michael said, "I would do anything for your daughter, Mr. Mathis. I'm just sorry that I wasn't able to get to her sooner."

"Please, call me Bill," her dad commented.

"Michael, this isn't your fault, either," Hannah's mom said as she touched his cheek . "None of you should have had to worry about your friend being attacked! It's not something you should have to go through so young! We appreciate what you did to help."

Michael thanked Hannah's mom as exhaustion washed over him.

Her dad continued talking, "We will meet with the police tomorrow to ask for an update and to let them know that we will be pressing charges against that young lady."

Everyone nodded their heads in agreement since none of them had much energy left. Seeing their exhaustion, Hannah's parents excused themselves to go to the hotel with the promise to return in the morning. Mrs. Mathis insisted on bringing breakfast for all of them and they couldn't refuse.

***

The next morning, Hannah opened her eyes and wondered where she was. The horror of the night before came flashing back as she sat up moaning in pain. Her body hurt all over.

That small amount of movement alerted Michael and he cracked open the door. "Morning," he said in a soft voice, and he rushed over as Hannah tried moving to the edge of the bed. "Let me help you," he commented as he helped her move her legs to the floor. Jackie and Michelle had finally gone back to the dorm to sleep in their own beds.

The three of them talked softly for a while and they left so that Michael could try to sleep.

"What time is it?" Hannah gasped the words from her pain.

"Around 6:30," Michael commented. "Here, drink some water." He handed her a glass and said, "The doctor said you were dehydrated from all that you went through."

Hannah gingerly took some sips as her hands shook from exhaustion. She moved to stand up, when Michael said, "Whoa, where do you think you're going?"

"Michael, I need to use the restroom," Hannah grumbled, but her legs were shaky.

"Okay, but I'm going to help you," Michael argued, not about to take no for an answer.

Realizing that she needed help, she allowed Michael to wrap his arm around her waist, wincing when his arm brushed the bruises. "Baby, did I hurt you?" His eyes were a cobalt blue from his concern and fear for her.

"I'm bruised where Rhonda kicked me, but I will be fine," she said, sucking in a breath as she took slow steps toward the bathroom.

Michael knew she would not like it, but he couldn't stand to see her struggle. He lifted her into his arms as soon as she stepped out of the bathroom and walked her back to his bed. Surprised when Hannah melted against him, he knew it was the right choice if she wasn't protesting or arguing with him. He put her on the bed and said he would be right back. Walking to the kitchen, he poured a glass of orange juice and took it to her. Her parents were filling the prescription for pain pills, so he couldn't do anything else for her pain until they arrived.

As he walked back in, fright filled him at the sight of Hannah crying in her hands. He quickly set the glass down as he sat beside her.

"Hannah, what's wrong? Are you hurting? Do we need to take you back to the hospital?"

Unable to speak, she shook her head as Michael carefully pulled her against him. He held her and let her cry. When she pulled back, she sobbed, "I'm sorry."

"Baby, don't apologize," Michael murmured against the top of her head while fighting his own tears. Knowing it would take some time for her to get past this trauma, he rocked her back and forth for a moment before he adjusted to where he could lean against his headboard. He pulled her back against him. "I know we've said it a thousand times, but I am so sorry that this happened to you."

Hannah (sniffing from the tears) snuggled against him, seeking comfort before she pulled back and said, "When I saw myself in the mirror, it all came back to me." In the bathroom, she had cried out in horror when she caught her reflection in the mirror. She looked like a raccoon with dark circles around her eyes. "Thank you again," she murmured as she gazed into his eyes and her tears continued to spill down her cheeks.

Caressing the cut on her lip with his thumb, Michael placed a gentle kiss on her mouth. It was barely a whisper of a kiss so that he wouldn't hurt her. However, Hannah leaned her mouth up to touch her lips to his again before Michael kissed her uninjured cheek and moved his mouth into her hair so thankful that she was alive and here with him. "I love you, Hannah."

Wrapping her arms around him as best as she could, she said, "I love you, too."

A knock sounded at the door just as Alex came out of his room. "Stay there, and I will get it," he said, opening the door to let Hannah's parents inside.

Rushing to her side, her mother gushed, "Good morning, sweetie. Did you get some sleep?"

"I just woke up a few minutes ago," Hannah said, but she didn't move away from Michael.

Her dad simply kissed her on the top of her head and said, "Your mother and I brought breakfast. Are you hungry?"

Hannah was surprised to realize that she was. "Can we call Jackie and Michelle so that they can come and join us?"

Alex was leaning against the doorjamb, and he said, "I'll give them a call" and he walked to the phone in their living room.

Not letting her walk again, Michael carried her to the couch thinking that it would be more comfortable for her to eat.

After eating a little breakfast, Hannah rested for the rest of the day and her friends skipped their Friday classes to be with her and assist her in any way. They struggled with their own trauma from what had happened and the need to be near was essential.

Hannah's mom brought her prescription for pain medicine. After breakfast, her back pain was increasing so she allowed her mom to give her one of the pills. Her mother also did all that she could to encourage Hannah to drink fluids. Normally, her mother's hovering drove her crazy, but she was thankful that she was there. While Hannah slept again, her parents went back to their hotel to rest. Michael spent some time studying next to Hannah on his bed, wanting to stay as close to her as possible. Jackie, Michelle and Alex dozed on the couch in the living room with the television playing a syndicated show.

At one point, Michael knew he needed to call home and talk to his parents. While Hannah took a shower, with her friends' help, he called them in his room and explained what had happened. He became angry with his mother when she was more concerned about him.

"Mom! Hannah was the one who was attacked! Stop worrying about my safety!"

"I'm sorry, Michael," she said. "But you could have been seriously hurt going after that lunatic!"

Michael sighed as he ran a hand through his hair. "Mom, I appreciate that, but what was I supposed to do? Rhonda intended to kill her!"

Letting out a breath as she showed slight remorse, Michael's mother said, "You're right. I'm proud of you for standing up to that crazy girl! Being your mother, I worry about you too much. I'm sorry for what Hannah went through."

Nodding his head even though she couldn't see him, he said, "I know, Mom. I just want you to know that Hannah and I are back together now. This situation made us realize that we don't want to be apart anymore."

"Are you sure that's a good idea? You told me you wanted to focus on your classes." Michael took a deep breath because he knew his mother would say this.

"Mom, my relationship with Hannah has nothing to do with that. We have different majors, so my time with her will not interfere with studying and school-work." He normally wasn't so bold, but he continued. "Please trust me that we are doing the right thing."

Silence was on the line before she said, "Okay, son. You're eighteen years old, so you're old enough to make decisions for yourself. Please tell her that I hope she feels better soon."

Thanking her, they ended the call with his promise to call her with updates.

For dinner that night, her parents brought pizza for everyone. It was decided that Hannah would remain at Michael's one more night where he and her parents could be there while she rested.

***

It took a week for Hannah's bruises to begin fading. Her eyes turned from black to a brown and purple color and the swelling on her nose subsided.

True to his word, Hannah's dad had visited the police station to press charges along with meeting with authorities who worked for the university. An officer stopped by Michael's apartment to get statements from everyone, strengthening the case against Rhonda.

Rhonda was expelled. Yelling at anyone who would listen, of her own inconvenience from her daughter's arrest, her mother took her back to her home after posting bail and awaiting a trial. The police reassured everyone that there would be a conviction and that she would serve prison time since she was no longer a minor.

Word had gotten around what had happened to her and students were compassionate and caring when Hannah began attending her classes again. Many of them had reached out, willing to help in any way that they could. Hannah's friend, Suzanne, made sure to take notes and get copies of any assignments that Hannah would need to catch up in her education classes along with kind notes passed along from her professors. The school had been happy to grant her a week off to recover from her injuries.

Angela, the counselor that Hannah had been meeting with, called and spoke with her offering her apologies. She told Hannah that she would be there whenever Hannah was ready to make an appointment to talk about her abduction along with anything else.

Her own brother and sister had actually called to check on her just as her Nana did. Hannah never wanted to be the center of attention, and it made her uncomfortable, but Angela encouraged her to be open to their willingness to be there for her. "You are more special and loved than you realize, Hannah. It's time for you to accept it and allow it to help you heal!"

Surprised at herself, Hannah actually believed that what Angela said was true. Fearing for her life had taught her how precious time with friends and family could be.

Michael devoted much of his time and attention to her, ensuring that she was getting rest and healing properly. It proved to Hannah that he was true to his word and that he was serious about her. Her trust in him was growing, but there were still slivers of doubt. She hoped to talk with Angela about her relationship with him to get advice.

Chapter 19

Once Hannah's parents went home, Michael convinced her to stay with him for a few more days. Hannah didn't want to put him out, but they wanted to be near each other. She had been struggling with sleeping in her room due to nightmares and knowing that they were keeping her roommates awake. She worried that they would never forgive themselves even though she and her parents had assured them over and over that the attack wasn't their fault. Unable to drive yet due to doctor's orders, she packed her bag and went to the lobby to wait because Michael was on the way to pick her up. She knew he would refuse if she offered to walk there. Coddling her brought him comfort and she didn't want to deny him that.

Lost in thought, the door opening brought her back to the present as Michael's face lit up with a smile at seeing her.

"Hey, beautiful!" he crooned. "Are you ready?"

Hannah snorted at the word knowing that she was anything but beautiful at the moment. "Please, wait a few more days before saying that!"

Leaning to kiss her softly, Michael murmured, "But you are!" Then, he reached for her bag and took her hand to walk her to his car.

"Thanks for inviting me to stay with you," Hannah commented. "I want Jackie and Michelle to get some real sleep without me being there."

"Hannah, I am happy you are coming, and this plan is to help you sleep." Michael's smile was gentle as he entwined their fingers together. He found that he hadn't been able to stop touching her ever since the attack.

Arriving at Michael and Alex's place, Michael made Hannah wait so that he could come around and open her door to help her out. Even though Hannah was walking again without pain, he held her arm to guide her inside.

Laughing softly, Hannah said, "Michael, I'm better now. You don't have to help me."

Kissing her uninjured cheek, he smiled into her eyes and said, "I know, but I want to." He was carrying her bag again and he walked into his room to set it down before turning back to her. Love flooded his gaze, and he pulled her into his arms, murmuring, "Come here." He intended a gentle and chaste kiss, but as soon as his mouth touched hers, he couldn't contain himself as he put all his feelings into it. The kiss was tender, but lengthy as she opened her mouth and his tongue danced with hers.

"Hmm..." she sighed with her eyes still closed as he rained kisses all over the side of her face without bruises. When she made that sound, it made him feel like he was on top of the world.

"Hannah," he breathed with want and desire. "Tell me if you need more time because I don't want to hurt you."

Pulling back, he saw his desire mirrored in her gaze and she said, "Michael, you aren't. I appreciate your gentleness with me, but I am ready for more."

Appeased by her words, he kissed her a second time. She kissed him back and he deepened it. Unable to stop himself, his hands found the soft skin of her back as they moved under her shirt. Hannah moaned as he continued kissing her when he felt her legs trembling.

"That's enough for now because you're exhausted," he murmured against her hair. He took her hand as she whimpered in protest. Ignoring her, he led her to sit on the couch after he grabbed a remote control. After switching on the television, he pulled her to where her back was resting against his chest and said, "Time for you to rest. Is there anything you want to watch?"

Michael's voice beside her ear was still causing shivers of desire and she felt frustrated from feeling so tired all the time when she was ready for more. She knew he would refuse to do anything else tonight, so she allowed herself to snuggle against him and leaned her head back, saying, "No." Completely comfortable in his warm embrace, Hannah dozed off while the movie was playing.

Tenderly gazing down at her, Michael grabbed the blanket off of the couch to cover her. Content with holding her, he finished the movie that they were watching before lifting her to carry her to his room. Hannah woke up and insisted on changing into her pajamas and brushing her teeth. Reluctant to let her go, he did the same as soon as she was finished.

Before assuming, he sat down beside Hannah, took her hand and said, "Are you comfortable if I join you in the bed tonight?"

With a gentle smile, Hannah kissed him and said, "This is your bed, so yes."

"I know, but I don't want you to be uncomfortable," Michael looked down with uncertainty.

Touching his hand and then his face, Hannah said, "Michael, I want you to hold me while we sleep." Hannah knew she said the right words to him when his eyes lit up. "I told you I'm ready for more."

Shaking his head, Michael tucked her against his side and moved against his headboard. He said, "Later, but tonight you need to sleep." Then he continued by saying, "I know you're not quite ready to go out on a date, but I'm bringing dinner here tomorrow night." He intertwined their fingers and said, "This is a 'stay at home' date. Now that we are back together, I don't want to waste any more time, Hannah."

Overwhelmed by his gentle treatment of her, Hannah moved her head so that she could look into his eyes and she said, "I'd like that. I don't want to waste any more time, either."

Lost in her gaze, Michael kissed her deeply for a long moment before he said, "I love you so much!"

Smiling against his mouth, Hannah exhaled, "I love you, too."

Michael groaned when he felt her breath, and he kissed her again. Laying down and pulling her into his arms, they were completely serene as they drifted off to sleep.

***

Surprisingly, Hannah slept the entire night without any nightmares. She knew it was from feeling safe and secure in Michael's arms.

The next day, they relaxed and rested. Michael knew that Hannah wouldn't unless he joined her. After lunch she insisted that they study for an hour or so. Michael agreed as long as she took a nap afterwards. She agreed as long as he joined her and they fell asleep again with him holding her with her back to his front.

Hannah woke up and stretched, noticing that Michael was no longer in the bed. Looking at the time, she was shocked to see that she had slept for three hours! Climbing from the bed quickly, she needed to take a shower and change her clothes for their evening at home. Not knowing that Michael had planned this, she only brought jeans, but she had packed a decent top to go with them. Walking out into the living room, she saw him sitting with a textbook in his lap.

He looked up and smiled. "Hey, beautiful." he said, crossing to her and kissing her on her cheek as he studied her face. "Did you sleep well?"

"I did," she smiled into his eyes. Then she asked, "What time are we having our home-date tonight?"

Kissing her eyebrow without the stitches, Michael said, "I placed a call a few minutes ago to the steak restaurant and told them that I would pick it up around six. I ordered a steak, baked potato and salad similar to what you ordered on our date at your parents' house. Does that sound okay? I can change it if you want something else."

Laying her head against his chest, Hannah said, "That sounds wonderful." Michael held her close for a minute before she continued, "I need to take a shower."

He didn't release her just yet as he kissed her on the cheek and said, "That's perfect because I have to request that you stay in the bedroom for the next little while."

Eyes narrowed with suspicion, Hannah asked, "Why?"

Kissing the top of her head, Michael said, "I have a few things I need to do before I go and get dinner."

Hannah chuckled as she said, "Alright." Then she disappeared into the bathroom.

***

An hour later, Hannah finished putting on her makeup and styling her hair. Straightening the top with her jeans, she took a final look in the mirror murmuring, "Well, I guess this will do." She had tried concealing most of the bruises with makeup and her hair was softly curled around her shoulders (she was thankful that she packed her curling iron).

A knock sounded on Michael's closed door and she opened it. A dazed look came over him and he took her hands in his and exclaimed, "Wow! You look gorgeous!"

Not wanting to ruin his compliment with negative thoughts about her appearance, Hannah said, "Thank you."

He looked wonderful, wearing the shirt that he wore on their first date. "You look wonderful as well." She realized that he had planned this and he must have gotten ready in Alex's room since he was away for the weekend.

Taking her hand, Michael's smoky gaze remained on her face as he said, "Dinner is ready."

Dizzy from the look he was giving her, Hannah let him lead her into the kitchen and she gasped. Michael lit two candles on the table (Hannah wondered where he got them) and there was a vase with a red rose sitting between them. Two plates, silverware and napkins had also been set on the table along with two glasses filled with iced tea. "Michael, it's so beautiful!" Hannah gushed.

With his eyes still on her, Michael murmured, "I'm glad you like it," Then, he confessed, "I might have had a little help from Jackie and Michelle." He reached down and turned Hannah's face up so that he could kiss her tenderly. With his hand still caressing the back of her neck, he whispered, "You are so beautiful." After one more kiss, he pulled out her chair.

Speechless, Hannah lowered herself into it and allowed him to place a napkin in her lap. He took her plate and placed her steak and baked potato on it. A small plate contained bread and butter, and he placed it in the middle before getting his plate. Before he joined her, he brought two more small plates containing their salads.

Dinner was delicious and Hannah thanked Michael profusely for it. As they ate, he confessed, "I learned serving skills when my church had a fundraiser to send my youth group to camp. We were taught how to pull out the lady's chair and place a napkin in her lap."

"I'm impressed," Hannah said with a loving smile. "This was wonderful!"

Holding her hand, Michael asked, "Are you ready for dessert or would you rather wait?"

"I'm so full," Hannah lamented. Her appetite had been sporadic since her attack, and she had lost weight. "Let's wait until a little later."

Michael stood, and quickly cleared their dishes into the sink. Then, he pulled out her chair and held out his hand to her. Walking her into the living room, he put up his hand signaling for her to wait. Taking another remote control, he turned on his stereo which was playing a beautiful love song.

He held out his hand again and he asked, "Will you dance with me?"

Unable to speak, Hannah nodded as he pulled her into his arms and began swaying. He held her so tightly against him as they moved together. Laying her head on his chest, his hands caressed up and down her back in a sensual manner and Hannah knew that this would be the night when their intimacy deepened. She tightened her hold on his neck as he nuzzled hers.

She leaned back, but Michael didn't let her go far.

His eyes were dark with emotion as he leaned down and took her lips in a gentle, but sensual kiss. Hannah couldn't help but gasp at the love that she felt from his lips. She didn't know if he had ever kissed her as intensely as he was now. It was as if he was making love to her with a kiss. She opened her mouth and invited his tongue in with hers. Shivers overcame her and he tightened his hold on her. He put all of his love and devotion into communicating to her with this deep kiss. His hands cradled her face by the time he was finished. Both of them could hardly breathe from the emotions washing over them. Hannah's arms were wrapped around his waist because her legs were trembling. It was then that she realized that they had stopped swaying together.

"Michael," she whispered as he continued to rain kisses down the good side of her face and to her ear. Hannah didn't know how to even put what she was feeling into words. She just knew that nobody ever treated her as special as he was treating her right now.

With her eyes closed in absolute bliss, she shivered again when he whispered, "I love you." One of his hands caressed her cheek and he gently pulled back. His eyes studied hers with an intense expression and then he said, "This was all I could think about today, even when I was trying to study."

With half-closed eyes, she said, "Me too. I was hoping for this when I was getting ready a while ago."

"I've missed holding you, Hannah," Michael's hands continued caressing her back down to the hem of her top where they slid underneath. Breathing against her ear, he whispered, "And, I've missed touching your skin."

Goosebumps arose as his mouth worked its way down her neck and she tilted it to give him better access. Pressing tightly against him, Hannah moaned as his lips found hers again and she opened wide for his tongue to dance with hers.

Michael groaned at her responsiveness as he kissed her deeply. Reminding himself to slow down and not go too fast, he laid his head on top of hers and said, "I want to finish dancing with you, but I don't want you to get too tired."

Melting against him, Hannah said, "I'm fine. I love you, Michael."

Her words just about did him in, but he made himself finish the song. Then he pulled back and said, "Are you sure that you're ready for this, Hannah? I don't want to pressure..."

Hannah put a finger over his lips before he could utter the word, "you," and she said, "I told you last night that I am more than ready for this." Then, she reached up and kissed him.

Groaning a second time at her willingness, Michael lifted Hannah into his arms and he carried her into his room. Putting her down, he closed the door and locked it. His fingers caressed her hair and then he pulled her close again for another thought-stealing kiss.

Then Hannah sighed as his hands were cradling her face and one hand was moving down her neck to her shoulder.

Upon hearing her sigh, his hand plunged under her hair to tickle the back of her neck and he followed his caress with his lips as he kissed down the side of Hannah's neck again. As he was kissing his way down, he breathed in the scent of her shampoo.

He murmured, "My word, I love your skin." He moved around behind her, and he lifted her hair to kiss the back of her neck as one arm wrapped around her waist from behind her. His hand was splayed across her stomach and those fingers found their way back under her shirt as they whispered across the skin on her belly.

Trembling with desire, Hannah's eyes remained closed as Michael's tongue joined his kisses, leaving wet trails on the back of her neck.

Hannah's pulse was haywire from the erotic sensations rushing through her. "Michael," was all she could coherently say as his mouth kissed her jumping pulse.

Michael pulled back to lift her shirt up over her head. Throwing it on the floor, his hands reached around for her breasts from behind as he continued feasting on her neck and her shoulders. His fingers slipped under her bra straps, and he lowered them as he breathed in deeply at seeing the curve of her breasts as they were bulging in the cups of her bra. "You are so beautiful." he whispered as his fingers rubbed the fullness of one breast.

Overwhelmed with so many sensations and emotions, Hannah sighed and she whimpered again from his light touch. She tried to reach around and release the clasp on her bra, but Michael's hand stopped her. The hand that was on her stomach drifted down to her jeans and his fingers slipped under the material tickling across the lower parts of her stomach.

"Please let me undress you," he said against the skin of her neck. His lips continued kissing every part of her neck and her shoulders.

Hannah whimpered a third time with frustration as she was unable to touch him. She attempted to turn around so that she could kiss him, but he said, "In a minute. I need to love you first," and he continued the slow torture to the point that Hannah was having a hard time remaining on her feet.

His fingers pushed one bra strap all the way down and off of her arm. Again, he reached around and caressed one soft mound as his eyes feasted on it.

He did the same thing with the other bra strap and finally, he turned Hannah in his embrace so that he could caress both breasts while kissing her deeply again. With his tongue plunging into her mouth, his right hand unclasped Hannah's bra and he watched it fall to the floor unveiling her breasts completely.

"Hannah," he breathed as if he had not ever seen her before.

Impatient with him, Hannah raised his shirt over his head and she threw it to the floor. Then, she pushed her breasts against his chest as she tried to get as close to him as she could, and Michael thought he might die from the sensation of her peaked nipples. "You feel so good, baby." he whispered as his thumbs rubbed across her hardened nipples.

His hands cupped them as his mouth found hers again. "So wonderful," he breathed against her mouth. His thumbs rubbed each nipple creating even harder peaks than before.

Pulling back, Michael unbuttoned Hannah's jeans and he pushed them to the floor. Then, he removed her panties along with his other clothing.

He gently placed her onto the bed and he climbed onto it. He gave her another open mouth kiss before he moved his mouth to one breast and he pulled a nipple into his mouth. Then he moved to the other breast feasting on them equally as Hannah writhed beneath him.

Gasping and sighing again, she caressed all of Michael that she could from his back to his chest, down to his stomach and below causing him to moan softly.

Michael kissed her breasts again and down to her stomach before moving back to her mouth. His fingers found her sensitive place between her legs as he gently moved his fingers back and forth and he felt her wetness as she grasped him, bringing a moan from his mouth.

He pushed her back and moved between her legs. Putting on a condom, he pushed into her, and they both groaned loudly. "Hannah," he whispered as he took both of her hands and interlaced his fingers with them. Pulling them up over her head, he pulled a nipple into his mouth as he began to move.

Michael made sure to thrust slowly to where he wouldn't come before Hannah did. His movements were gentle motions, but he created enough friction that both of them were gasping in pleasure. Even during sex, he was worried about her continued recovery, but she urged him with her hands.

He felt Hannah tighten around him and he continued thrusting and encouraging her orgasm before his own exploded. Careful of her injuries, he gently rolled to the side and took care of the condom before gathering her close.

"I love you," they both said at the same time, and they laughed softly together. Michael pulled Hannah against him as he kissed the top of her head.

"That was absolutely exquisite," he commented, slightly out of breath. "It felt like it was our first time together."

Leaning back to look at him, Hannah said, "In a way, it was. I mean, it was our first time since getting back together."

Smiling at her, Michael's hand rubbed up and down her back. "I think everything that we have been through has deepened our relationship. Baby, I hated to see you get hurt and I was terrified when I couldn't get to you. But I know for sure that I want to be with you and only you."

Hannah lifted up onto her elbow, causing beautiful cleavage between her breasts. "I want to be with you, as well. Michael, I know that I've had my doubts and fears. But they went away when you did all that you could to rescue me. Rhonda could have easily killed you as well, but you did it for me!"

"I know I've said this already, but I will go to the ends of the earth for you, Hannah Mathis. You are the love of my life!" His gaze fell on her cleavage as he ran a finger between her breasts and he whispered, "You are beautiful like this!" His other fingers joined in as they rubbed the sides of her cleavage and his eyes darkened. Moving her underneath him, he deepened the kiss as his hands stroked up and down her body. Her hands were caressing him the same way.

Her sharp inhale was his undoing and with a groan, he reached for a condom. Her hand stilled his and she said, "Remember, I'm on the pill."

With wide eyes, he said, "Baby, are you sure?"

Her answer was to pull him down where she kissed him passionately. Sliding between her legs again, he pushed in all the way, and he loved hearing her soft moan and his eyes rolled in the back of his head from his own sensations. His motions started out gentle, but her hands urged him to move faster.

Afterward, he pulled her against him and he said, "Are you ready for dessert now?"

"Hmm..." she breathed softly. Snuggling against him, she said, "This was the best dessert." Michael couldn't argue with that. However, he insisted on getting them water so that she could hydrate since she was still recovering. After brushing their teeth and drinking the water, he pulled Hannah close again where they fell asleep in each other's arms for the remainder of the night.

Chapter 20

T he rest of the weekend was wonderful. Feeling ready to go out in public, they went out to breakfast on Saturday morning where Michael sat beside Hannah in the booth instead of across from her.

With his arm around her, he shared things that she had not known about him before. Michael talked to her about one of the reasons that he chose to go into being a choral director in a high school. His own choral director was a mentor in his life. His leadership and passion for the students that he taught inspired Michael to follow in his footsteps. He even told Hannah about the pressures that he sometimes felt from his mother which is why he made the mistake of breaking up with her. He didn't want to disappoint his mother. Hannah's eyes were filled with compassion as she kissed him gently after he confided in her and she understood a little more the pressure he felt to please his mother.

She shared with him about what she was learning from her counseling sessions with Angela. Eyes focused on hers, he idly traced circles around her opposite shoulder as she talked about her relationship with her family and how it affected her outlook on life. It was encouraging for Michael to hear because he needed to call and set up his own time for counseling. It helped that they both came from parents who did not understand the helpfulness that came from seeing a professional.

Eventually, they got up from the table in the restaurant. Michael drove and parked at the campus where they took a walk, hand in hand, and continued talking. The more time they spent together, the more they realized that this was a relationship with a future.

As they were walking back to his car, Hannah said, "Would you mind dropping me by the dorm for a few minutes? I want to check on Jackie and Michelle and I need to get a dress for church tomorrow."

Kissing her fingers on the hand he was holding, he said, "No problem."

***

The weekend flew by with Hannah and Michael growing closer. Stopping by their room to check on their friends, Hannah could tell that Jackie was slowly healing but Michelle continued to struggle with all that had happened. Hannah was gentle with her in suggesting that she go to the counseling center with her the next day on Monday just to see what was offered to her.

Michelle was reluctant, but thankfully Jackie helped to persuade her by saying that she would go.

When Hannah was checking on her friends in their room, she also called her parents before going back to Michael's. They were fine with her staying there during her initial recovery, but they would not be happy if she was continuing to stay with their archaic ideas of not having sex before marriage. Never having wanted to before, Hannah didn't mind it. But now she and Michael couldn't keep their hands off of each other after last night. They enjoyed another time together just that morning before getting up for the day.

That night, Alex came back from his mom's house and he didn't have a problem with Hannah staying there for a few more nights. The people-pleaser in her made extra sure that it wouldn't be a problem, and she even cooked dinner for them on Sunday night. Michael and Alex had wholeheartedly voted for spaghetti and Michael drove her to the store to buy the ingredients.

"I can make two things," she commented as she was browning meat in a frying pan. "My mom taught me to make tacos and spaghetti."

Both guys offered to help out. Alex tossed a salad while Michael boiled water to cook the pasta. Hannah added jars of sauce to the meat and warmed garlic bread in the oven.

Hannah was surprised and pleased with herself when the meal turned out well. Both guys complimented her and thanked her for it. She topped it off with ice cream sundaes for dessert.

***

The next day, Monday, felt slightly strange as Hannah walked to the dining hall with Michael and Alex. All three of them had morning classes, but Michael would meet Hannah for lunch so that he could walk with her to the counseling center before his afternoon class and practice session. His midterm would be a vocal performance in front of his professors and he was making plenty of time to prepare for it.

At breakfast, Hannah reminded Jackie and Michelle to come to the counseling center after lunch as well.

***

Hannah, Michael, Jackie and Michelle walked into the counseling center to see Mark and Angela standing behind the desk.

"Hannah," Angela's eyes teared up. She walked over and gave her a gentle hug. It was her first time seeing her face to face. All of their conversations had been over the phone in order to give Hannah plenty of time to rest and recuperate from her injuries.

Mark followed Angela and gave Hannah a hug from the side. Stepping back, he addressed all of them. "How are all of you doing? I know it's been difficult for all of you." As he looked around, he noticed open expressions on all of their faces except for Michelle. Then he continued, "I'm glad all of you are taking the first step in working past the trauma."

Hannah looked at Angela and said, "I want to make sure that they have appointments before coming back with you."

"No problem," Angela commented walking with all of them to sit on the couches in the lobby.

Mark explained what they hoped to accomplish, and Michael immediately wanted to set up a session with him. They walked to the desk to schedule an appointment on the calendar for the next day. Saying he needed to get to his next class, Hannah gave him a hug before he left.

Angela was asking Jackie and Michelle if they wanted to sign up for appointments as well. Jackie nodded immediately, but Michelle hedged saying, "I don't know."

Angela's face was gentle and kind as she said, "We aren't going to force you to come until you are ready."

Michelle's face was guarded as she said, "Thanks."

"However, I will say that it will become harder for you to face your struggles if you continue to bury them," Angela was direct in her words.

Being someone who appreciated honesty, Michelle eventually nodded and said, "Okay, I guess I need to make an appointment as well."

She explained that she would meet with her and Jackie together as well as separately since they were together when Hannah was abducted. Then, she went on to explain that both she and Mark wanted to meet with everyone who was involved as a group.

***

After Jackie and Michelle left, Angela ushered Hannah back into her office saying, "I have to be honest that this will be difficult for me, as well. I consider you as a friend, Hannah. I know I'm supposed to be objective and impartial, but I was terrified when I heard about your abduction. Mark called me that night to tell me what had happened and I was sick with worry."

Hannah's eyes teared up at hearing how much Angela cared about her. "Thank you."

Angela continued, "Rhonda had been meeting with our other counselor and I saw her come in a couple of times. It makes me sick that she was coming to sessions and plotting this the entire time!"

Inexplicable emotions filled Hannah after hearing what Angela told her. Looking down, she said, "Maybe it was my fault and I created this situation."

"Hannah," Angela said gently as she touched her arm. "It was not your fault. Rhonda was not my patient, and I wasn't privy to her information. But I can share my thoughts about her without getting into any trouble. I honestly believe that she has mental issues that were never identified within her childhood and adolescence."

A few tears leaked out as Hannah looked down and her breath whooshed out.

Angela continued by saying, "Now that you are physically healed, we need to work on your inner pain. You won't like this at all, but I want to hear from you everything that happened, word by word."

Shaking her head in denial, Hannah continued looking in her lap as she said, "I don't know if I can do that. I would love to forget about it."

"Hannah, look at me," Angela said. "I know you think that's the best way to handle this, but it will continue to haunt you until you face it. As painful as it will be, you need to feel each pain and sit with them. It will involve several sessions. It's why you've struggled with sleeping. Along with Mark and I meeting with all of you, I am going to teach you meditation and deep breathing exercises to use on a daily basis. I also want you to continue to write everything down. Your deepest feelings will be expressed in the journal I gave you during our early session and you can share only what makes you comfortable with me. But we will talk about one part at a time and take our time going through it."

"Okay," Hannah's mind was spinning and it felt like it was out of control. Rolling her eyes, she said, "You're right. I won't like that at all."

Taking a breath, Angela said, "This is the best way through all of this. Today, I want to talk about that first moment when Rhonda came up behind you when you went into the bathroom."

Putting her hands on her face, Hannah shook her head in refusal of what Angela was asking her.

Touching her arm again, Angela said, "I'm sorry, Hannah. I know this will be awful, but I promise you that I will just listen. There is no judgment because this is not your fault. And I will be here to hug you when you have talked through it."

Hannah was silent for a few moments, and she continued looking down. Angela didn't say anything, giving her time. She wouldn't force Hannah to talk and she would be there when she was ready. Deep down, Hannah knew that Angela was right.

With many tears, she revealed her feelings when Rhonda came from behind the bathroom door with the knife. She was angry with herself for not listening to her friends when they wanted to come in with her.

Angela hugged her again and she told her that she did a great job. As they stood, she said, "Your homework is to write down all of what you are feeling from this session. If you want to write more of what happened that is fine as well."

Exhausted, Hannah nodded in agreement, but she was surprised when she felt like a load had been lifted from her.

Hugging her one more time, Angela said, "You did well today, my friend."

When they walked out to the lobby, she was surprised to see Michael waiting for her. Rushing to him, she flung herself into his arms as Angela said, "See you on Wednesday."

Michael held her tightly against him as his eyebrows drew closer together. Pulling back, he brushed the hair from her face and said, "Baby, are you alright?"

Looking into his eyes, she smiled and nodded before saying, "I'm just glad to see you. Why are you here? I thought you would be practicing."

"I'll go back over there in a few minutes, but I wanted to be here for you when you came out of your session." Michael kissed her gently on her mouth and then on her cheek.

Continuing to smile, Hannah said, "It wasn't easy, but I do feel better from it."

"I'm glad," he murmured, noticing peace in her eyes.

She said, "I'm supposed to write everything in this journal. I don't know how good I will be at it."

Nodding his head, Michael said, "Are you ready? I can walk you back to my place and then go practice."

"Yes, I have an exam to study for," Hannah said as he kissed the side of her head and they walked outside.

***

The next afternoon, Michael was apprehensive over his own session with Mark. Hannah had a class after lunch, so after walking her to her building he went to the counseling center where Mark was waiting for him.

After sitting in his office, Mark asked him preliminary questions about his family and background. Then, he asked Michael to share what happened. With an anguished expression, Michael explained his version of it.

"How did you feel when you learned that Hannah was missing?" His voice was gentle as he asked, but Michael couldn't help the anger coursing through him from it.

With a heated voice, he said, "Why is this necessary? Hannah's the one who needs the help and attention."

"I disagree," Mark observed. "You feel responsible for this, don't you?"

Michael continued with an angry tone, "I should have realized that something could have happened when Rhonda came to the game that night. Then, when it did happen, I was in the locker room during halftime. I didn't even know it until I saw Jackie and Michelle trying to find her!"

Mark shifted his position and said, "Michael, look at me." When his troubled gaze focused on him, Mark said, "This was not your fault. You weren't responsible for Rhonda and what she did and you weren't even responsible for Hannah. The only one you are responsible for is yourself."

"I should have been there!!" he yelled, kicking a leg of the coffee table in front of him. "I should have protected her!! When I found out she was gone..." his voice drifted off and moisture filled his eyes. "I was terrified that I would never see her again!"

With a deep breath, Mark said, "I know, and I understand. When I heard what happened, I had the same feelings."

Tears were rolling down Michael's cheeks as his eyes focused on Mark. Then, he put his head in his hands and allowed himself to sob.

Mark didn't say anything, but he sat quietly while he cried in anguish. Eventually, Michael lifted his gaze and leaned back against the couch in exhaustion.

"That's the first time you've cried, isn't it?" Mark asked.

Nodding his head, Michael whispered, "I wanted to be strong for Hannah and I didn't want her to see."

Smiling, Mark said, "It's okay if she does see it. You can be honest with her about what you were feeling. It might help her through her own trauma if she can share in yours. It might be something you can share with each other which will also help the healing process."

As they finished up their session, Mark handed Michael his own notebook with instructions to write down his thoughts and feelings for the next time. Understanding what Hannah meant yesterday, he was shocked at how much lighter he felt. As he walked out, he spotted her sitting on a couch waiting for him just as he waited for her the day before. Pulling her up into a tight hug, he was comforted by her warmth. It filled him with more love than he ever realized he could feel for someone else. And he knew he never wanted to let her go.

Chapter 21

Two months passed and the counseling sessions helped all who were involved, even Michelle. It had taken a while longer for her to come around, but each of them shared their entries in their group sessions. Hearing Hannah's anger had hurt, but it was therapeutic for her to hear the honesty behind her true feelings, reassuring Michelle that she and Jackie had been forgiven and released from any responsibility in her attack.

Sharing the journals with each other had also drawn Hannah and Michael closer together. The two of them found comfort in reading each other's thoughts and feelings.

***

Hannah's parents had invited Michael home with her between Thanksgiving and Christmas. Her parents were more than willing to accept him as a part of their family because of his heroic efforts to rescue their daughter. Her mother even went to the trouble of purchasing a Christmas present for him and she made him open it with them sitting there.

He wasn't able to meet Hannah's sister, Denise, but he met her brother, Peter. The day that it happened, Hannah's mother had just told her about how feeble her grandmother was becoming and her dad spoke up to say that she had been to the emergency room a few times in the past couple of months.

Hannah left the table and went upstairs, saying she needed to brush her teeth. The truth was that she wanted some time to process what her mom had said. Her grandmother had been like a second mother to her and her siblings.

In his gentle way, Michael came up a few moments later and asked, "Are you okay?"

Unable to speak, she nodded as he pulled her against him. He was content to hold her as long as she needed. They sat there for a few more minutes before hearing the loud and rumbling noise of a truck outside and then the front door opening.

"My brother's home," she said softly. "Come downstairs and you can meet him."

Michael leaned down and kissed her softly before saying, "I'm glad to finally meet him," He kissed her forehead once more before standing up and reaching for her hand.

Walking downstairs, Hannah steeled herself for her brother's grumpy nature.

They walked into the den and Hannah's mom said, "Michael, please meet Peter, Hannah's brother."

Michael walked over and shook his hand. "I'm glad to finally meet you!"

He shook Michael's hand and surprise was in his gaze as he looked at Hannah and said, "How did you land a guy like this, Hannah?"

Michael felt Hannah tense up beside him, and he spoke again, "I'm the lucky one to have her as my girlfriend. She's an amazing person!"

His arm went loosely around her shoulders as he said the words. Even though he spoke in kindness, there was steel in his voice as he addressed the rudeness of Peter. She had never felt more protected and adored in her life and her eyes thanked Michael.

Peter studied him for a moment, surprised at Michael's protection of his younger sister.

Michael didn't say anymore, but he agreed with Hannah's many descriptions of her brother. He was an ass because it was apparent that he didn't see his sister for who she truly was. They sat together on the couch and Michael placed his arm around Hannah, pulling her close in a protective embrace.

The conversation led to a discussion on the classes he was attending at the local university in their town. "That class is going to kill me," he was commenting as he glanced over at Hannah and Michael sitting so closely together. He did have the manners to ask, "So, Michael, where are you from?"

Michael answered him in his easygoing manner and Hannah was filled with immense pride for his confident nature as it collided with her brother's arrogance.

A while later, Hannah announced that they were going to her grandmother's house. They walked to her car and he opened the driver's side door to help her inside. As he did, he glanced at the window and saw her brother watching them. He gave him a slight wave and walked around to the passenger side.

Hannah pulled the car up slightly in the curved driveway and he put a hand on her arm and said, "Wait a minute."

Since they were out of sight, Michael's hands cradled Hannah's face and he kissed her tenderly.

"What was that for?" she asked, pulling away as she looked at him in confusion.

"You know you're beautiful, right?" He murmured as he continued kissing down the side of her face and one of his hands moved to the back of her neck into her hair. "I just wanted to remind you."

As she was pulling the car out, she reached for his hand and said, "I love you, Michael Davis."

"Baby, I love you, too." Michael responded as he entwined their fingers together.

They stayed at her Nana's for about an hour. Her grandmother insisted on serving them homemade pound cake and sweet tea even though they tried not to go during a meal.

Hannah insisted on cleaning their dishes and Michael helped her. The two of them had their few dishes washed, dried and put away in a matter of minutes before hugging her grandmother goodbye.

The following day at church, Michael suggested that they sit beside her grandmother for the service. She sat in a group of her friends and she had ridden with one of them so that she could attend Sunday School. Her parents opted to spend the morning at home with Hannah and Michael.

They walked into her grandmother's row, and Hannah gave her a warm hug before she sat beside her. Nana's face beamed with pride that her granddaughter was sitting with her. She introduced Michael to her friends and they commented on how good-looking he was which caused him to laugh self-consciously and blush beet red.

As they sat, Hannah leaned over and whispered, "I totally agree with them, but I think I have some competition now!"

Michael grinned down at Hannah and whispered, "Some of these ladies don't look half-bad even at their age." Hannah playfully slapped at his shoulder and he laughed softly before kissing her cheek and rubbing his fingers down the other cheek at the same time. Hannah's eyes softened with love as she gazed up at him.

Hannah's brother, Peter, happened to be walking over to their side to also sit beside his grandmother. Michael caught him as he watched them and the look in her brother's eye was one of respect.

He shook hands with Michael and surprised Hannah by hugging her and then his grandmother. Astonishment swept over Hannah's face, and it was obvious that hugs didn't happen much at all. She mumbled, "Hey, Peter" to him and sat back shaking her head in bewilderment.

Michael took Hannah's hand and entwined their fingers in support of his understanding. He hoped it was a turning-point for their relationship.

Peter wound up joining their family for lunch and it was a pleasant time all around.

***

After Christmas, Hannah drove to Michael's home so that they could celebrate New Year's Eve together. While she was there, it was a wonderful time with his family. It also seemed that the abduction had brought Michael's mother around to accepting her as a part of their family. Hannah didn't know it, but Michael had confided to his mother that Hannah was the woman he would marry. His mother surprised him by touching his cheek and told him again that he was nineteen and adult enough to make his own decisions. After that, she didn't say anymore about it. His mother also bought Hannah a Christmas present, and she cherished the classic video of an old movie that she loved.

One of the best parts was that she got to know his sister, Jenny. Michael had gone with his mother on an errand regarding his car so they had a few moments alone to talk.

Both of them found common interests and then the conversation moved to Michael. Hannah heard many stories and antics of them growing up as children. She was filled with laughter and joy at hearing about him as a small boy. Jenny pulled out some photo albums for them to look through.

Hannah moved to the topic of his manners and Jenny's eyes widened. With extreme sarcasm, Jenny asked, "Are you talking about Michael Davis?" as her eyes filled with disbelief. Hannah said yes in agreement and Jenny was overcome with shock causing Hannah to laugh again. "Hannah," she said. "You must be bringing out the good in him because he most definitely didn't ever do that at home!"

"Did you ever see him out on dates with other girls?" Hannah inquired as jealousy shot through her at the thought.

Jenny had a thoughtful look on her face as she answered Hannah's question. "He didn't see, but I watched him. He never brought any girls home, but I saw him with a girl that he was dating at church. Believe me, he did not open her car door or touch her when they walked inside. She was a rather mean girl at church, so maybe that's why he didn't do those things with her. She treated him horribly a couple of times during our youth group meetings and he eventually stopped dating her."

Hannah couldn't describe the feeling that swept over her at Jenny's words and her breathing became erratic. As she was sitting there, her mouth pursed and a shaky breath came out of it.

Michael and his mom pulled into the driveway and he walked inside. He made a beeline toward Hannah and he joined her on the couch.

Jenny walked back into her bedroom to get ready, because she was going over to a friend's house for the night. Michael's mother disappeared in the back of the house as well.

Hannah reached up and kissed Michael on the mouth, taking him by surprise. She deepened the kiss because she was overcome with the need to kiss him after what Jenny shared with her.

Michael pulled back, keeping his arm around her and said, "Wow! What was that? Not that I'm complaining!"

Hannah looked into his eyes and said, "I love you so much, Michael Davis. I just needed to show you how much."

Michael's other hand stroked her face as his voice lowered, "I would love to continue this demonstration a little longer, but my mom could walk back in at any point." He did pull her against him in his favorite position with his head resting on top of hers and his eyes closed in contentment while she melted against him.

After visiting his grandmother, Michael drove Hannah to the mall. Surprisingly, his grumpy grandmother had given him twenty dollars to spend on Hannah for lunch.

As he drove, Hannah teased, "Jenny and I talked about you while you were out."

"Really?," he said. "What did my sister tell you?" Her hand was in his as he drove.

Hannah's face became serious, and she commented, "She told me that you didn't show manners to any other girls like you do with me."

Michael made a right turn and said without looking at her, "She's right." He was matter of fact in his answer.

"What makes you do it with me?" Hannah asked, overcome with curiosity and trying not to let her face mirror the joy she felt when all she wanted to do was pump her hands with joy.

Michael's face did a double take in glancing at her as he tried to stay focused on the road. "I can't believe you don't know why." Then, he continued as he tightened his hold on her hand. "Hannah, I've told you multiple times about how you make my heart race."

"Even that first night we went out? You went out of your way to be so thoughtful that night." Hannah spoke with amazement in her voice.

"Baby, you have mattered to me from the first time I put my eyes on you! You are beautiful on the inside and the outside. Seeing how kind you were with that guy who had special needs from your hometown showed me your kind heart. You also carry yourself in such a ladylike manner. Watching you walk into a room puts my heart into overtime! The girl that I dated in high school couldn't hold a candle to you!" Michael glanced at her as he was pulling into the mall parking lot. "I know I was stupid when I doubted us and broke things off, but those feelings never went away."

With her eyes shining, Hannah exclaimed, "Michael Davis, when you park this car, I need to kiss you!"

Anticipation filled his expression as Michael pulled into a parking spot. He quickly put the car into the parking position, and pulled Hannah close. Gazing into her eyes for a long moment, he noticed she was looking at him with a similar expression and he whispered, "Come here."

They kissed deeply and with passion as Hannah tried to get as close to him as she could with the console in the way. "Well, shit," Michael commented, making Hannah giggle at his frustration. Then, he pushed his seat back as far as it could go and he pulled Hannah over on his lap and she straddled him as he kissed her thoroughly.

She pulled back and said, "I didn't think I could love you any more than I already do, but I am over the moon for you, Michael Davis."

Giving her a hard kiss which quickly deepened, Michael mumbled, "I will never stop loving you, Hannah." She sighed, a sound that he loved, and their kiss deepened as their hands found each other. Rearranging their clothing, they stepped out of the car to go into the mall.

***

That evening, Michael and Hannah were going out to dinner to celebrate New Year's Eve. Hannah took a shower so that she could get ready, and she took her time rolling her hair and applying makeup while Michael got a shower in his parents' bathroom. At five o'clock, she walked into the living room where Michael, his sister and his mom were sitting.

She heard him mumble, "Oh my word!" when his eyes feasted upon her. Her heart quickened at the look of desire in his eyes.

"Hannah, you look so pretty!" Michael's mother said in a sweet compliment to her.

"Thank you," she muttered with her gaze still on him. She saw Jenny glancing at Michael and his sister dipped her head low so that she wouldn't laugh at his dumbstruck expression. Hannah wanted to chuckle at his sister's reaction.

She was dressed in a soft, red dress that was tight on her torso. It accented her breasts, her waist and flared out. The dress stopped right before her knees where she had on panty hose and black heels.

She smiled at Michael in appreciation for his unspoken compliment.

Michael came beside her and calmly asked, "Are you ready?" causing Hannah to automatically nod her head in agreement.

Jenny did snicker at that moment causing him to frown in her direction. Hannah couldn't help smiling at how amused his sister was with the situation.

Michael's mother insisted on taking a picture of them with her camera before they left, causing Michael to grumble in response.

Walking out to the car, he opened her door like the gentleman he usually was. When he got into the driver's side, he yanked Hannah to him and kissed her hard. "Woman, you know how to drive me crazy! How on earth am I supposed to sit beside you and eat dinner when all I want to do is kiss you senseless?" He exclaimed the words as his eyes feasted on her face, her hair, and her dress. Hannah's heart fluttered at his words.

"I'm glad you like this outfit. My mom and I went shopping the day after Christmas and I found this to wear for this moment." Hannah smiled and she happened to look toward the house, and she saw Jenny laughing in the window. "I'm afraid we have entertained your sister this evening!" she said laughing at him waving her away from the window.

As he drove, Michael's hand was on Hannah's leg because tonight he wanted to do more than hold her hand. Truthfully, he wanted to take her into his room, shut the door, and have his way with her. Knowing it would scandalize his family, he refrained from it.

When they got to the restaurant, Hannah learned that Michael had made a reservation for a booth. The greeter led them to their table and in his typical manner, Michael sat on the same side of the booth as she did.

Unable to help himself, he pulled her even closer to his side and kissed her slowly and reverently before pulling away to glance at the menu.

They had a lovely steak dinner and Michael finished the rest of hers. Hannah didn't know, but he had ordered dessert ahead of time. The server brought it out and she saw a tray with chocolate covered strawberries and some sort of chocolate dessert that looked delectable! Again, Hannah was blown away by his thoughtfulness.

"Michael," Hannah breathed. "You shouldn't have done all of this."

"I wanted to," he said, kissing her again. They fed each other strawberries before sharing the other dessert on the tray. Watching Hannah lick the chocolate off of her lips made him even more crazy for her.

There was a dance floor, so after dessert, Michael led Hannah out to the farthest corner where people wouldn't see them as he kissed her. He looked into her eyes and said, "Did I tell you that you look beautiful tonight?"

"You didn't have to," Hannah said with a dreamy smile. "I could see it in your eyes earlier. You look amazing, too."

Michael had on a red, button-down oxford shirt and black slacks. He looked extremely hot in Hannah's opinion.

He pulled her as close as he could and he kissed her for the entire song that played. Hannah was out of breath and shivers were running down her spine because of his caresses up and down her back. Another slow song began playing. Hannah put her head against his chest while he placed his head on top of hers in their favorite embrace and he sang the words softly in her ear. She could hardly remain standing from the effect he was having on her.

When they left the restaurant, Michael paused before starting the car. Puzzled, Hannah glanced at him and his face looked pale. "Michael? Are you alright?"

Nervously, his hands fidgeted in his lap before he looked at her. "I have something for you."

"Michael," Hannah argued. "We gave each other Christmas presents before we left for the break." She was in love with the lovely necklace and earrings set that he gave her and her hands reached up to touch both of them. Her gift to him was tickets to go and see his favorite band when they came back for the second semester.

"I know, but this isn't a Christmas present," Blowing out a nervous breath, he reached into his pants pocket, and he put a small package in front of Hannah. He said, "We've officially been back together for three months now, and I know that you are the one for me, so I wanted to get you something."

Hannah looked into his eyes and then down at the package as she opened the gift to reveal a jewelry box. When she opened it, she saw a lovely ring with a pearl on the top. "Michael," she breathed. "It's beautiful."

"I know we are meant to be together, Hannah Mathis. But we are only Freshmen in college and we are still very young, so will you wear this promise ring?" Michael's eyes were a teal blue as he gazed into her eyes with love.

Tears were shining in hers as Hannah exclaimed, "Yes, yes, I will!" and he pulled it out of the ring box and put it on her left hand. His hand stroked over the beautiful pearl and then he leaned in and kissed her softly. The kiss deepened for a while longer and Hannah was practically in his lap when they pulled apart. As he drove back to his house, she couldn't help but gaze at the lovely ring on her left hand. Deep within, she knew that he was the one for her as well.

Later that night, he snuck into his sister's room and the two of them made love without making any noise. In Hannah's mind, it was extremely sexy.

Chapter 22

One year later...

As Hannah pulled into the driveway of her parents' house, Michael's palms began sweating profusely. The two of them had been talking regularly about a commitment to get engaged and he planned to find time this weekend to speak with Hannah's dad. Even though they had been talking, he wanted the conversation with Hannah's father to remain a secret in order to surprise her with the perfect proposal.

They made short work of pulling their bags out of the car and walking them upstairs. Hannah's mother had met them at the door and hugged them tightly, chattering away about their plans for the evening. Michael found himself half-listening. Even though Mr. Mathis was still not home from work, intimidation filled him. He had a deep respect for Mr. Mathis from what Hannah had shared as well as how he managed their family's wealth and well-being. Knowing he had large shoes to fill made Michael quiver inwardly.

After setting their things down, they walked downstairs to catch up with Hannah's mom.

"Mom, is your year going better?" Hannah asked.

Her mother had talked about several students who were difficult for her this year. By Christmas break, she was completely fed up.

"It is going better," her mom said. "I called one of the student's parents and we had a parent conference. He's been much better since then."

"Mrs. Mathis, Hannah has told me what a wonderful teacher you are!" Michael was complimentary as he sat on the love seat beside Hannah and his arm was loosely around Hannah's back.

Hannah's mom smiled. "Thank you, Michael. I'm getting too old to teach for much longer, though! I just don't have patience for children who are disrespectful."

"My mom says the same thing," Michael said. "She's the principal's secretary and she has to keep an eye on students who have been sent to the office until the principal can meet with them. She has many stories to tell!"

They continued talking for a few minutes more when the garage door opened and Hannah's father walked into the kitchen.

"Hi, Dad," Hannah said as she walked over and gave him a hug.

Bill Mathis pulled her close and kissed her on the cheek. "Hey, sweet girl," he said. Then, he turned and shook Michael's hand as soon as he had walked up to greet him as well. "Michael, it's nice to see you again."

As Michael shook his hand, he hoped the older man didn't notice the perspiration on his brow. Thankfully he didn't as Hannah's mom walked back into their bedroom with him.

They sat back down, and Hannah took the remote control and turned to a rerun of a show they had both watched many times. Michael's arm was up around her back again as they laughed and watched together.

At one point, Hannah's mom walked out to witness how they were looking at one another. She was taken aback as she witnessed Hannah's smile as she gazed at Michael and he was smiling back at her as he idly rubbed her forearm. As Hannah was talking to him, he looked as if she was the only person in the world at the moment because he was completely engrossed in the words she was saying. Anita Mathis observed how Hannah's eyes conveyed a love that showed permanence and forever.

Tearing up at the lovely scene, Anita's heart broke a little bit. It was beautiful to see them together. Her overprotective nature fought a little at the thought of her baby growing up, but she couldn't imagine a better man than Michael for her daughter. He had already proven to them that he would take care of her in any situation.

***

Saturday morning involved a leisurely breakfast with Hannah's parents and a visit with her grandmother.

Once they were back, Michael noticed Hannah's dad out in their flowerbed and he said, "I'm going to see if he needs help." He knew it was a lame explanation, but he was trying not to tip Hannah off on his intentions. Thankfully, she seemed elusive as she said, "Okay, I will get my book to read for a little while."

Michael touched her cheek softly before letting go of her hand and walking over to Mr. Mathis.

"Hey, Mr. Mathis. Do you need some help with this?" Hannah's dad was in the flower bed and he was cleaning out the old pine straw.

Even though it was February, he said, "I always do this a month and a half before spring." He handed Michael the rake and went to the garage to get another one before scooping some of the old pine straw into a lawn bag.

Michael raked at the old straw and said, "I wondered if you had a moment for me to talk with you."

"Sure, what do you need, son? And you can start calling me Bill." Hannah's dad said. "You have earned it by taking care of our girl at college."

Michael smiled and said, "Thank you, sir. I want to let you know how much I love your daughter. Her happiness and health are beginning to matter to me more than anything else. She inspires me to get out of bed every morning and become a better man."

With a gentle smile, Hannah's dad commented, "She is special."

"What would you think about my asking her to marry me? I've come to realize that she is the one for me. I know we are still young, and we will probably wait another year before actually getting married," Michael was looking at the straw he was raking as he spoke.

"If you plan to wait, why the rush to ask her?" Bill Mathis didn't say the words in an angry tone, but he asked with concern in his voice. His hands had stilled as he held the rake without using it.

"This past January, she and I spent six weeks apart because I stayed home to work at a part time job instead of attending the January term. Those were miserable weeks for me because I missed her more than I can describe! I realized that I don't want to ever be apart from her again like that." Michael shook his head before finally looking Hannah's dad in the eyes. "She is the love of my life and I plan to love her for as long as I live."

Bill Mathis paused as he thought about Michael's words. "I can't say that I'm not concerned about how young the two of you are, but you have already proven to me that you will take care of her." Smiling slightly, he continued talking. "It's been a while, but I also remember young love. My only concern is that you both need to finish college. How would you support her and yourself if you are still in school?"

Michael did not take offense at his question. He knew that Hannah's dad was concerned about Hannah's welfare, and he had already thought through the answer. "Sir, I have been thinking about that. I want to let you know that I have been paying off some credit card debt that I accumulated when first getting to college. I plan to apply for an internship at the local high school as assistant choral director. It won't pay much, but it will help. I have applied for a part time job at the university for these next few months before beginning the internship next Fall. I will save as much of what I make as I can and I believe that I will be able to work both jobs, if necessary," Michael's expression was earnest as he spoke to Hannah's father. "I also want to help my parents with paying off the loan they took out for me to attend college."

Bill Mathis looked at Michael with respect and said, "It sounds like you have done quite a bit of thinking about this. Have you talked to Hannah about it?"

"She and I have talked about it, but I didn't want to assume anything until I had a chance to speak with you and Mrs. Mathis." Michael said as he saw even more respect in the eyes of what he hoped was his future father-in-law. "Hannah has bragged about how well you do financially. I am open to advice from you about managing my money before I even think about asking Hannah."

"I will be happy to help you with that, Michael," Hannah's dad said as he held out his hand again. They shook hands and Michael continued to help him gather the rest of the pine straw. After Bill thanked him, he headed back into the house to take a shower and clean up for supper. Michael followed him inside to take his own shower before seeing Hannah.

***

The Tuesday after Hannah and Michael returned from visiting their parents, Valentine's Day, he called her room to ask her to go for a walk with him. When he got to her dorm, she was waiting outside on the swing for him. Wiping his sweaty hands on his jeans before trying to hold hers, he approached as she stood with a gentle smile. Alex knew what he really had planned for this evening and so did Jackie and Michelle. They were hiding in one of the buildings where they could watch his proposal.

Strolling hand in hand, they came upon a beautiful gazebo in the middle of the campus and Hannah had no idea why she had never noticed it before.

"Let's go inside and sit," Michael said and she nodded her head as they walked inside.

Immediately, Hannah saw what had to be a dozen roses in a vase on the ground in the middle of the small building. Gasping with joy and shock, she turned and saw Michael getting down on one knee. He had a jewelry box with a gorgeous diamond ring inside of it. Tears sprang to her eyes as what they had imagined was now becoming true.

Gazing up at her, Michael said, "Hannah Mathis, I love you so much! You didn't know, but I spoke with your dad last weekend and received his blessing to propose to you." His words were spewing out quickly from his nervousness. Taking a breath, he continued, "Will you do me the honor of marrying me?"

Paralyzed by joy and happiness, Hannah finally nodded her head, and she said, "Yes, Michael, I will marry you!"

Michael jumped up to hug her tightly and then he pulled back. He took the promise ring and moved it to Hannah's other hand before sliding on the engagement ring. One tear escaped as she hugged him tightly again before he kissed her.

Pulling back, she whispered, "I love you so much!"

Within seconds, they were surrounded by their friends yelling their congratulations.

Holding up a camera, Michelle said, "I even got a few pictures so that you can look back and remember!"

Overcome with how blessed she was, Hannah hugged her friend and then held out her left hand so that they could admire her ring.

***

Michael and Hannah were married a little over a year later in May. The wedding was a ridiculous affair handled by her mother, but it included all of their friends and family at the church where she grew up. Once they actually stood up with one another and recited their vows in front of the large congregation, the moment made all the headaches from planning their wedding disappear. At one point, Hannah's dad had pulled them to the side and offered to pay for them to elope because of how stressed her mother had been with the planning. Hannah and Michael had been tempted, but they persevered through the mayhem of going to school and planning their wedding.

They had one more year of school left before graduation. Hannah had done her part in adding to their savings because she had to complete her student teaching for her final year. She spent the past year and a half with a part time job and adding to the savings account that her father had encouraged them to open.

After they returned from their honeymoon and got into a daily routine, she had never known such contentment! She could have never imagined all of the events of beginning college, moving away and the trauma with Rhonda would lead to meeting the love of her life and her best friend!

Epilogue

Hannah sighed in contentment as she remembered that wonderful day so long ago. They had two wonderful children who were grown and living on their own. She turned her head as she heard the garage door opening.

Michael walked in the door and her heart skipped. She remembered wondering if she would get excited at seeing him after being married for many years and she was happy to realize that those feelings were still deep inside.

With more lines on his face and more gray hair, he smiled as he walked toward her.

"Hey, beautiful!" he said as he leaned down to give her a kiss.

Hannah breathed out happily as she kissed him back, and she was so thankful for those early college years where they developed the best friends they had ever known. Even though they lived in other parts of the state, their group made time to get together. It was a yearly reunion planned on the same weekend every year.

Thanks

Thank you to my husband and best friend in life. Without him, this book would not have been possible. Thank you to my two kids, Hannah and Caleb, for your support in my pursuing this as a dream. There were times I bounced ideas off of all of you and appreciated the feedback you were able to give me. Thank you to All Write Well for your mentorship through this overwhelming but exciting process. I appreciate your guidance throughout all of it.

About the author

About the Author:

Liz Hamilton lives with her husband in central Georgia. Having spent most of her life growing up in Texas, she was able to use her experience of living there to help in writing this series of books. She has two children, Hannah and Caleb. She has two dogs, Walter and Chloe. Balancing a full time teaching position as a middle school Language Arts teacher, she was able to use her passion for writing to publish her first book and she hopes to make this a second career when she retires from education. Her hobbies include reading, cooking, walking her dogs and traveling with her family.

Also by

Also By Liz Hamilton:

Life Lessons: A New Love (ETC Mystery 2)

Connect with me

Connect with Me:

Follow me on my Liz Hamilton Facebook page or lizhamilton0801 on Instagram.

Find my paperback using the QR code.